Sow the Wind

A Political End-Times Thriller

The Whirlwind Series
Book 1

Gary W. Ritter

This book is a work of fiction. Names, characters, places, and incidents are either the product of the author's imagination or are used fictionally. Any resemblance to actual persons, living or dead, or to actual events or locales is entirely coincidental.

Additional Scripture where noted for Psalm 23 is taken from the King James Version of the Bible.

Version 2016.09.01

www.GaryRitter.com

Give feedback on the book at my Author page:
www.facebook.com/gritter3390

ISBN- 10: 1530680549
ISBN- 13: 978-1530680542

Books by Gary W. Ritter
Available at Amazon.com

The Panic (Omnibus)
The Panic
Flying Dollars
Spa Treatment
Zapped!

DEDICATION

First and foremost, I want to thank my Lord and Savior, Jesus Christ. Without Him I would have no life, and this book would not be possible.

Secondly, I'm exceedingly grateful for my wife Dalia. The Lord has graciously given me a partner evenly yoked. I'm thankful for her love and support in all my endeavors.

ACKNOWLEDGMENTS

I'm want to thank those who made this book possible. Shann Hall-LochmannVanBennekom, although it was a rough road, thank you for your perseverance. Your editing made all the difference. Ken Raney, thanks for your great cover design. Dalia, a day doesn't go by that you don't help me in some way.

Gary W. Ritter

They sow the wind...

- Hosea 8:7a

Prologue

September 11, 2001
Idaho

Sweat coursed down the faces of the two hikers, staining deep Vs on their shirts. Panting, they labored in the early heat as they trekked along the hard-packed trail. Approaching the forest, James Glazier picked up the pace. Behind him, his fiancée, Janna, was eager to reach protection from the relentless sun. Turning around, he motioned. "Come on, honey, you can do it. Only a few more steps."

A fine haze wreathed the tops of higher hills in the distance. As Janna labored upward, James waited, glancing around in evident appreciation at the beauty of the clearing. Late-season wildflowers bloomed showcasing brilliant purples, golds, and reds. A breeze tickled the grasses bordering the trail, teasing the hikers with momentary relief from the oppressive heat. The buzzing of flies, bees, and gnats brought the only disturbance to the peaceful vista.

Once Janna caught up with James, he reached for her hand while swatting at an insect that landed on his ear. “You doing okay?”

“I wish I had longer legs.” Several inches shorter than his six feet, Janna usually had to increase her pace just to stay even with James. She gulped air while he drank from his water bottle. His fingers lingered, touching hers when he passed it to her.

James wiped his brow, pushing back dark brown hair that spilled over his forehead. “Steep back there. I don’t recall that kind of grade going down.”

“That was at the beginning of our hike when we were fresh.” Janna smiled. “But you love it.”

His eyes sparkled. “You ready to finish it out?”

She nodded. James straightened his glasses, pecked her on the lips, and grinned. He took off with Janna following close behind as they attacked the last of the hike in the relative cool of the woods.

It took another twenty minutes to reach the top. Emulating a trail horse that knows it’s heading home, like he always did, James increased his stride. Behind him, Janna muttered, “Wish you’d remember I can’t keep your pace.”

He slowed so she could catch him. “I’m sorry. I get lost in the moment.”

She jabbed his arm with a playful punch. “Mr. Enthusiastic.”

“Yeah, but I forget your needs. I have to keep it fun for you, too.”

She shrugged. "I know you love me. It takes time to learn how to bring out the best in each other. It's hard, though, because of our pasts. We’re growing, and our faith is still new. But we'll make it. I know God put us together for a reason."

When they emerged from the trailhead, the couple collapsed on the grass near their car. Janna fanned herself with the bottom of her T-shirt while James tipped his water bottle over his head. At his sigh of pleasure, Janna splashed water from her own bottle onto her cheeks.

James climbed into the driver's side and situated himself. Janna sank into the passenger's seat and tugged at her seatbelt until it clicked. She kicked off her hiking boots as the first blast from the air conditioner surrounded her.

Pulling out from the parking spot, James maneuvered the car down the long dirt road, away from the federal land they'd been hiking.

Once they reached concrete, the road wound around the mountain toward the bottom at an easy grade. While chatting about their early morning adventure, Janna saw brake lights immediately ahead around a bend. James was looking at her. She shouted, "Watch out!"

At her cry, James braked hard to avoid rear-ending an SUV. Janna sighed in relief as the car stopped mere inches from its bumper. She placed a hand on her chest. "That was close. Wonder what's the problem?"

Color had drained from James' face. He touched her knee. "Sorry. Looks like a traffic stop of some kind. There's a couple of uniformed officers."

Inching forward as someone waved on the cars one-by-one, they didn't have to wait long. Despite the short delay, by the time they reached the head of the line, three more cars had stopped behind them. A female officer walked up to their car. Her eyes darted between the two of them before she scanned the back seat. "May I see your driver's license please?"

James reached into his rear pocket to extract his wallet. "What's this all about, Officer?"

She examined his license, peered at Janna, and nodded. "You haven't heard?"

Perplexed, James accepted his license back. "We've been hiking. Heard what?"

"There's been a terrorist incident in New York. We've been commanded to perform a security check."

"Not to be a smart-aleck, ma'am, but this is Idaho. What's anything going on in New York have to do with us here?"

"Planes flew into the Twin Towers. The authorities put police on immediate alert all over the country."

Janna shivered as goose bumps rose on her arms. She rubbed them vigorously as she slowly rocked back and forth in her seat.

"You folks can go." The officer patted the roof of the car, and James drove off.

Janna turned on the radio. She fiddled with the dial, but got only static. She threw up her hands in despair. "There's no reception here."

The radio's search feature finally discovered a station after they turned from the remote mountain road onto a larger one.

She locked on it in as an announcer continued in the middle of his explanation. "...the North Tower at 8:46. Then another plane struck the South Tower at 9:03. We don't know if this was deliberate, a planned attack. The authorities...oh, my God!...Oh, oh...I just can't. These...the tower's collapsing. I can't believe this." He began to sob.

James looked at Janna in astonishment. "Oh my gosh."

She mirrored his shock. "I think we should pray." Janna grabbed James' free hand. He kept his other on the wheel and his attention on the road. Janna softly prayed as tears welled up and spilled down her cheeks. "Lord Jesus, I don't even know what to ask. This is too horrible to imagine. Please, help everyone involved in this disaster. Might they turn to You in their distress. Be with them, Father. Bring them hope and life." Looking up she saw James' reddened eyes. He hiccoughed with a half-caught breath and wiped away the moisture on his face.

Eager to return to the resort where they'd been staying for the past week, they listened to the radio in silence. Once at the hotel, they grabbed their gear and raced up one flight of stairs to their unit and turned on the television to Fox News. Glued to the screen, they watched the planes striking each tower over and over. The visual drove the tragedy home. The first tower collapsing, followed by the second, ran continually. Fire and smoke billowed forth. The commentators' repeated descriptions of the horrendous scene rang in their ears. Their voices droned on as the towers came crashing down. Witnessing the drama replayed for hours left the couple limp.

Any thoughts they might have had about their scheduled flight home in two days were lost. The beginning of their last year in seminary, where they'd met a year ago, became a distant memory.

Twenty-five hundred miles away James and Janna felt an integral attachment to the power of the moment. The camera zoomed in, and a person at a window leaped to her death rather than face the flames consuming the floor at her back. On the streets below, billowing black clouds of dust and debris rose from the two buildings, overtaking and devouring people sprinting from the scene.

The horror of it left Janna weeping into the night, long after the actual destruction occurred. In those hours, they held each other as though afraid to let go. At one moment of shuddering emotion, Janna whispered in James' ear, "I wish we hadn't vowed to remain chaste until our wedding night. It's nice to have your arms around me, but it doesn't feel reassuring enough." She paused until resolve returned. "But nothing, not even terrorists will make me break my oath to God. I've been through too much."

James nodded his agreement. His story was different, yet the same. Janna knew he too had overcome a sordid past with great deliverance. Neither had any desire to weaken what they'd received as a gift from the Father.

The next day James located a Wall Street Journal and the couple spent several hours reading its extensive coverage. One major concept shone brightly through the thousands of words the paper published. This was an attack by a major, unknown foe. The United States had entered a new era.

Chapter 1

27 Years Later
Late August 2028
Western Michigan

Only the ticking of the heart monitor and the soft whoosh of the automatic blood pressure device interrupted the silence of the room. The partially-closed curtains created an unnatural darkness on this bright August day. Faint cries of children at play in a nearby park contrasted with the somber atmosphere inside. The smell of antiseptic wafted in from the hallway through the open door. A nurse bustled in. She gave James Glazier a sympathetic smile, checked her patient's vitals, straightened the bed sheets, and left without saying anything.

What was there to say? The nurse couldn't heal; all she could do was provide care. There was little hope, so why waste words? The doctors had done all they could do. Now it was simply a waiting game.

The book on James' lap began to weigh heavy, and he set it aside. He touched the brown leather cover and closed his eyes for a moment, listening. His wife's breathing, erratic at times, was slow and steady. So today was the beating of his heart. Lately his fears had taken control, bringing him great anxiety, despite knowing it wouldn't make a difference.

Focusing on the present, James scanned the monitor readouts that showed Janna's vitals were stable. He reached to brush from her face a strand of blonde hair that had begun showing streaks of gray. Her unlined skin felt cool to the touch. She slept peacefully today and didn't look to be in pain; for that he was thankful.

He pondered how quickly the years had fled. In his mind she was still the beautiful young girl in her early twenties he had fallen for, never thinking for an instant he was worthy of someone like her. Vibrant, healthy, a woman given over to God. How could her life have come to this?

Checking the time, he saw that he needed to go. He kissed Janna's cheek and stood quietly, listening for another minute. With a sigh he turned to leave.

The familiar hallway seemed longer than usual today. The patient rooms, some occupied, others not, the various offices and nursing areas, they all spoke to him of troubled humanity. How much people suffered in this life. How great an effort in a place like this to alleviate that distress.

The elevator bell dinged, and the door slid open. A woman stepped out. "Oh, Pastor James, I was just going to see Janna. How is she today, and how are you?"

Sylvia was one of the faithful prayer warriors in the church he pastored. He couldn't give her any good news of Janna and didn't feel much like talking. With the platitudes most people speak when not interested in conversation, he begged a time constraint. He waved at her as she turned away to carry out her visit to his dying wife.

Back near the church, James heard the familiar, faint buzz in the heated air above him. Wiping sweat off his forehead from the excessive heat that had permeated the area most of the summer, he knew what the sound was without looking. They were pervasive these days. He remembered the time drones had been a novelty with Federal Aviation Administration concerns about airspace encroachment and the privacy advocates warning of Big Brother. The apprehension by the FAA disappeared during the final years of the Obama Administration. Suddenly it wasn't a problem after all. As to Big Brother, he had certainly come onto the scene. One could hardly go anywhere without a drone flying nearby. The loss of privacy was shocking, but as with most annoyances, James, along with most people, had gotten used to the intrusion.

Alone in his office, James faced the first of his many tasks. He had a sermon to prepare. It was Friday, and he knew he had to get busy. Once again it seemed necessary to speak on faith. He'd made that a frequent topic over the last year. With good reason. When the doctors initially discovered the malignant tumor in Janna's breast, it had been difficult for the couple to rationalize. They'd been faithful servants; it didn't seem right. The subsequent rounds of tests, scans, radiation, and finally chemo had tried their faith week after week. None of the doctors' ministrations had proven of use, but to date, neither had the seemingly endless prayers.

Janna and he prayed at great length for her recovery, and the congregation—or at least a portion of it—had continually lifted them up in prayer. There were many around the country, even some overseas, who reported that Janna was before them constantly. Yet the cancer metastasized, spreading to other organs of her body.

Throughout this period they never lost faith, even as doubt crept into James' mind. They believed that God could and would heal her. That meant they weren't bartering with Him or trying to manipulate Him, simply that healing was integral to His nature. In His sovereignty, God would heal if that action was according to His purposes.

There was a knock at James' office door. Glancing at the clock, he saw it was after five. His secretary left at noon on Fridays, so he usually dealt with whatever came up after that by himself.

"Come in."

Joe Bennett entered, and James waved him to a chair. He was a deacon and a fixture of the church for many years, long before James arrived on the scene.

"You got a couple minutes, Pastor?" Bennett sat tall in the chair, his angular body not seeming particularly comfortable as he shifted in the seat. He fiddled with the dark hair at the back of his neck spilling over his collar.

He didn't have the time, but James tried, within limits, to always make room for personal interaction with his board members and individuals in the congregation. He nodded his assent while trying to penetrate the man's depthless, brown eyes.

"There's something I need to tell you."

Before Bennett opened his mouth again, James had a premonition. Whatever he was about to say wasn't good. James focused in on the deacon more closely.

"You know there's talk going round." Bennett paused, rubbed his hands on his jeans, his fingers continually busy, his discomfort palpable.

James was aware of the talk, but decided to hear him out. "Go ahead."

Bennett squirmed in his chair. "There's talk you don't have enough faith, and that's why Janna hasn't been healed." He lifted his hands in a helpless gesture.

"What do you think, Joe?"

"Me? Why, I don't know. The rest of the board is kind of restless about it, I'll tell you that."

"Restless in what way?"

"Look, I don't say I necessarily agree with this, but I was elected to bring you the message."

"So, you're the sacrificial lamb. And the message is what?"

He pursed his lips. "Well, it's...it's an ultimatum."

James raised his eyebrows and tilted his head, feigning surprise. He removed his glasses and set them on his desk. Anticipated or not, Bennett had his attention.

"Right. An ultimatum." Bennett pursed his lips. "If Janna doesn't get well, if she...you know..."

"Dies?"

"Yeah, right." His face turned red but he soldiered on. "The board, with the backing of the congregation I hasten to add, think we—the church—would be best served if you resigned." Beads of sweat appeared on his forehead. A drop trickled down near his right eye. He swatted at it with his sleeve.

There'd been rumors. James had heard them, but they seemed nonsensical. "You're telling me that my position as pastor of this church hinges on whether or not God chooses to heal my wife? Is that really what you're saying?"

"Because of your faith."

James strained to hear the mumbled reply. "I want to make sure I understand this. It's my faith, rather than God's will, that's at issue?"

"You can put it any way you wish, Pastor. I'm just the messenger." Bennett stood and took a step toward the door, then turned back. "One other thing." He rubbed the stubble of his beard, clearly collecting his thoughts. "You've been here eight years. We—the board—expected more from you." He jammed his hands in his pockets, his jaw clenched in the resolve of his statement.

"You can tell the board I got the message loud and clear." James turned to scan his bookshelf in dismissal. "Please close the door on your way out."

Chapter 2

On Sunday morning James felt rather odd standing in front of the congregation. He had an out-of-body sensation of hovering over the church, looking down at a man he didn't know gripping the pulpit, speaking to a roomful of strangers. He'd pastored three other churches, spending nine years in the one prior to this. When he and Janna had come to this community, he'd hoped this would be their home until he retired. They loved the seasons and the countryside in this locale on the western shore of Lake Michigan halfway up the mitten. Better still, Lighthouse Christian Church appeared to be a perfect fit.

Poised for growth with one hundred thirty regular attendees, in a conservative corner of the state, and with a Board of Directors seemingly willing to let him preach in whatever style and direction he desired, James felt he'd finally found the place he truly fit.

Looking directly at his congregation while he preached this morning, it seemed like the connection he'd had with them had vanished. Perhaps it was just the sense of having been abandoned, but he didn't think so. Some still supported him, but the love affair had soured after only eight years in the pulpit here. For all the Sylvias who continued to come alongside him, there were many in opposition. His soul-searching had been in vain. Nothing made sense.

He spoke once again on faith and healing. Pushing past his feelings of hurt, James preached about how Jesus came to both heal and save, with deliverance in both of these areas integral to the atonement. "The Greek word *sózó* means both to heal and to save and is used in many passages. Look at Isaiah 53:5. 'But he was pierced for our transgressions, He was crushed for our iniquities; the punishment that brought us peace was upon Him, and by His wounds we are healed.' There the Hebrew word for healed is *rapha*, meaning complete healing of body and soul, the same as the Greek *sózó*. Jesus is Jehovah Rapha. He is truly the God Who Heals."

James stressed that one day all true believers will be perfect and healthy. "With many people God decides to wait to give that bodily perfection only when they've passed from this life. He allows the sin in this world to bring us tribulation so as to allow our faith to grow stronger, and so that we can identify more closely with Jesus. He doesn't always answer the prayers of His people for healing right now, as much as they desire that He do so. His decisions in this regard are a mystery, one believers have to accept knowing He is God and far greater than them."

As he continued, it seemed as though a filter of some kind stood between the people in the pews and James on the altar. Were his words—his message—having any impact? Maybe his feedback loop was faulty, but he didn't think so. The heart of the content of his sermon wasn't reaching them. All he could do was pray for the Holy Spirit to penetrate the veil separating him from them. Again, James' prayer went unanswered. The static in the room made him wonder if he stopped in mid-sentence and stepped away from the microphone whether anyone would notice. He almost did it, but cautioned himself that he was called to a higher standard than that.

Few people spoke to him after the service. Sylvia, the lady he'd met at the elevator in the hospital, clasped his hand and leaned in. "I feel an opposing spirit among the people today. It disturbed me and made it difficult to listen to your sermon."

James knew she was one who had the interests of the Lord and the wellbeing of her pastor at heart. "Thanks for your discernment. Please continue to pray for us." She nodded, and he knew she'd follow through. At least she was one on whom he could count.

A couple who had been faithful through the years and good friends, Mark and Beth Nelson, caught up with him. "We so appreciate your encouraging word on faith and healing. We've been praying for you and Janna and will continue to do so." Mark placed a hand on James' shoulder. "In fact, can we pray for you now?"

They gathered close and prayed for him right then. He needed that. They left him with a rare smile on his face.

He saw a cluster of deacons talking. Every now and then one would glance his way, as if concerned he might come near and overhear their conversation. James steered clear of them. When most of the crowd had left, he headed back to his office.

Once inside with the door closed, he sighed. Here he was among friends. Surrounding him were the books he'd learned from in seminary and used in his preaching and teaching. This was his personal sanctuary, a place he could relax, think, and pray. He set his Bible down on the edge of the desk and patted its brown leather cover. With bowed head he rubbed the bridge of his nose where his glasses rested. The Word. It was life. He needed all it had to give; yet something was missing. He wished he knew what.

With so much happening around him: his wife's terrible illness, the church crumbling even as he stood in its midst, and those things outside in the world that he hadn't given much thought to of late, he realized how much stress he was under.

It didn't seem like it would let up any time soon.

Chapter 3

Light reflected off something ahead of James as he walked toward his meeting, the heat of the morning already oppressive. The summer months had been so dry, and nothing in the forecast spelled relief for weeks to come. Pausing for a moment, he looked up to see a workman on scaffolding chiseling at the stone above the courthouse steps. When he saw what the man was doing, he halted, his feet impossibly frozen to the overheated pavement.

Whenever he'd passed this particular spot, he tended to read the inscription put there long ago. The words and intent inevitably put a smile on his face and gave him confidence this nation would endure despite challenging times, a belief he'd carried since his days in seminary. Events of the last two decades had caused him to rethink that optimism.

The words from Isaiah 9:6 written in stone were: "And the government will be upon His shoulders." That prophecy had been written over 700 years prior to the coming of Jesus.

It was as true then as it was now and would be as far as the eye could see. James mused that the road to that future, however, could be rocky and winding.

One more blow of hammer striking chisel and another letter from that Scripture disappeared. A part of him died inside as he watched. The city council, bowing to the demands of atheist groups, which had threatened unrelenting lawsuits, had finally ordered the removal of this verse.

"Separation of church and state." James knew that was so bogus as to be ridiculous. The context of the phrase came from a letter Thomas Jefferson had written to the Danbury, Connecticut Baptists, who had complained about the infringement of their religious liberty by the state legislature. The statement wasn't in the Constitution and meant exactly opposite what many declared it meant. But the argument continued to make inroads in every municipality around the nation as it had for years. Government bureaucrats wanted God written out of the fabric of the nation's existence. The way people framed it today, Church-State separation was a false argument. The founders intended that America's government not impose religion upon the people, not that religion was to be absent from the public sphere. But the fabrication resonated with more and more people who either didn't know any better or who had an agenda for the country contrary to how it was intended. James passed on in mourning, certain he'd never see the institution of government again in the same way.

Arriving at his destination, he entered the church conference room and sat down at his accustomed seat. Several other members of the Ministerium trickled in, and the meeting started on time.

This was another of the seemingly too frequent gatherings of people with whom he disagreed. It's been said that if a person has issues with everyone around him, maybe he's the issue. James couldn't discount that. There were few situations he was involved with these days where he was in agreement with the majority of those in a room. The real problem for James, as he saw it, was his struggle to consistently stand against what was wrong, to boldly voice his position that differed from that of others.

He'd wondered at times why he bothered to attend these meetings. Should there be a point at which he threw in the towel? Up till now he'd justified his ongoing attendance as vital to keeping in touch with the community and other like-minded leaders. Given his tentative hold on all things he held dear, maybe his thinking on this should change.

He looked with envy at Bob Sanders. Clear-eyed and outspoken in what he believed, he was so many things James wished for himself. James kept up regular exercise at the health club and on the hiking trail, but Pastor Bob burst with vitality. James asked him once what he did to get so fit, but Sanders had waved him off. From everything James had observed about the man, he was modest as well as rock-solid in his conservative, strongly biblical convictions, a man dedicated to his family and the church. That confidence gave him a faith that many hated and even ridiculed, all the more apparent when he went toe-to-toe with the other ministers in this meeting. As much as James wanted to emulate Sanders' self-assurance, he couldn't pull it off. When others started arguing, James inevitably backed down, leaving Bob Sanders to stand alone.

Naïve at first when he'd begun attending Ministerium meetings, James, like most people, wanted love and approval. He hadn't said much for or against the concerns that were discussed. Because he kept his mouth shut, the members viewed him as one of their own, even thinking him wise.

In contrast, after a period of time, Bob Sanders' resolve against much of what the Ministerium stood for became evident. He'd told James once that he spoke out because the sentiments of the other ministers violated his personal covenant with God.

James yearned to exhibit a similar tenacity. God had delivered him through great distress and despair in his previously sinful lifestyle, even as He had redeemed his wife in hers. Without Christ, James would have died because of his foolishness. Because God had been faithful, he and Janna made certain promises to Him that they both intended to keep. Speaking up and taking a stand were an outgrowth of James' covenant with God. Except he couldn't do it.

The Ministerium was a group of ministers in the community who met every two weeks. The intent was to lift up the Church in their area, pray for souls, and work toward the common good of the community through their respective congregations. Part of the charter of the Ministerium stated that individual churches would work together on common projects that would give God the glory He deserved. All good as far as it went. What that glory was to look like had mutated over time.

The purpose this week was to develop a new initiative. Because of the difficult issues facing James and Janna, and his struggles within the church, he hadn't spent any time thinking about potential joint projects. As they got down to business, it was clear some of the participants had.

The twelve ministers came from a variety of denominations. How they dressed in large part provided insight into the person and the church tradition each came from. Some dressed in business casual: slacks, button-down shirt, sweater or sports coat. Others wore ministerial collars: starched, white, authoritative. James used to go the business casual route. As he'd come to have less respect for the group as a whole, he'd begun dressing down to jeans and polo shirt. Inevitably he'd get that look from one or two indicative of their disdain. Counting on God not worrying about what they wore when gathered in His Name, James ignored the veiled sneers.

But James' attire was nothing compared to that of Pastor Bob. Today he wore shorts, a well-used polo pullover, and no socks with his deck shoes. This summer he'd come a couple times as if from the gym, wearing sweats and a sleeveless tee. That had really gotten the Ministerium wags on their high horses, but Sanders just shrugged his shoulders and grinned when others muttered about his holy disrespect for God.

"I've been much in prayer," Reverend Phyllis began after the preliminaries and snide remarks about Sanders' dress habits had been dispensed. Dark hair, glasses, stylishly dressed and with a white clerical collar, she led one of the mainstream denominations in town. An outspoken, married lesbian, she boasted that God was working in and transforming her congregation to be relevant to the culture. It left James scratching his head as to God's intent given her flaunting of His natural order in marriage and family. At one time her church laid claim to having most of the prominent leaders in the community as members. It still had a substantial trust fund that would sustain it for a long time, but its number of attendees had dwindled in recent years.

"We have a sizable Muslim population in the area," she continued. "We've done little to reach out to them. We must be more ecumenical in word and deed. It's about time we do that."

One of the two black pastors, Deacon Jones, waved a hand in assent. "I couldn't agree more that we must bring the Gospel to these neighbors. I will correct you, though, Reverend Phyllis, in that my church has been engaged in prison ministry to incarcerated Muslims for some time."

Around the table discussion ensued with each minister contributing ideas or comments. James almost found himself nodding in agreement with many of the thoughts expressed. Sanders sat back in his chair with arms folded, a sardonic smile playing at his lips. It didn't take long for the hammer to drop, making James glad he'd withheld comment.

The leader of the largest church represented, Pastor Tom Hall, PhD, sat forward to weigh in. "After hearing what's been discussed this morning, I'd like to volunteer my church for this initiative." Seating as many as fifteen hundred in every service, this offer of his church got their attention.

Slender, thoughtful in demeanor, and wearing a well-cut, dark blue, herringbone suit, Pastor Hall stood up to address the group. "I've studied Islam for some years now, and I believe we have much to learn from our Muslim brothers and sisters. Because of my extensive research, I'm convinced we must come together jointly to worship our God. Think of the glory we could give Him as our ranks swell and our voices rise to the heavens in unison. Many other communities around this great nation have come together in ecumenical unity. It's about time we joined with them.

"To start this proposal off on the right foot, I would be pleased and honored to invite the local imam to hold a joint worship service in my church. From there we could have our Muslim friends come to each of our churches for similar services."

Deacon Jones stood and applauded. "Brother, that's what I've been hoping and praying for ever since I went into those prisons and saw my persecuted brethren turning to Islam. I said to myself, 'Deacon, you got to bring these men together in one holy place to worship the one, true god, the god of us all.' You got it exactly right, Pastor Hall. Might I accompany you to speak to the imam? I know him well."

"Of course," Hall said. "Your experience with our Islamic brothers is welcome."

Pastor Bob Sanders finally broke his silence. "This is not wise. Jesus commands us not to be unevenly yoked. Perhaps—"

"Pastor Bob," Reverend Phyllis interrupted, "that verse only refers to believers and unbelievers. Clearly that's not the case here. Muslims believe in god."

"They believe in Allah. He's different from the God of the Bible."

"Rubbish!" The good reverend grew indignant. "God is God. There's no good reason we can't celebrate our respective faiths together."

At this rebuke Pastor Bob rolled his eyes and didn't say another word.

Not able to stand it any longer, James knew he had to speak, contrary to how he'd always operated in these meetings. He raised his hand. Reverend Phyllis looked at him, but continued the argument she had started. When she paused, James steeled himself and interjected.

"Excuse me, but you're wrong about Allah being the same as our God."

Some at the table squinted hard at him as he continued.

"I've read a little about Islam, and I know this one thing. The Qur'an definitively says that Allah is not a father and does not have a son. It denies the deity of Jesus and through that implicitly denies the Trinity. Muslims are not believers as the Bible defines us. Either we are in Christ or we're not. We must be born again in Christ to see the kingdom of God. To share a service with followers of Islam is to bring in a leader of their faith who will specifically denounce Jesus as the Son of God in his prayers, which he'll recite in Arabic so that no one knows what he's saying. This is not a good idea."

James saw no point in continuing. He'd issued his warning. Better yet, he'd actually exhibited some boldness. He noticed Bob Sanders glance at him with new admiration while the room sat in silence. That seldom happened in this gathering where one of the participants always had a word to speak.

Deacon Jones broke the stillness. "In my ministry, Pastor James, I've dealt with many Muslims." His tone was full of sorrow. He spoke to James like one might talk to a child. "Muslims are fine people, and we should not judge them. I've learned that they'll quickly and easily accept Jesus even while still worshiping Allah. I find nothing wrong with that. I challenge you to soften your heart; give this initiative a chance."

"Deacon," Bob Sanders said, "It's well and good you want to be inclusive, but the truth of the Gospel is that it's not inclusive; in fact it's extremely exclusive. Jesus must be on the throne. To include a different god in our worship, which is what Allah is, is to corrupt the Christian faith. You're defining the essence of syncretism, the combining of two or more beliefs into one to make something more palatable. What you're talking about is *Chrislam*. That's heresy and exceedingly dangerous, especially for us as leaders and shepherds. God will judge us more severely if we take people off the true path to salvation."

"Oh, how I hate this talk of judging!" Reverend Phyllis pounded both fists on the table. "Please, James, Bob, stop it right now! You're simply not operating in a spirit of love. This is so disappointing."

"She's right, you know. It creates disharmony and bad vibes." Pastor Hall's condemnation had the weight of a final word.

James glanced over at Pastor Bob to offer a little support. Sanders shrugged and mouthed the word, "Vibes."

After this dressing down of Bob Sanders like a wayward child, there was little James wanted to say, but a question bubbled up inside him that he had to ask. "Reverend Phyllis, you're a committed lesbian. How do you think Muslims view homosexuality?"

She tightened her lips into a thin line and stared hatefully at him before finally speaking. "The ones I know have no problem with it." James mouthed a silent prayer for God to forgive her of her arrogance.

Once again Bob Sanders interjected. "Whenever anyone throws out numbers, the usual count is that there are something like one point six billion Muslims in the world. Of those, it's estimated maybe ten percent are fundamental, or radical, if you please. These include active members of Islamist groups such as ISIS, al-Qaeda, Boko Haram, and others, along with many so-called lone wolves who agree with their ideology, but aren't members of a group for one reason or another. That ten percent equates to about one hundred sixty million terrorist types. To rephrase James' question another way, how do you think those one hundred sixty million fundamental-radical Islamists would view your homosexuality, and what do you think they'd do to you if they got their hands on you?"

"This is just so pointless!" Reverend Phyllis threw up her hands. "We're not talking about all those terrible ones out there. What they do is not Islam. Islam is a peaceful religion. We're dealing with our brothers and sisters in our community. Why must you two persist in such nonsense?"

"I wonder how many of these brothers and sisters, as you call them, agree with the ones trying to destroy Israel and the United States?" Once Sanders got going, James loved to hear his hard reasoning.

"It's not pertinent. We must reach out to them."

"We do them no favors by accepting their faith and coddling them. These are lost souls, not Christian brothers and sisters."

Reverend Phyllis stood up with hands on hips. "Is there anyone else in this room who thinks this discussion would go much smoother without such dissent?"

There were a bunch of sheepish nods. No one looked at the two pastors who had made the atmosphere in the room so uncomfortable.

Bob Sanders sadly shook his head, gathered his things, and left the room without a backward glance. The others looked expectantly at James. He swallowed, bit his lip, and followed his fellow dissenter out the door.

Chapter 4

Washington, D.C.

The burly man entering the White House ignored the guards. He didn't care whether they saluted or acknowledged him in any way. They were beneath him and not worth a glance. Arnold Rickards hadn't made it to the top of his profession worrying about the little guy, and he wasn't about to begin now. He took the elevator to the second floor, ignoring the greeting of one more peon in uniform and stepped into the Oval Office.

Frowning, Luisa Parker, President of the United States, glanced up from some documents she was signing. She quickly straightened her pink pantsuit to hide the bulge of weight Rickards noticed she'd gained, and grinned at him. "I didn't expect you so quickly, Arnold."

"I do not waste time," Rickards said, his German accent making the 'w' sound like a 'v'.

"No, you don't." Parker patted the dyed-blonde hair that framed her face with its heavily Botoxed contours. "That's what I like about you."

"My handsome face is not what attracts you to me?"

Rickards was immaculately dressed in a custom-tailored gray suit costing well over ten thousand dollars, as did all his suits. He was, however, anything but handsome. He'd cursed his fate more than once. The swarthy skin of his cheeks was pockmarked, and his bulbous nose was the first feature to grab one's attention.

Parker laughed. "Mary Ellen doesn't have to worry about a thing."

The first out-and-out lesbian to run for and win the presidency, Parker had flaunted her homosexual proclivities from the first with Mary Ellen, the woman who became her husband in a highly publicized wedding as she ran for her initial term. It made her the darling of the media and progressives throughout the nation, leading to a romp through the primaries. The American public, more and more enamored with gender activism, had overwhelmingly embraced her and the LGBT politics she'd espoused in the general election seven and a half years ago.

Before Rickards had a chance to sit, a knock on the door turned his head toward the dark-skinned man striding his way. "Abu, it is good you are here. The better for us all to strategize."

The genius of Luisa Parker's two presidential runs was her pick as VP. Vice President Abu Saif, a devout Muslim, had rounded out the ticket and assured victory. The American public had been told repeatedly by the mainstream media that anything less than electing a lesbian and a Muslim to the highest office in the land would be homophobic and racist. The hapless Republican opposition running another moderate white guy who shied away from any kind of ideological criticism of Parker or Saif had no chance. The political differences between the parties had lessened with the Republicans becoming Democrats-lite. Both parties wanted bigger government. As a result there was little the

Republicans could articulate as to why American voters should choose them. Hence the Democrats commandeered another victory.

That was then. On the cusp of another election, as Parker's tenure drew to a close, the rip currents incessantly pushed politics further leftward. Parker was constitutionally unable to run for a third term. She had often laughingly stated that if it weren't for the 22nd Amendment she'd love to do so, the Presidency being her dream job. Gracefully bowing to the law in her public appearances, and continuing to surf the progressive wave, Parker had endorsed her current VP, Saif, as the person to continue the good times. With the election only several months away, the strategy had provided a solid lead in the polls. Barring disaster, Abu Saif would become the next U.S. president. At the center of it all, strategically and financially, stood Arnold Rickards. Little wonder he effectively owned the White House when he visited.

"The campaign is going well," Rickards said, after the three of them had settled into a corner cluster of over-stuffed chairs. He pointed to the American flag standing in the far corner. "Soon we will make history."

"For a country founded on the whim of rich, dead, white, Christian Europeans," Saif said, "who disrespected people of every economic strata, color, and religion, the changes we're implementing can't come soon enough." His gravitas, the dark good looks of his Egyptian heritage, and his tasteful attire drew people to him.

"We're building on the shoulders of our predecessors, and they were giants," Parker said. "If it hadn't been for the example and actions of Barack Obama and his administration beginning twenty years ago, we'd have never known what was possible. Who would have thought the Republican Congress would totally cave as Obama issued executive order after executive order gutting congressional authority and amassing more and more power to the Executive Branch? Who could have imagined he'd make treaties with nations long considered our enemies and emasculate congressional approval of those treaties? Best of all, how is it possible he almost completely alienated Israel, a nation previously thought to be inviolate as our closest ally? Obama paved the way for us to close every door of reconciliation that we might soon abandon that noxious country. How delicious!"

"In all modesty," Rickards said, "you'll recall I played some small part in all those initiatives in the Obama administration."

"Arnold," Parker said, "you've been my hero in that regard for years. Gun control, healthcare, IRS investigations, you name it; you're a one-man wrecking crew against conservative ideals." She laughed in glee and reached over to squeeze Rickards' forearm. "You have an amazing brain. Now, Abu, it will be your job to carry on to finish the task."

Saif settled back in his chair, steepled his fingers, and nodded assuredly. "I've been speaking with my campaign leaders in every major city. The invasion of illegals that Obama initiated is about to come to fruition. The next president after him didn't stop it, and you certainly didn't in your two terms. Of course, I'm leading in the polls, and that all looks good, but I would never want to count on the American people. They're foolish and exceedingly ignorant about governing, and the proper role of government. Too often they change their minds at the slightest provocation—an October surprise—or some other negative news. The beauty of the tens of millions of illegals in the country, and how they've been dispersed and infiltrated in every Republican stronghold like Idaho, Tennessee, and Texas, is that by definition they're under the radar. No pollster can get an accurate count of them or determine which way they might vote—if they could vote, which they can't legally do."

Saif smirked and sat forward, excited. "As you both know, because the Obama administration orchestrated the dispersal of the illegals, his people knew who they were and where they went, and that work continues. His people did this work because they believed in it. A labor of love. Allah be praised! Those people deep within the bureaucracy now work for us, and we have maintained accurate records of the whereabouts of 95% of the illegals. Most importantly, we have also made a way for them to vote. Voila! An extra twenty million votes coming from nowhere countering any last minute rise in Republican voters will assure my victory."

"It will be the final proverbial straw that breaks the camel's back," Rickards said. "We will bring to completion the transformation of America that Obama began. We will bring about the downfall of America as we know it, paying it back richly for its many sins, and complete its descent into anarchy."

Chapter 5

Western Michigan

James went straight to the hospital from the Ministerium meeting with a heavy heart. Mercifully, Janna was awake. Her bright smile greeting him was such a blessing that tears came unbidden. With a gentle hug he felt the frailness of her body, the weakness that had set in from the many rounds of radiation and chemo treatments.

"Just came from a Ministerium gathering."

"You look like it." She knew him well. It was hard for him to hide much from her, which he didn't want to do anyway. They'd learned that being open and honest with each other was the best policy. Secrets created wedges in a relationship. There were enough problems in the world without causing more in the most intimate relationship they had.

James didn't feel like discussing the meeting, but Janna deserved to hear what was going on in his life. First, though, he got her to relate the little she had to share from the doctors and nurses who'd visited her since he'd last been there.

It seemed a round of highly-contagious MRSA superbugs were sweeping area hospitals. MRSA stood for *Methicillin-resistant Staphylococcus aureus* and was an extremely antibiotic-resistant bacterial infection. Worse, it killed. Knowing that Janna could be exposed to this on top of her cancer made James nervous. The light in her life was already flickering out. If a MRSA infection got in her bloodstream, with her already weakened immune system, he hated to even contemplate how quickly she'd go.

The thing of it was, Janna was more sanguine about her condition than James was. She had told James that she wanted to stay alive and be with him, but she also knew who she was in Christ. That meant she could look forward to death, knowing it was really the beginning of eternal life in His presence. Death had no hold on her; she didn't fear it at all. She had come to accept it as a stepping-stone to something amazing.

Even though James knew all this and likewise believed, the thought of losing her in this life was hard to contemplate.

Getting past the bad news of MRSA, Janna encouraged James to talk about the Ministerium, asking, "What do you think is going on with all these churches and their leaders?"

"It's discouraging, but not unsurprising. We've been seeing this descent from biblical Christianity going on for years now. I think one of the major ways people stray from the Truth is to allow sin into their lives and into the church.

"If someone is righteous and in good standing with God, like Job, Satan has to ask permission to harass and oppress him. Jesus echoed that principle with Peter when He told His disciple that Satan had asked God if he could sift him like wheat."

Janna frowned in thought. "What you're saying is that Satan is subject to God's rule in that if a person's relationship is right with Him, then Satan isn't free to hurt that child of God whenever he wants?"

"There's nothing hard and fast in the Bible that says that. We only get to that understanding by inference in the Job and Jesus incidents. On the other hand, it's pretty clear that when someone sins, he opens a door for Satan to step through. Satan sticks his foot in at that opportunity and can then twist his knife, so to speak, to create mayhem and pain. Unless there's repentance, the crack widens and Satan has more and more leeway to do harm."

"What do you think happened with the pastors in the Ministerium?" Janna had always been fascinated at the interplay in these meetings.

"Obviously only God knows the full story, but since Christians have the obligation to judge other Christians or so-called Christians, we can speculate. I believe that somewhere along the way, these people sinned. They didn't get right with God through repenting and turning from that sin, and through Satan's intervention, the sin has magnified. It's led them down the road of heresy and apostasy. That's why we see acceptance of homosexuality in the Church and this ecumenical melding of Christianity and Islam that's taking place. It's crazy and sad, but the Bible prophesies all this would happen."

Janna was quiet for some time. "I guess all we can do is pray for them, so let's do that."

Chapter 6

September

While these personal issues swirled around James with gale-wind force creating uncertainty in his life, events in the country and world continued to unfold making for highly disturbing news—news that affected him and every other citizen in the nation.

This came home to him when James visited his doctor for a routine examination. Dr. Mason's sheepish expression was out of character. "I'm sorry to have to ask you this, but the healthcare rules force medical providers to get into aspects of peoples' lives we'd rather ignore. This has been a long time coming, and I've held off as long as I can. If we don't ask for and provide responses in every electronic medical record, the government has declared it will withdraw our licenses to practice."

His statement took James aback a moment. He blinked rapidly trying to process what he'd just heard.

Dr. Mason continued in a monotone. "The regulations demand that we ask whether or not you own one or more firearms." His jaw tightened. "Do you?"

James gave a nervous laugh. "You've got to be kidding."

The doctor's rigid posture accentuated his response. "I'm afraid not."

"What if I refuse to answer?"

"It gets ugly. If only three of my patients refuse to provide this information, black marks go against me. If I accumulate seven such marks, the licensing authority will shut me down."

"That's absurd," James said. "That's the stuff of police states."

"Tell me about it. It gets worse—for the person who won't answer."

A great wariness came over James. "How's that?"

"I mentioned the electronic medical records. The IRS has initiated a direct link to every doctor. They'll see your denial and enforce the mandate against each patient. I'm not sure what they'll do, but it'll probably be unpleasant. Perhaps audits or other harassments."

Being a minister of the Gospel didn't mean James was a pacifist. They lived in a rural state that valued its freedom and independence, and he owned guns. However, the federal government knew that already. After all, to purchase a weapon required a background check from the dealer. The purchaser also had to send a copy of his concealed carry permit to the local governing authority—police or sheriff. Nobody could tell James the information wasn't available in some secret database. He found it hard to believe that all this personal data collected wasn't stored somewhere to be used at an appropriate time.

Yet here they wanted more information again in another form, and he wasn't about to comply. As much as he regretted being the cause of black marks against Dr. Mason's right to earn a living, James was fed up with the ever-growing number of intrusions the government was making into everyday life. Call him non-compliant. Call him rebellious. There was too much going on with the nation's overweening government. Darned if he was going to help them take away his Constitutional rights.

He looked at Dr. Mason and shook his head. "I'm not going to answer the question."

Dr. Mason shrugged his shoulders and slumped in his chair. "I thought you might say that. You're certainly not the first."

"I'm sorry, Doc."

"That's alright. I'm getting along in years and was thinking the hassle of being a doctor was more than I've been enjoying it these days."

He completed the exam, and pronounced James fit and healthy. They shook hands. James wasn't sure if he'd see Dr. Mason in this capacity again.

Chapter 7

Immersed in sermon preparation for the upcoming Sunday, James didn't even look up when he heard the knock on his office door. "Yes?"

His secretary, Delores, poked her head in. "Your counseling appointment is here." Delores had come with the ministerial position. A long-time member and employee of the church she did her job competently enough, but James had the impression she put up with him out of duty rather than personal affection. It had never been a problem for James even though he would have preferred a more cordial relationship with the woman.

"Show him in."

"Her." Delores never had qualms about correcting James.

"Oh, right." James set aside his notes and looked up expectantly.

He hadn't had any real interaction with the female who entered. She and her husband had been attending Lighthouse Christian Church for several weeks. They had spoken to James only once in passing as they exited following service. Delores had given him his calendar of appointments for the week, and he hadn't recognized the name. The accompanying note indicated she desired to speak to him regarding marriage counseling.

Delores began to close his office door after she'd shown the woman in, but James had a rule. "Please leave that open, Delores." She should know better. James had always insisted on transparency when counseling a woman, and always made sure Delores or someone else was nearby. The last thing James ever wanted was for there to be the appearance of impropriety.

In her twenties and extremely attractive, the woman who entered the room wore a short dress and a low-cut blouse. James noticed these things in passing and did his best to keep his eyes averted

"I'm so thankful you agreed to see me. I'm Sheri Woodley." Her blonde bob-cut hair bounced as she moved her head while talking. Her green eyes contrasted with her ruby-red lipstick. She reached across the desk to shake hands with James, revealing more of her cleavage than he preferred.

Many people new to the Lord often continued to dress the way they had prior to finding their way to a church. Until people began reading the Bible and sitting under preaching and teaching they simply didn't know any better. James accepted this fact. Until the heart changed, the life wouldn't change.

After they'd chatted for a couple of minutes, James got to her reason for seeing him. "You're here about your marriage? Tell me what's going on."

"Nelson and I have been married for two years..." She gave him some particulars and began to describe some of the troubles they'd been having.

James listened, asked questions, and took some notes. He quickly realized Sheri had little understanding of what it meant to have a personal relationship with a loving God. Her conception was of a distant being, stern and judgmental. Apparently her husband Nelson periodically abused her.

"Just last night Nelson forced me to go to bed with him." Sheri got up from her chair and came around the desk next to James. "Look at these bruises on my legs." She lifted her skirt to reveal black and blue marks on the inside of her thighs. "Feel them. Can you believe it?"

James hadn't expected this close encounter that Sheri initiated. Immensely uncomfortable, he pulled back. "I believe you. Please sit down, Sheri."

But she was insistent. "Really, you have to see what Nelson did to me." Practically on top of him, she bent down and grabbed his hand forcing it to her thigh. Her lips brushed against his through her unlikely advance.

It was too much. James tried to push her back while at the same time sliding his chair away from her. His face flushed with heat. "Sheri. Stop it! What are you doing? You're going to have to leave." She retreated back to her chair as he called out, "Delores? Delores, please come in here!"

When Delores didn't appear, James made a wide circle around Sheri and strode into the hallway to Delores' office. She wasn't there. Frustrated, he stood outside his door. "I want you to leave right now!"

Sheri pouted and straightened her dress. "Can I see you again?"

Astounded, James said, "Not without your husband."

"Fine." She had to pass by James to leave and leveled her green eyes at him. As she did, a smile played on her lips. "See you, lover boy."

After the sound of the outside door closing reached him, James shook the tension from his clenched hands. He'd had his share of flirting women and veiled invitations over the years, but his love was for Janna alone. Thankful that womanizing was one vice he didn't struggle with, he wondered what had happened to Delores.

She didn't reappear until several hours later, claiming she'd had a personal emergency with which she'd had to deal. She hoped it didn't inconvenience him much.

***

Around the block, Sheri got into the waiting car. "Did you get them?"

The man at the wheel tapped his intelliphone with its advanced camera functions and grinned. "Sure did."

Chapter 8

The end of the week brought the quickly arranged but heavily promoted Christian-Muslim event to be held in Pastor Tom Hall's megachurch. In the meantime, Janna had been moved to a nearby nursing home and given over to hospice care. The hospital had done all they could for her. Since its marching orders were to rush patients out the door to generally maximize reimbursement rates from Medicare, Medicaid, and insurance companies, shorter stays were in the financial interests of most hospitals. The doctors had determined Janna soon would die. In that case, no sense in wasting a good hospital bed.

In the church James had taken a wait and see attitude. He performed his duties, continued much in prayer, and wondered how God would manifest Himself in the situation.

Friday was the day of prayer for Muslims. To honor them Pastor Hall invited the imam and his congregation to use Hall's two-thousand-seat sanctuary that day for their joint Christian-Muslim service. Although James disagreed with the concept, he figured he had to see it for himself to appreciate the full scope of his opposition.

Being somewhat embarrassed to even be associated with this dishonoring of God and His Son, James donned dark sunglasses and a Detroit Tigers baseball hat to go incognito. In his pocket he stuck his intelliphone with a high-quality recording application. He felt a little ridiculous, but that was the price he paid to see how bad this debacle would be.

It turned out to be every bit that. People flocked in the doors early, no doubt wanting good seats. It may have been that members of the congregation were told in advance that a portion of the seating would be removed to provide space for the Muslim worshipers to spread their prayer rugs on the floor in the very center of the auditorium near the front. That put all other attendees behind and to the sides of the Islamic followers.

That was ironic in a way, or perhaps purposeful coming out of the negotiations Pastor Hall and Deacon Jones had with the leaders from the mosque. Islam demanded that all other religions were subservient to it, so for its followers to be front and center was appropriate.

As people took their respective places, James wondered if there had ever been a single instance in which a mosque had hosted a strong Christian pastor giving him the opportunity to preach Jesus. He knew the answer: none. It was a rhetorical question.

James stayed near the rear in order to observe, and had his fill from that distance. At one point he thought he spotted Pastor Bob Sanders, likewise being discreet in attending.

The Muslim call to worship, the adhan, began the service. The muezzin sang it out in Arabic from the altar as he would have for every prayer and worship event at his mosque. It was haunting, and terrifying that it should come from the pulpit of a Christian church.

It all went downhill from there. A couple of Christian worship songs were sung. They had an oddly flat quality to them. James thought of the incident recounted in the Bible in 1 Samuel. Eli the priest had two ungodly sons, who nevertheless also served as priests. The wife of one of the sons, while she was pregnant, learned that the Philistines had killed her husband, Phinehas. At that time the enemy captured the Ark of the Covenant. When she gave birth, and before she died moments later, she named her son Ichabod, saying, "The glory has departed from Israel, for the Ark of God has been captured." In this time and place James had the distinct impression that the glory of God had departed from this church.

The imam continued the service, speaking parts of it in Arabic and some in English. Not being a scholar of languages, James had no idea what he said in those obscure parts. Other than a few Arabic speakers who might be among the Muslims, he suspected that no one else understood him either. Because he'd come into this service highly suspicious of the proceedings, James recorded what the imam had to say. Later, he sent the recording to several independent translation sources and learned more than he wanted. The imam praised Allah and defiled the church by proclaiming that all who worshiped any god other than Allah as the one god alone was a blasphemer.

When he subsequently reflected on the imam's proclamation, James realized the man had effectively denounced the deity of Jesus. In doing so, he proclaimed the spirit of antichrist in the church itself. If nothing else, James had read his Bible and knew the Word of God. It said that whoever denied Jesus is the Son of God was a liar and hated the Father. In allowing this proclamation from the pulpit, Pastor Hall facilitated and allowed the desecration of his church. It nauseated James to think about it.

As the event proceeded, there was much excitement among the congregants from Pastor Hall's church and the many who attended from the Ministerium members' houses of worship. It seemed that the ecumenical atmosphere and demonstration of diversity in action was a wonderful thing. The pastors involved all bowed when the imam prayed and cheered themselves as more tolerant than other church leaders. James sensed the pride and arrogance that arose, hanging like a darkening cloud that enveloped the sanctuary. When Pastor Hall gave his sermon, he extolled the virtues of living together, Christian and Muslims, as brothers in faith.

While watching this self-congratulatory activity, James kept reminding himself that these were the actions of lost people. It was easier to see the Muslims as lost and without life or hope because they had never known the One true God manifested in His Son, Jesus Christ. For the pastors leading their flocks down this road of falsehood and deception, and the congregations that followed these men, it was harder for James to love them as Christ said he must to all who are lost and without Him. These were people of the Book. They had the Bible as God's inerrant, inspired, infallible Word. How could they have read the Scriptures, presumably preached them each week, and not known that this was an abomination to God? What were they thinking?

Toward the end of the service, the pastors encouraged the men of their joint congregations to join their brothers on the prayer mats in the front where both Muslim and Christian bowed toward Mecca. They asked the women to congregate in an area to the side. James knew that apostasy would rise and the love of many would grow cold as the time neared for the return of Jesus, but he never realized he'd see it close up.

When he couldn't take any more, James slipped out the rear of the church, saddened more than he could say.

Chapter 9

In the coffeehouse down the street, James sat and contemplated what he'd seen. He prayed for the Muslims, that God would supernaturally appear to them, as He had so much in recent years to their brothers in the Middle East. From many reports he'd read, in those dreams and visions Jesus Himself had often come and spoken His message to them: He is the way, the truth, and the life. From receiving those appearances, many Muslims came to deep repentance and real, committed faith, ready to die for their Savior.

Likewise, James prayed for those Christians and those who called themselves Christians who were willingly going astray. He asked God to give him a soft heart, not hardened, but with a desire to warn and show them how far from God they were traveling.

James was in an out-of-the-way corner of the shop with a view of the door. As he took a swig of his now tepid tea, he recognized the person who had just entered. The man turned, and James waved to him. Gadi Benjamin held up his index finger, giving him a "hold on" sign, ordered from the counter, and came over with a worried smile.

They greeted each other with a handshake and affectionate hug. Gadi settled in, and they caught up with each other. What he had to convey wasn't good.

Gadi was a Jew from Israel in the U.S. on a work visa. With dark hair and Semitic features, few would think him other than Jewish. He and James had met one day by the side of the road. James had seen someone struggling with the tire of his car, and on a whim stopped to help. In a freak occurrence the car had run over a discarded motorcycle helmet. It had rolled up and gotten stuck in the wheel well, causing the car to stop moving. The man was trying to free the remains because it had frozen his tire in place.

James wasn't the handiest of men, but he did have experience changing flat tires. It appeared this guy didn't. James had helped him jack up the car, loosen the lug nuts, and eventually remove the tire to get at the mangled helmet. They got it all back together and Gadi couldn't enthuse enough in thanking James. That began a friendship.

Gadi's outlook, like many Jews, was secular. He accepted there might be a God, but it didn't sway him one way or another. In learning James was a pastor he didn't shy away from him as some people did, rather it interested him. He was open-minded, and they began meeting and talking. James had been happy to witness to him, particularly emphasizing Isaiah 53, which Gadi had never previously read. He hadn't converted yet, but Gadi listened and interacted with great attention.

For the last several years, Gadi had been involved with high-tech software development. He leaned forward and said, "Have you heard today's news?"

"No. Been busy this morning." Seeing his friend's somber demeanor, James mirrored Gadi's posture.

Gadi ran his hands over his face. "It is terrible. I have worried about this for some time seeing the attitude of this president and previous administrations toward Israel."

James shared his concern. The President of the United States had an apparent active hostility toward Israel, America's only true ally in the Middle East. They both agreed that if relations worsened it could only lead to trouble. Gadi came at this situation from his non-faith perspective, geopolitical in nature. James saw it through the lens of Scripture. The Bible stated clearly that any nation that blessed Israel would itself be blessed, a nation that cursed Israel would be cursed. The U.S. had always been a friend of Israel, and the nations had deep ties that had come back multiplied as blessings. That had changed of late. America had begun treating Israel as an enemy, supporting those whose fervent desire was its elimination, to drive its people into the sea.

Gadi could hardly speak the words. "This morning the president severed all diplomatic ties with Israel. She recalled all embassy personnel and stated that every visa here would be revoked. She set this nation on a hostile footing with the only democratic country in that area. It is crazy!" His accent thickened. "But there is more." His agitation turning his face red, Gadi told James the rest of what had happened that morning after the president's announcement at the United Nations.

When Gadi finished, James reacted in stunned silence. Unable to find any other words, he finally said, "That's incredible. Horrible. What's it mean for you?"

"It is unbelievable. She gave us a two-week deadline to leave the U.S." Gadi rubbed his neck. "The president doesn't care about our families, our jobs, how we leave, just that we do. She said anybody who is still here after the deadline will be apprehended by the authorities and imprisoned."

James had little to say in response. The morning's events were beyond the pale. What had happened was an abomination. It was harsh, unrealistic, and more dangerous than the president and most people in the country could imagine. This would invoke God's wrath even more than what had previously been done with the multitude of national sins such as promoting abortion, embracing the homosexual agenda, abominating the marriage covenant, and many more. The nation was in real trouble. It left him feeling helpless.

They spoke at some length until James needed to leave. The lunch crowd had come and gone. Surprisingly, Gadi let James pray for him and their two nations. They parted ways, with James not sure—just like with his doctor—if they'd see each other again.

Chapter 10

Washington, D.C.

The presidential announcement at the U.N. that Gadi Benjamin had reacted to so strongly had likewise stunned Israel. Severing all diplomatic ties between the two nations was bad enough; the aftermath proved tragic.

Two hours after personally making the declaration in an address at the United Nations, President Luisa Parker watched the TV monitors back in the White House with great satisfaction. Talking heads on Fox, CNN, and all the other major news outlets blathered on in astonishment; most expressing admiration for the president's courage for this significant diplomat move, yet ignoring the elephant in the room that had occurred during worldwide television coverage.

In its follow-up reporting, the media uniformly expressed the view that time had long passed for the U.S. to abandon this much-hated nation. Time and again it had demonstrated its intolerance and racism toward its Palestinian neighbors who yearned only for a place to call home. Obama, in his stint in office some twenty years prior, hadn't forsaken Israel completely, although he'd made noteworthy movement toward that objective. The succeeding president likewise hadn't made the final move in a four-year term, but under pressure had edged away a little further.

President Parker similarly hadn't undertaken this earlier in her two terms. The reason for her hesitation had been the subject of much speculation because of earlier campaign promises. Was she preparing the way for further actions by her vice president, Abu Saif, when he presumably won the election and entered the Oval Office early next year, leaving the ultimate split to him? Would the U.S. create a stronger diplomatic alliance with Iran as a follow-up to earlier treaties that literally opened the door for it to pursue its nuclear weapons program unfettered by economic sanctions? The scramble by all the pundits in their search for truth made Luisa Parker chuckle in glee.

The truth of the matter was simple, yet hidden from all but those closest to her. At the very core of her being, Parker hated Jews because she hated the concept of a God who would judge her. If this God existed, He would judge the decisions she made and the lifestyle she lived. That was unacceptable. As a loudly declared out-and-out married lesbian advocating to one and all the virtues of judgment-free love, she couldn't stomach the idea of a God who condemned her for the choices she made about her lifestyle. Because this God had come from the Jews—from Israel—her antagonism and wrath focused initially on them. She had bided her time, complaining nightly of her frustrations to Mary Ellen, but not willing to play her hand too quickly. Now she determined was the right time. Once she'd taken care of Israel, the Christians would be next on her agenda.

In the U.N. meeting, once the president had taken her seat following her proclamation, a stunned Israeli Prime Minister had risen heavily when recognized by the Secretary-

General and walked slowly to the podium. A chorus in the U.N. chamber of hisses, boos, foot stomping, and table pounding accompanied him. After allowing himself thirty seconds of silence before speaking by simply gazing at the people in the room, he began by denouncing the president's statement as one that would lead to greater instability in the Middle East and the world as a whole. Shouting began with men and women standing and shaking fists at him. The clamor and chaos rose to fever pitch among the delegates. Several threw shoes at the prime minister. The tumult became so great that he stepped away from the microphone. Anger at Israel and its representative peaked with the diplomats of four of Israel's neighbors rushing toward the front, rage filling their faces. Alarmed, the prime minister shouted at the security guards for help. They didn't move. They stood casually with arms crossed as though they'd been told to rest at ease.

The men reached the dais and clambered toward the object of their loathing. The prime minister found his route of escape blocked by two guards who stepped into his way. He tore at the men's shoulders to cast them aside but they didn't budge. The attackers came upon him from behind and threw him to the ground. Three held him down while the fourth kicked him again and again in the ribs, groin, and face. By this time the prime minister had stopped struggling. The men switched positions and another began taking out his hatred in the most physical way he could.

From her seat above the fray, Luisa Parker had watched the spectacle with grim delight. Blood spattered the stage and the clothing of the four men. The raw lump of flesh that was the Israeli Prime Minister, shapeless and unrecognizable in his once-immaculate suit, lay still where he'd fallen. Panting hard from their exertions, the men left the platform. Many of their colleagues gave them high-fives as they returned to their seats. At a nod from the Secretary-General the guards dragged the lifeless body away. Business resumed as if nothing untoward had happened. The long-standing hatred of this august body toward the most despised nation in the world had finally given vent to action.

Reviewing the scene in her mind, Parker nodded to herself as the rightness of it all convicted her once again. It was one of the reasons she had bonded with Abu Saif when they'd first met. He wanted nothing more than for Israel to be driven into the sea, completely ruined and forgotten as a nation. Little by little the U.S. had inched toward that objective. The time was nearly here. Parker, in her role as president, desired that as her legacy. Just as Reagan was known for destroying the Soviet Union, she wanted the destruction of Israel as hers; that, and the final takedown of the United States as a superpower in the world. Once all her plans came to fruition, that goal would also be achieved.

Chapter 11

As a pastor, James regularly visited members of the congregation who became hospitalized, as well as the few elderly shut-ins at their homes. It felt different being in the hospital without Janna there.

He first stopped to visit Marge, who was recovering from heart surgery. The doctors said she'd handled it well since she was previously healthy and only in her early sixties. Although weak, she smiled when James entered and pointed at the chair. "Sit down, Pastor, and tell me all the happenings in the church. Sylvia came yesterday and filled me in on some, but I enjoy hearing it straight from the horse's mouth."

James sat down and arranged the chair so she could see his face. Despite his best intentions, the news upset the sweet lady. The monitor showed her blood pressure spiking, and he almost pushed the nurse call button. Instead, he took her hand as inspiration came to him. "I want to pray for you, Marge."

She nodded and closed her eyes.

"Lord, Jesus, we ask that your peace surround this dear sister. I pray your health and healing in her life."

As quickly as he finished, her blood pressure moved back into normal range. She settled back against her pillow with a contented expression on her face. "I love prayer. You know, it's ridiculous that your position should be predicated on the move of God through Janna's healing. What you just did, that was the act of a shepherd for one of his sheep. I so appreciate you, Pastor James.

"I can't tell you how much that means to me. Sad to say, I think you're one of the few willing to buck the growing consensus that I'm a failure."

She asked him to read the Bible to her. He finished with Psalm 23, reading it in the King James Version, knowing her preference that other translations didn't do justice to the depth of expression and lyrical quality in this version. After giving her a hug and gently kissing her forehead, he left.

From the hospital James made his way to Janna in the nursing home. The cancer had progressed to a point of no return, yet today she looked so much better that he began to hope the doctors were wrong and indeed God would do a miracle.

The doctor had placed Janna under hospice care to assure her comfort. In hospice treatment for disease stopped, while medication to ease pain became the priority. Janna's pain reduction seemed dramatic in relation to her condition. James had a brief gloating moment as he projected Janna's return to church in perfect health, while the elders and deacons stood with downcast eyes, ashamed of their disbelief. Sometimes thoughts like that came from nowhere and he'd say to himself, "How did that happen?" But he knew the truth. Many times they originated with Satan, outside of himself. The enemy constantly wanted God's creation to swell with pride or arrogance as part of his deception and war against the One he would usurp. Because of his hatred toward Jesus, Satan would do anything to take people out of relationship with their Father in heaven.

James shook it off, asked the Lord to forgive him, and turned his attention to Janna. He brought out Scrabble, and they played several games. As usual, she beat him. They were both strong in English, but most of the time she was cleverer with words. He didn't mind losing. He enjoyed that he could be with her in any capacity.

Her meal came, and James sat with her while she ate. Later, he took his leave. He held her face, looked into her eyes, and told her he loved her. He kissed her on the lips. She drifted off to sleep as he waved goodbye from the doorway.

Chapter 12

Maryland Shore

The two men stood on the beach facing each other. The excessive heat over the past months had roiled the Atlantic more than usual. The ocean's waves crashed in with a thunderous roar, pounding the sand and eating the shoreline. The encroaching water struggled to grab at the men's shoes. So intense was their discussion, the sea's invasion didn't faze them.

Abu Saif was not pleased. The excuses General Wylie, the top ranking officer in the U.S. Army, had given were unacceptable. "You know this purge began way back during Obama's tenure. You had no problem implementing it then. Why this sudden fit of moral clarity?"

"Sir, I've had a change of heart. These are good men. They've served their country well. I've seen their records, talked with their commanding officers, spoken with them, played with some of their kids. They don't deserve to be exposed and left hanging."

Saif jabbed his index finger into the general's chest. "You will do what you've been commanded to do."

General Wylie straightened his shoulders. Even his military jacket couldn't hide the impressive physique of the man. "What if I don't?"

"You'll be court-martialed like some of your underlings who refused to comply. Your glorious career will be in ruins."

"And here I thought you might shoot me like you've ordered my men to fire on innocent U.S. citizens."

Clouds overhead skipped across the sky, fueled by overheated air currents. Saif glanced up at a squawking seagull hovering in the thermals. His jaw tightened. "You will not disobey direct orders from the Commander-in Chief."

"With all due respect, sir, I've had enough. That woman has no business running this country. I'll no longer allow the Executive Branch to gut the military and for you people to mold it into your personal, ideologically pure, security force. I will not let my men be used as pawns so that you can assume control of this country through dictatorship. My men who oppose this, as do I, will not give in to this suborning of our nation's principles. It's pathetic how few men are left in the armed forces that will stand up as true patriots and defenders of the Constitution. You've destroyed it with your social experiments. You've created robots that jump at your progressive orders. I'm telling you, no more!"

"You're not getting the message, General. You have no choice."

"I actually do, Mr. Vice President. I'm going to the conservative media with this. You may control the major news outlets, but you still can't prevent talk radio from getting this out, let alone conservative bloggers and websites. Your administration has whittled away at their numbers with all your *fairness* initiatives, but enough are still out there to convey the message. It may no longer be fair to hear anything but your progressive dogma because anything else is intolerant, but people around the country will hear about this, and you'll be stopped."

"That's your last word?"

"Yes, sir."

Saif shook his head. "So be it. You're dismissed."

General Wylie saluted and turned, walking at an angle across the beach toward his car. Saif caught the eye of one of his Secret Service detail in the rise of a dune peppered with brush. He made a slashing gesture across his throat. His protector raised his eyebrows questioningly. Saif nodded, giving assurance of his intent, and the man melted into the dune scrub.

Chapter 13

Western Michigan

The culture wars had taken direct aim at Christianity, getting much worse over the prior two decades. James worried about his friends who owned a small photography studio. Mark and Beth Nelson had dedicated the business to the Lord when they'd first opened and had adhered to their faith in their work. Unabashed Christians, they had decorated the studio by bordering each wall with Bible verses. Someone coming in couldn't help but know where they stood with God. To make it even more apparent, they didn't let an opportunity go by to witness to anyone gracing their premises. These were people who lived out what they believed. It was exactly these kinds of folks that the homosexual lobby had focused their sights.

Every day for years the news brought word of a Christian provider—florist, baker, photographer—who had denied celebrating a homosexual couple's wedding. Inevitably, their heavily financed litigation partners targeted the Christians. In the course of normal business the provider served the homosexuals without restraint or bias. Because God was clear that homosexually was a sin, just as much as lying or stealing, many Christian business owners had determined they wouldn't violate God's standards and their own faith by participating in such a wedding. The Supreme Court had ruled that gay marriage was the law of the land. It implied that the First Amendment freedom of religion was a lesser right. When Christians pushed back in denial, homosexual activists brought out wrath, rage, hateful words, and even deeds.

Thus far, Mark and Beth had slipped under the radar of the activists. They provided loving, gracious service to everyone. They had biblical principles they refused to disobey. As attacks mounted throughout the nation, James had wondered how long it would be until the Nelsons were targeted with the inevitable. He found out when he answered his cell phone.

Mark got right to the point after a brief exchange of greetings. "It's started."

They had talked about this many times. James knew where the conversation was heading.

"A longtime gay customer came in with his partner wanting us to photograph their 'wedding.' I told them I loved them, just as Jesus loves them, but God's standard is that we don't facilitate or celebrate sin, which is what a homosexual lifestyle is. Our original customer took it okay, but his partner went ballistic. Yesterday we were served notice of a lawsuit. This morning, we've been the object of an intense Internet attack. Every social media platform has erupted against us. Our website has been hacked. It's like the whole world is targeting us. We're receiving death threats. People are saying they plan to burn down our building. I don't know what to do!"

James had been on his way out the door to the hospital. He immediately reversed course. "I'll stop over. See you soon."

Beth appeared calm when James arrived; it was Mark who was frazzled. Yet James experienced the same sense of peace entering the studio as he always did. There was a presence of the Lord there that few places had. God had blessed the Nelsons in that business. He had multiplied their reach and provided for them financially. They had given back to the work of the church through substantial tithes and offerings, helping people in need, and even opening their home to those in distress. There were few on the Left for all their preaching about tolerance and love who gave and helped like Mark and Beth.

Besides the Bible verses, as with most photography studios, many photos lined the walls: individual portraits of smiling families and individuals, wedding and graduation shots, glorious photographs of beautiful sunsets, mountains, and beach shores. There was always something lovely to look at in their place.

James saw they already had a tech guy working on their computers. They talked about the situation and what the future might hold. "What about the various threats?" James asked.

Beth was resolute. "We can't—we won't—allow them to make us afraid. Our fear is in the Lord; He has instructed us not to fear man. Whatever happens we're going to trust Him."

Mark nodded in agreement, but James knew his heart. If it came down to it, if something happened to the business, so be it. His concern was for Beth and her safety. He knew his role as a man of God was to protect her and their children.

"What about your kids?" Their two children were ages twelve and fifteen.

"We haven't heard of any problems today so far," Mark said. "I've been asking God to keep them safe." They were at a vulnerable age, subject to intense peer pressure. With something like this, it was impossible to know how their friends and acquaintances would react.

From a rational perspective it was difficult to understand how decent people could be on the receiving end of such vitriol. Fortunately, Scripture made it clear. From the beginning of James' walk with the Lord, end-times prophecies had fascinated him. Numerous passages declared how the morals, ethics, decency, and love of people would decline drastically. Things in the world would be turned upside down as the time of the return of Jesus grew nearer. One of James' favorite passages, in the book of the prophet Isaiah, proclaimed graphically what was happening before their very eyes: "Woe to those who call evil good and good evil, who put darkness for light and light for darkness, who put bitter for sweet and sweet for bitter. Woe to those who are wise in their own eyes and clever in their own sight."

Remembering the verse, James reflected on the sad state of mankind. "The world really is turned upside down. Men pretending to be women, and vice versa. Pedophilia on the rise and proclaimed as healthy for children to get in touch with their sexuality. It never ceases to amaze me how prophetically accurate the Bible is. Paul says in Romans, regarding those who fall prey to this thinking and dive into the sin of homosexuality, that God gives them over to a depraved mind. Think about that. A depraved mind! I wanted to understand that better, and looked up the word 'depraved.' It means corrupted or evil. I think about that when I consider what's going on here and what these people have done to other Christian businesses around the country. It's evil, and it's sad. The tragic thing is that these people who are doing this are forever lost and subject to God's wrath, judgment, and eternal damnation unless they repent and turn from this to a life of trust in Jesus Christ. We have to keep praying for them."

"That's why we dedicated the business to God as we did," Mark said. "He saved us from that awful fate. If He can do it in our lives, He can do it in the life of anyone willing to come to Him."

James hugged them. "You're both great." No customers came in, and they spoke several more minutes. Before James left they prayed. He told them, "One way or another, this will all work out."

Beth's final words were a tribute to her faith. "It always does with God in control."

Chapter 14

A hot, dry wind blew sandy grit into his face. James shielded his eyes, wondering when he'd been transplanted into the Sahara Desert with its strong Sirocco winds. True, these blustery blasts came from the west over Lake Michigan and its sandy shoreline, but he'd not experienced anything like this in his years here. People were worried about the tinderbox the area had become. Normally September brought moderating temperatures and the hint of winter to come, but nothing like that was in the forecast.

The few thin and fragmented clouds high in the sky raced from one side of the horizon to the other. The sun beat down its relentless heat. The only joy experienced in these conditions was by those who ventured into Lake Michigan. Because of the depth of the water, its temperatures reacted to the winds and weather. When moderate temperatures prevailed with mixed winds, the surface of the water often had a chill even in summer. For the water to be comfortably swimmable in September wasn't typical.

Breathing harder than usual against the onslaught of wind rather than from the exertion itself, when he reached the hospital from the far end of the parking lot, James detoured into the hospital bathroom. He rinsed his face and held wet fingers pressed against his eyelids to cool himself down. With eyes still closed he fumbled to grab a paper towel from the mechanical dispenser. He worked the lever and got…nothing. He opened an eye and saw the darkened, opaque box was empty. With a sigh, he turned to the electric hand dryer. He bent and stuck his head under the hot blast of air with only minimal success.

He made his way to the fourth floor to find Marge from the church, hoping her heart condition had continued to improve. At her room James peered in and saw the bed was empty and made up. Confused, he double-checked the room number to assure he had the right one. It was correct.

He asked at the nearby nursing station where Marge was. The young woman gave him a smile and spoke in a European accent, "I was off the last couple days. Let me check."

She tapped away at her keyboard, frowned, tapped again. "She's been taken to an isolation unit on the third floor."

"Isolation?" James said. "What's the problem?"

She glanced around the area. "You're the pastor, right?"

"Yes." He began to pull out his ID card.

She held up a hand. "That's okay. I'm not allowed to divulge information except to family, but she talked about you in such glowing terms, I think that qualifies. The notes in her record say she has an infectious case of MRSA."

His reaction to her kind words halted at the bad news. "I saw her yesterday, and she was fine."

The nurse nodded. "Looks like routine blood work confirmed it. It says here she experienced a severe outbreak of symptoms on her skin, and she developed shortness of breath, among other things. It's a serious case."

"Oh my. What room did you say?"

He found Marge's room and learned he had to wear a gown, latex gloves, and a mask to enter. She was sleeping, but restless. Her head rocked back and forth. He heard her mumbling, but couldn't make out the words. James stood by her bed for a while, thinking of this good woman and reflecting on how she'd been faithful in the time he'd been at the church. She had supported Janna and him, and for that he truly appreciated her. Because she loved the 23rd Psalm so much, James read it again to her. Whether she heard it in her sleep, he didn't know.

Chapter 15

Wednesday, September 11, 2028
Minneapolis

The morning dawned clear and bright, much like a similar day twenty-seven years prior to this one in New York City. Rachel Oswald kissed her husband, Derek, goodbye, and bundled their three children into her minivan. School had started the week before, but in one of those maddening events that Rachel never understood, the school system held a teachers' institute day the following week. That meant kids' classes were canceled today as the teachers gathered to be instituted, or something. Rachel thought it was the silliest thing to begin immersing the children into their schoolwork, only to take them right back out of it. Regardless, she figured she'd take advantage of the situation. Since Derek wasn't much on going shopping, let alone at the Mall of America, and for the fact that he had to work, he'd said, "Better you than me." Besides, he complained, "Too much stuff. Too many choices."

That was true. The mall boasted five hundred some stores and had almost five million square feet of store space. It comprised a small town in itself with over twelve thousand employees and its own zip code. Rachel thought, *How could someone not love it?*

Despite their kids having started school, Rachel considered this excursion a final fling of summer. The children were twelve, ten, and nine; Amy, Patrick, and Donny in that order, plenty old enough for her to keep them in tow without losing them. Just in case, she'd previously purchased special GPS kid tracker units that she attached to chains and hung around the kids' necks. She admitted that in a place this large, though they were well-behaved and usually stuck close to her, the possibility existed for the family to be separated. The trackers gave her the means to reunite if the unexpected happened.

The parking lot had already begun to fill when they arrived at 10:30, a half hour after the mall opened. They made their way to the entrance, waved goodbye to the outdoors, and entered wonderland. Because the kids loved their Legos, they first made their way to the huge Lego Store where they gazed in awe at the massive creations whose bright reds, blues, and yellows dominated the interior. Dinosaurs, castles, fighting robots, princesses in distress, it was a place for imaginations gone wild. After taking their turns at helping to build a life-size military helicopter, Rachel agreed to purchase another Lego set the children could share.

Leaving paradise, they meandered their way along the endless line of shops, gawking in store windows, each child exclaiming how wonderful such and such a dress, book, or toy would be. Rachel had heard it all before but smiled at her children's exuberance. She made them wait while she tried on several pairs of running shoes. They sat together and good-naturedly argued about who got to play with their new Legos first. They usually behaved themselves well, which was one reason Rachel inevitably looked forward to a day like this spent in their company. She wished Derek had more tolerance for the mall, but couldn't fault him too much. He made up for it by taking the children to sporting events and other activities that held little attraction for her.

"You hungry, kids?" Rachel asked as they left the shoe store. They responded with a chorus of "Yeah!" and she led them on the hike to the food court. As they entered the huge area with dozens of eateries, the insistent buzz of hundreds of diners assaulted them. Rachel surveyed the tumultuous scene and saw that some take-out places already had fifteen to twenty people waiting in line. The sit-down restaurants, far out of her budget, also had lines snaking out of them.

"Amy and Patrick, see that area over there? Looks like there might even be an empty table or two. I'll take Donny. Okay, no argument. Today we're having tacos."

Patrick opened his mouth to object, but Rachel silently pointed her index finger at him, and he stopped before uttering a word. "Go, you guys." Her two oldest said, "Yes, Momma," and scampered in the direction she had indicated. She grasped Donny's hand, and they waded into the crowd toward the takeout taco place she'd selected.

The ten-minute wait to order passed quickly as she people-watched. The mall attracted all sorts, and it never failed to amaze her what people wore and how they comported themselves in public. She had gotten used to the massive influx of Muslims who had come to the Twin Cities area to make their homes. Having reached this Mecca of freedom and capitalistic enterprise, it was their lack of assimilation that disappointed her.

Rachel watched the Muslim women in their hijabs. Why would they wear such constrictive head coverings? There was even a woman in a full-body burqa. Goodness! How could she do that? Rachel considered herself as tolerant as the next person. As such, she welcomed one and all. But hadn't many of these people escaped highly questionable conditions in their trek to America? Weren't they trying to get away from a lifestyle that promised nothing other than more poverty? Why then, Rachel wondered, would they willingly live in segregated, government-funded enclaves? Why would they congregate in crowded conditions when they had the entire United States in which to spread out? She didn't understand Islam and all its rules. It made no sense to her.

Strange tongues rose all around her. Rachel struggled to comprehend why these people couldn't, or wouldn't, speak English. Numerous newspaper articles had informed her that many of the immigrants to Minnesota made no effort to learn the language of their new land. To her thinking, it was almost as if they wanted America to accommodate them with their ways and traditions rather than they change to meld into the American way of life.

She had read newspaper articles noting that some cities had set up parallel judicial structures after Muslims had pressured their governing councils. The response of those in charge had been to allow the implementation of Sharia law courts side-by-side with the traditional court system. This allowed Muslims to be tried according to Islamic dictates and outside the jurisdiction of American law. Rachel wasn't well-versed in these matters, but she felt instinctively there was something wrong with this.

At this myriad of thoughts, Rachel sighed and took her place at the counter to order their meals with Donny at her side. He had been quiet most of their wait but now tugged at Rachel's sleeve. "Momma, Momma, look at those men up there!"

"Wait, Donny. I have to finish ordering."

"But, Momma..."

"Shush!"

At that moment, bursts of gunfire from automatic weapons erupted overhead with amplified shouts of "Allahu Akbar!" More gunfire began coming from every compass point around her, then a series of ear-splitting explosions. Rachel looked in the direction of the first sound and saw Donny's finger pointing that way. The floor above ringed the massive food court, and at the railing stood a number of masked men wearing black and firing down into the crowd around her. Screams erupted. A hail of bullets cut many cries short. Bodies fell all around her. Rachel shrieked for Donny to get down even as she pulled him to the ground and covered his body with hers. Fire and smoke rose around her. Dying moans and free-flowing blood assaulted her ears and eyes.

In that next instant, she remembered Amy and Patrick and panicked. She tried to push herself up from the floor and realized someone had fallen on her. Gunfire pulsed in the air of the food court but began fading out. Explosions rocked the ground beneath her, but the sounds seemed to indicate the gunmen were on the move. Rachel's hand slipped in the puddle of blood at her side. She crashed back to the concrete with an "Oomph!"

Letting go of Donny's hand she wriggled out from the dead weight of the man who lay inert on her. She pushed him away and freed Donny from the man's body, grabbing his shoulder. "Come on, Donny. We have to find Amy and Patrick!"

He didn't respond. "Donny! Come on. You've got to move. You have to be brave." No response from the boy laying face down. Rachel's chest heaved as her eyes widened in fear. She cried out, "Donny?"

With a quick jerk at his shoulder, she turned her son over. At the sight before her, she raised her face to the ceiling far above her and wailed, "Noooo!"

Bullets had riddled the entire left front of Donny's chest. His face was constricted in a painful last grimace. Tears flowed down Rachel's cheeks as sobs arose from deep within her. It was more than she could bear. But she still had to find Amy and Patrick.

She covered her face with her bloody hands. Pulling them away, she saw the gore that had spattered from those lying slain around her.

On shaky legs she teetered over and around the fallen men and women near her. With a desperate glance back, she saw Donny's broken body and forced herself to search out her other children.

The layout of the food court had changed. Everything lay in shambles with hundreds of dead resting uneasy in varied positions alone and heaped one on the other. The explosions from earlier had cratered the floor, leaving large holes she had to skirt to make her way. When she thought she'd found where she'd earlier directed the children, she scanned the area. The massive toll of death weighed upon her, but she couldn't yield to that despair. Her children came first. Where were they? In a moment of inspiration she pulled out the GPS tracker to help locate them.

Wherever it appeared someone lay over someone else she ran to push, tug, and pull the mass to reveal what was beneath. Over and over again she came up empty. Her little strength ebbed in hopelessness. She moved one final corpse and gasped.

Beneath a large man Amy and Patrick lay grasping one another in a death hug, part of each of their heads blown away. Rachel sank to her knees, not conscious of the pain as they struck the hard floor.

Her shoulders slumped, her life, her love gone. Rachel beat her chest and ripped at her clothes. Her words echoed in the killing field around her, "Why, God?"

Chapter 16

Western Michigan

James pulled up outside the nursing home where Janna had been taken. He halted at the sight of an ambulance. It triggered a panicked memory. The last time he'd seen Marge was right before she exhibited the symptoms of her MRSA infection. His heart caught in his throat. "Lord, don't let anything more happen to Janna."

The heat soaked his shirt as soon as he exited the car. He wiped his brow at the door of Janna's room. His fears had been realized. James watched from a corner as the EMR personnel prepared to take her back to the hospital. This morning she had displayed MRSA symptoms. Despite her being under hospice care, the nursing home wanted nothing to do with the problem and had called her doctor. She was now on her way back to the very place the MRSA had originated.

And that was the problem. James was certain he'd been the carrier bringing it from Marge to Janna. Why hadn't he gotten it? He remembered reading about MRSA, recalling that it struck the weak whose immune symptoms were compromised. James was healthy, but he was the transporter. Typhoid Mary. MRSA James.

Back in his car following the ambulance, James balled his fists and beat on the steering wheel. *I'm the cause. It's my fault Janna has this!* He could barely breathe thinking he could be the instrument of her quicker death.

James waited with Janna in the ER for hours until the hospital assigned her a room. Just like Marge, Janna didn't look well. Seemingly overnight she'd shrunk as the illness consumed her. Periodically she would rise to consciousness, say several indistinct words while trying unsuccessfully to focus her eyes, and slip back into deep sleep. The time went by slowly. It gave him much opportunity to reflect, pray, and wonder about the future.

Janna and James had been married twenty-six years, having tied the knot the spring following 9/11 after they graduated from seminary. James took his first church that fall. They had no children, and both their parents were deceased. Before she died, Janna's mother professed saving faith in Christ. To the best of their knowledge their other parents had died without Him.

Over the years, James and Janna noticed that a longtime trend in many churches had been to proclaim someone who attended church and died as being with the Lord. After much study, discussion, and prayer, they didn't agree that was necessarily the case. They believed the Bible clearly informed the reader what was necessary for someone to go to heaven. Reading more deeply, they saw it commanded believers to look at the fruit of someone's life. No one could know the heart of another, but those walking with Jesus could certainly see how another person lived out his life, whether it exalted the flesh and the things of the world, or Christ Himself. If that person didn't live as though fearing the Lord, the conclusion they'd come to was that individual should be seriously concerned for his eternal destiny. Janna and James tried to help their parents understand and live this, but they never saw the repentance and turning to God that would have convinced them their parents personally knew Jesus. They could only sadly assume they didn't, and that James wouldn't see his parents nor Janna her father when they themselves went to heaven.

As a pastor, James knew this concept angered many people. They wanted the unconditional love of God but not the flip side of Him as a righteous judge who condemned people in their sins if they hadn't been cleansed by the blood of Christ. He could only tell them, "Read the Bible."

An attendant eventually rolled Janna's bed to a room. The whole scene was depressingly familiar. James had hoped that Janna wouldn't have to return here. MRSA was the number one killer of patients in hospitals. It was scary to think people came to these places to get well, and that very environment killed them. He remained until visiting hours were well over and left with a heavy heart.

Chapter 17

Police officers put their lives on the line every day. Sometimes the bad guys defeated them, and they lost their lives. The funeral of a policeman who died, particularly in the line of duty, often attracted many law enforcement officers from nearby communities as they paid tribute to their fallen comrade.

The policeman who recently lost his life had found it some years previously. He was a Jew who had come to faith in Jesus Christ. The Messianic Jewish congregation he attended was small, not really equipped to handle the overflow of men and women from the local and neighboring police forces that came to pay their last respects.

Although James didn't know the slain officer, he had heard about his final battle and respected him. James showed up at the modern, one-story church building late because of visiting Janna at the hospital. He saw he wouldn't be able to get inside for a while. The line of officers waiting to say goodbye snaked out the door and down the sidewalk. He resolved to wait in his car until the line dwindled somewhat. It was a good thing he did.

The heat was relentless. It hadn't rained for months. The humidity wouldn't leave. James found it amusing that Washington elites no longer hesitated to use the term "global warming" once again versus the previously preferred "climate change" when temperatures weren't so steamy. The foolishness of labeling weather as climate continued unabated.

James parked down the street with a view of the church and the mixed crowd of police and civilians, presumably members of the congregation and other friends. A man with a swarthy complexion walked past him toward the church. For such a hot day, he wore a heavy jacket that was out of place.

As the man passed James, a strange sensation seized his gut. It spoke of danger. With heightened concern, James watched the man approach the crowd. The need to cry out in warning drove him to action. He struggled to unfasten his seatbelt and reached for the door handle. The man pushed his way through the uniformed mass to the outraged cry of several. He paid no heed.

James emerged from the car and took two running steps toward the church. He was about to yell an alert when he heard a faint echo rise. "Allahu Akbar!"

He shouted, "No!" and was lifted off his feet as a horrendous blast erupted from inside the church and moved outward with the force of a tidal wave. The explosion threw James across the street.

His ears rang with deafness. A kaleidoscope of red, black, yellow, and gray overwhelmed him, but he couldn't hear a thing outside his head. Smoke and fire poured from the building.

Entangled in a rosebush, he pushed away as sharp thorns caught him. They jabbed his bare arms, drawing pinpricks of blood. He brought his hand to his forehead. The blast had knocked off his glasses. He found them in the rosebush and settled them on his nose. That action brought a sense of normalcy, and he realized the thorny insult of the rosebush was nothing. His eyes stung, and with another swipe of his hand recoiled at the stickiness of blood. Feeling around he found a gash on his head bleeding copiously. But his injury, compared to the mayhem around him, was trivial.

Bodies lay everywhere. Mangled blue uniforms lay scattered like bowling pins. The church itself had half its front wall and part of the roof blown away. Flames licked at anything flammable. Many human torches writhed on the ground. Hearing came back to James like the snap of one's fingers.

From a distance sirens howled. In minutes, multiple fire engines and ambulances arrived. James staggered closer and saw the mangled bodies missing limbs, faces half torn away, blood everywhere. He couldn't comprehend the carnage.

He tried to pull himself together. He needed to. That was his job. James was one who could provide emotional support now and later. As awful as it was for him to see the slaughter, the psychological damage to those still alive and to the families would be much worse. He raised his eyes to the heavens and implored God to provide him the strength to give of His comfort.

Toward evening, the effort of coming alongside people throughout that day had exhausted James. They needed to talk, to cry, to lament, to express their anger, even their hatred for the perpetrator. He tried simply to be there for them. Few words could bring reassurance in a time like this, and he spoke little. The need was to hold a hand, hug someone, or just sit next to a grieving, questioning person, being a physical presence.

Word had spread about what the attacker screamed in his last moments. Every person there knew he had acted in the name of Islam, the so-called religion of peace. Not so shockingly, as had been their practice for many years, the media reported that the motive of the bomber was unclear. City officials joined the club and disavowed any Islamic involvement. It was a maddening repeat of the willful blindness that had so often been the official response.

The problem contradicting this ludicrous obtuseness was the rash of similar attacks throughout the nation the same day. Shopping malls, police departments, Jewish centers, and churches had all been targeted on this celebratory day of Islam's greatest victory against the U.S. A proud pronouncement came forth from a group claiming to be affiliated with the Islamic State terrorists that had run roughshod over the Middle East. It warned they would soon destroy the United States and Israel. Their official announcement stated they had accomplished three objectives in this attack. The first was to destroy Jews, the second to annihilate Christians, and the third to decimate the law enforcement structure in the U.S. That many capitalistic business enterprises had also been devastated in a number of the attacks was an added bonus.

The president of the United States commented that no verifiable proof had come forth indicting Islam. She stated that she had decided to withhold judgment until the FBI had made a thorough investigation. One of the memes that subsequently went forth was that Christian radicals had staged the various events to frame Muslims. In mere hours, many segments of the public called for the burning of Christians at the stake. The Republican presidential aspirant, to the continued disappointment of most in his dwindling base, refused to "apply labels", while the Democrat candidate, the current vice president, wondered out loud when Christians would be held accountable for their many atrocities throughout the centuries.

Locally, the story that eventually emerged and took hold was a confluence of the various narratives. The attacker had a personal vendetta against the police because of a recent run-in he'd had during a routine traffic stop. His Christian beliefs twisted his moral compass causing him to kill as many police as he could. Like Hitler and all other Christians, he hated Jews. The funeral became the opportunity to exercise his perverted rage. As James listened to all this, he knew it was absurd to the point that one had to either laugh or cry, or both, at the deliberate ignorance behind the assertions. Either way, tall tales were being fed to the public, which largely swallowed the lies.

In looking past the media template to the terrorist group's statement, James had to admit they'd made a pretty good start with this target. It was a brilliant attack in the sense that they'd gotten a triple play, with all three of their goals achieved. The Messianic Jewish congregation held to their Jewishness, yet proclaimed Christ as their Lord. Because the funeral attracted a large number of policemen, they'd wiped out many with a single blow.

Despite the Islamic acknowledgment of culpability, the powers-that-be refused to change their song. Islam was misunderstood and peaceful, a religion that built up rather than destroyed. Anyone contradicting this storyline obviously didn't understand Islam and were racists. Because most people didn't like being labeled as such, particularly opposing politicians, the description continued to circulate that Christians were the malcontents and a threat to the well-being of the United States. It was despicable, and those who refused to turn a blind eye could only shake their heads in disbelief.

A further outrage came with the Ministerium calling for a Day of Repentance for Christians who held ill will against Islam. The issue became one in which guilt was placed on the shoulders of those to whom the harm was done, while the responsible party—Islam—became the victim. A city-wide call went out to all Muslims and Christians to attend the service once again held in Pastor Tom Hall's megachurch.

James couldn't bear to observe that one, but later heard it was a great "success." The ministers present jointly apologized to the good people of Islam for the unfair characterization that so many Christian congregations around the country heaped upon them. They vowed to work more closely with Muslims and their communities to bring these two great faiths into harmony.

The distressing aspect of this to James was that Islam worshiped a false god. Allah was not the god of the Bible. To promise Christian unity with Islam was to unite light with darkness, the One true God with the spirit of antichrist. Rather than delivering a lost people from their deception, the Ministerium, and all who supported their initiative, were calling Muslims into further darkness and causing Christians who didn't know better to fall into the pit of false teaching. This wasn't a loving action on the part of these ministerial leaders; it was demonic.

Chapter 18

The flurry of activity ministering to the hurting kept James busy over the next several days from early morning until late at night. Periodically he would look at a clock and see that once again he had failed to make time to visit Janna. The doctors had declared no hope for her recovery, and he couldn't even spend what were likely her last days with her. In the midst of his demanding schedule, he began slipping into a shallow depression. Hours would pass, and he'd kick himself because he couldn't break free. Someone always needed him, and James felt the obligation to be there. Yet, didn't Janna need him, too? Didn't he need to be with her?

Late at night James would drag himself into their home, his body rebelling at the strain, his eyelids drooping from lack of sleep. He felt guilty on another front as well. It had recently become apparent their cat wouldn't last much longer. She'd been with them from her infancy—twenty years. Pepper had gotten slower the last couple of weeks, not eating much, and beginning to drag one of her rear legs. She'd always been Janna's cat, despite their having gotten her together. Pepper had bonded with Janna and seemed to express perpetual bewilderment as to why this strange man lived in the same house with them. The situation led to many amusing encounters over the years. Now Janna wasn't here; Pepper was also dying, and James could do nothing for either of them.

During this crazy time, James managed to call Janna several times but reached her only once. Every other time she didn't answer the bedside phone, perhaps asleep or somewhere in the hospital for further tests. The one time he caught her wasn't satisfying for either of them because she could barely stay awake. She had to hang up abruptly as she dropped off. He held the cell phone in his hand, saw the terminated call, and uselessly said, "Janna? Janna?"

Later that same day, James received terrible news. Sylvia, the prayer warrior and faithful visitor to those who were ill, called him. "Pastor," she said, "I'm at the hospital."

His heart beat faster as he envisioned the worst for Janna.

Sylvia began sobbing. "I went to see Marge. You know she had the heart problem and then got MRSA? Her bed was empty, and I asked at the nursing station where she was. The nurse got this look on her face and said, 'She died a couple hours ago.' Oh, Pastor, I missed the chance to see her!"

His emotions swirled at the report. He was greatly relieved for Janna, but grieved at Marge's passing. "She knew the Lord, Sylvia. That's our consolation. Surely she's rejoicing right now in His presence."

"She was a good woman."

They spoke several more minutes, both of them reflecting and sorrowful. James expressed his gratitude for Sylvia's faithful service to the Lord and His church. Inwardly he wished more people in their congregation had her heart and wouldn't submit to gossip and a critical spirit.

At the call's conclusion James had a revelation that struck to his very core. He realized he was a major part of the problem. As the shepherd of the flock, what had he done to quench this dissension? If people gossiped and criticized, shouldn't he as the pastor have discerned it earlier and stopped it immediately? He was guilty.

Upon grasping that truth, James fell down on his knees. Covering his face as tears flowed, he repented. A wrenching gasp for air doubled him over in the pain of his sin. The congregation had only done what he allowed it to do. "God forgive me," he whispered.

This was a difficult time in his life and in the culture, but he had no excuse. Yes, the church needed people to focus more on Jesus than the distractions around them. James, because of his position, needed to do that more than anyone. He could only ask God for His mercy for his spiritual blindness.

Pushing himself up from the floor, James' mind flitted back to the death of Marge. He vowed to see Janna the next day, regardless of the needs of anyone else.

Chapter 19

Marge's family asked James to perform her funeral. He was already having trouble keeping up, yet it was right that he should lead the celebration of her homegoing. Somehow, he sandwiched in time with her family to learn their anecdotes and fond memories. Her husband had died several years ago. Her children recounted their cherished recollections. They cried, prayed, and planned.

Many from Lighthouse Christian Church, along with other friends and family, attended the service. In their grief, they recognized a life well lived and all gave praise for it. James had the opportunity to preach the Gospel and drove the message home.

"When a believer dies, that person knows where she's going. Marge knew without a doubt. She'll be with the Lord forever. What a joyful certainty! What about you? Do you wonder what's next after this life? Are saved by the blood of Jesus?"

Following the service a longtime friend of Marge approached James. The older man hadn't stopped weeping since the end of James's message.

"Your words struck at my heart, Pastor. When I'd speak to Marge, she always impressed me with her passionate trust in Christ, but I couldn't bring myself to renounce my life of sin." He paused with a sob. "But if I don't, where will I end up? Not where Marge is. Will you help me?"

A younger man whom James knew to be a nephew of Marge had joined them. His voice breaking, he said, "Sir, me, too. I need God in my life. What can I do?"

"Truly repent of your sins and trust Jesus with your life. It's as simple, and as hard as that."

The three spoke for several more minutes, with both coming to new life in Christ. James thanked the Lord as they departed, knowing that for a minister of the Gospel, there's nothing better than a person's salvation.

In contrast to these whose hearts had softened, some had attended the funeral from his church whom James had seen watching him closely. He'd discerned that critical spirit he struggled against so much himself. Here, it was directed toward him. He sensed the same issue that had put his pastorship at the church in jeopardy. These people had concluded that he'd failed at his job. Why? Because the Holy Spirit's healing power wasn't present. In the view of his critical congregants, he must be at fault for the lack of the gifts of the Spirit in their church.

Afterwards, James deliberated again on that possibility. He paced his living room at home and argued with himself. *I'm the leader of this Body. It's my responsibility to encourage the flow of the Spirit. I have to have the faith that He'll rise up and move among us. But does everything have to fall on me? Don't the people of this church have to exercise faith?*

It left him conflicted. Without that faith, how could they please God?

That begged the question: Why wasn't faith present that led to the supernatural move of the Holy Spirit? James considered the nature of sin and the work of the devil. Many times he'd read the writings of the Apostle Paul. He wrote that believers effectively open a door for Satan to enter into their lives when they sin living as carnal Christians.

Great sadness overcame James. No doubt the sin of gossip and a critical spirit had infected the church. *We've invited Satan to the party.*

How much harm had been done? How much was that damage inhibiting the flow of the gifts of the Spirit? James feared it was more than they knew; yet because of that, the focus fell on him as the shepherd of the flock.

He settled in bed that night, alone and downcast, with only a weak and dying cat for company.

Chapter 20

Brrrinnnggg. Brrrinnnggg. James struggled up out of a deep, dark place at the electronic warble of the phone. With a groan he reached in the dark, fumbled with the receiver, and got it close enough to croak, "Hello?"

"I'm sorry to disturb you, Pastor."

"Yes?" James squeezed his eyes shut and rubbed his face, wading through the fog of sleep to place the man's voice.

"Pastor, it's Mark Nelson."

Nothing clicked. Still not registering the caller's identity, he repeated, "Yes?"

"Somebody torched our photography shop tonight. Destroyed it—burned it to the ground. Deliberately! Police said there's no doubt. It's arson. They found gas cans."

James' mind snapped into clarity. "Someone made good on his threat."

"I'm afraid so."

"Mark, I'm so sorry. Are you and Beth okay?"

"Physically, yes. But they wiped out our business. Records, client lists, negatives, everything—destroyed." A sob stopped the flow of Mark's words. He coughed before continuing. "How are we going to survive? They took away our life's work. What am I supposed to do to take care of my family?"

James heard the tremble in his friend's voice; he clenched his fists in anger. It was hard to reconcile. People got so incensed by the Nelson's refusal to celebrate a homosexual union with their services that they'd eradicate their livelihood. Despite the man's turmoil and sense of helplessness, Mark's next statement blew James away.

"Pastor, this has shaken us to the core, but somehow God will provide. It's the person who did this that grieves us most. Beth and I are already praying him. The perpetrator is someone so deeply obsessed with the thought that homosexuality is right that he's lost his moral sense. He needs God's help."

Mark was right. James hadn't gotten to that place in his thinking. He didn't know whether he could even get there. Mark and Beth had. That was the mark and Spirit of Jesus in them. James could only marvel.

A couple of hours later he stood on the street in front of the burnt-out shell of the Nelson's photography studio. He thought about the Bible verses that had adorned the walls, and God's promises of protection. But James also remembered that He never said the lives of Christians would be easy. In fact, Jesus said that because He was persecuted, His followers would be also. A life of following Jesus Christ was filled with spiritual riches; the truth was that the riches of this world were only temporary. This latest development in Mark and Beth's life demonstrated that clearly. Regardless of how faithful one was, earthly possessions could easily come and go.

James made sure the Nelson's had what they needed for their physical well-being and returned home by noon. Flipping through the mail, two pieces caught his attention. One came from the IRS. He opened that first.

In bureaucratese, with which the IRS typically communicated, the agency informed James that he was in non-compliance with a reporting requirement. The violation required him to submit certain paperwork within seven days. There were times when James read a letter of this nature, his mind wandered, and the gist of the words on the page totally escaped him. That happened now.

He shook his head, grabbed a glass of water from the faucet, and tried again, this time reading more slowly. With comprehension came outrage.

He recalled his visit, where Dr. Mason, effectively under duress, had queried him about the firearms James owned. Upon his non-cooperation, Dr. Mason had warned him of repercussions. This appeared to be the beginning of that.

The IRS declared its knowledge of his owning weapons and demanded an accurate accounting. It ominously stated that further actions would be taken by the agency if James did not comply with the exact specifications of this letter.

He thought of the doctor who said his medical practice might be in jeopardy if enough people like James refused to provide answers in the medical context. He muttered, "That's so wrong."

Irritated at the demands, James tossed the letter on the kitchen table. He paced throughout the house fuming. In the bedroom, Pepper, their old cat, lay curled on her fluffy, pillow-like bed. He stroked her gently after ascertaining she was still alive. When he'd calmed down a little, he returned to the kitchen and to the letter.

He didn't need to think too much about this. He'd come to the point in watching the degradation of the laws and the very Constitution upon which the country was built that he knew he had to resist. He remembered the old Star Trek series with Captain Picard who encountered a massive invasion force known as the Borg. They were a collective, interconnected society intent on destroying everything in their path. In a way their culture was like government gone wild: overweening, overpowering, and impossible to counter. The phrase they uttered to Picard became a classic.

"Resistance is futile!" Resistance to the IRS had the same feel. James knew it would ultimately be futile, but he couldn't comply with their demands. In the next several moments he shredded the letter to confetti.

Turning back to unopened mail he spied an envelope without a stamp, with simply his name typed on the front. The typed note inside said, *Meet me tomorrow at 5:00 PM River Road Park by the bridge*. There was no signature.

That was odd. James couldn't remember ever having received a mysterious letter like this. With no idea who sent it, he figured the writer would see him and identify himself—or herself, assuming he went. His curiosity got the best of him. Why not?

He made the time that afternoon to visit Janna, continually regretting how little opportunity he'd had to be with her. It wasn't right or fair; James had let her and himself down because of all the other obligations of late that he'd undertaken.

Too weak to sit, she smiled up from her pillow. It pained him to see her in this condition. A nurse and an aide came in to help turn her; she was so feeble she couldn't do it herself. They treated the bedsores she'd gotten, those inflamed sore spots from constantly lying down. James' knees trembled, and he had to sit and look away for a moment to gather his composure. He swallowed and wiped away the tears.

They talked a bit—well, he was the one mostly talking; Janna had little strength to even do that. He brought her up to speed on all the events going on: the Ministerium-Muslim service, Marge dying, the fire that destroyed the Nelson's business, and the peculiar note for the meeting the next day. So as not to upset her, he didn't mention the IRS letter.

Despite her weakness, with a flash of prophetic insight, Janna said, "The Ministerium is more deeply involved than you imagine."

Janna had often operated in the prophetic with dreams and visions. James knew the revelations came from God because they always exalted Jesus, and they came true in a verifiable way.

"What do you mean?" James couldn't fathom what she meant.

She gave a frail shrug. "That popped into my head. The Holy Spirit has been with me a lot as I grow closer to entering the presence of the Lord. He brings me peace. He's also given me Words of Knowledge for the workers taking care of me."

The statement she made that James heard most clearly was the one about entering the Lord's presence. Her admitting she was soon going to die caused him to shudder. Neither of them had shied away from the reality, but her speaking it was too much. "I can't bear the thought of losing you!" he cried. "How can I go on without you at my side?" James lowered his head and sobbed. She touched his hair gently and rested her hand alongside his cheek.

"The Lord has something special for you. He's shown me a picture of you standing upon a crumbling wall with a bullhorn to your mouth. The sun is about to be eclipsed by a cloud. The skies in the distance are dark and threatening with bolts of lightning streaking down to the earth. People in the field look up at your amplified voice in alarm. Some are running toward you, others away."

"What does that mean?

"I don't know."

Chapter 21

Wall Street – New York City

Surrounded by rows of earnest young men and women yelling into headsets and typing furiously on computer keyboards, Arnold Rickards waited for the expected shouts of triumph. Tension rose within him, but he was used to it and kept it well under control. Eyes throughout the room darted back and forth between the two large screens occupying their desks. Wall Street trading had been hectic that day. It was about to become more so.

The man standing beside Rickards in a trim, gray Brooks Brothers suit with a red-checked Brioni tie twitched his fingers at his sides. Rickards noticed his companion's apprehension from the corner of his eye. "Remain calm, Edward. I have faith you'll come through."

"Yes, sir, Mr. Rickards. I'm sure everything will work as planned."

In a low voice, Rickards said, "You have much riding on this."

Edward gave him a grateful smile. "You've placed much trust in me."

"I chose you because you're very good at what you do. I only hire the best people. And I pay them commensurately."

Edward lifted his wrist. "Thirty seconds." He waited several beats. "Almost there."

The men watched in silence while the clamor continued all around them. Simultaneously the major news networks lit up on the many monitors placed strategically around the trading floor. News anchors on Fox, CNN, CNBC and every other outlet that carried financial news began babbling about a major software hack of each of the largest airlines in the country. United, American, Delta, and Southwest computers had all been infiltrated. Flight control systems in every plane owned by these companies had been compromised. Each of the airlines had shut down operations immediately. All planes were grounded indefinitely. The only thing experts agreed upon was the disruption to travel in the U.S. and the financial toll it would take on the entire airline industry.

The anticipated shouts erupted throughout the room from the eager young people at their computer consoles. "They're going down!" "Look at United plummet!" "They're dying like quails!"

Rickards nodded his head at the news. "Congratulations, Edward."

"Russian hackers have proven to be very skillful. From the time we first made contact, they had their strategy and software completed in a month. Quite impressive."

"Indeed. The results speak for themselves."

One monitor on the wall showed the rapid share price decline for the four companies singled out in the news. They had lost from $7 to $12 per share. Rickards recalculated in his head what he had done many times before. By selling each stock short with the massive number of shares he'd acquired, the price decline made him hundreds of millions. Soon his boys would close out the trades; Rickards would take his profits, and he'd move to his next financial coup. He didn't mind leaving a little money on the table by exiting the trade earlier than some would, but he wasn't greedy.

More shouts from around the room. "I'm out!" "Closed here down!" "Big day for the kid! That Porsche 918 Spyder is mine!" Each of the traders knew the commissions they'd racked up for this day would more than pay for the toys they enjoyed.

"What about you, Edward?" Rickards asked as they made their way back to the Executive Suite. "Do you have your eye on something for this day's work?"

"I'm buying gold and silver."

"Really? Why is that?"

"You've said it yourself, Mr. Rickards. Events happening in this country will lead to greater instability. Best to be prepared. What better hedge in a time of uncertainty that the currency of the ages?"

"Very wise, Edward. You're a bright young man, but you know it because I've told you that many times. You continue to impress me. Keep up the good work. You'll go far."

"You're my idol, Mr. Rickards. I couldn't ask for a better and more successful mentor."

They parted at the door to Rickards' office. "Keep your eye on the prize, Edward." Rickards winked at Edward and watched him as he walked away down the hall. Trust was a fragile commodity. Despite Edward's current fealty Rickards knew such faith wasn't necessarily forever.

Chapter 22

Western Michigan

The leaves on a smattering of trees in the park had begun to turn with the approach of fall. The continued heat and lack of rain had kept the color change at bay, but the season was changing despite the thermometer. Some gold, some red, some orange, leaves on a variety of trees speckled the landscape with their array of colors. James sat on the stone railing of the old bridge that crossed the creek and enjoyed the solitude. His melancholy mood dissolved as God worked in his heart with this short time spent in the beauty He had created. It made James remember that God was in charge; regardless of what happened, those in His will would always have the privilege of His presence. James needed that assurance after spending the time yesterday with his dying wife.

Deep in his reverie, he didn't hear the footsteps on the bridge until the person stood right beside him. He glanced up to see a familiar face.

"How are you, James?"

He blinked, surprised to see that his mysterious visitor was Pastor Bob Sanders. The two of them hadn't spent much time together outside the Ministerium meetings. Sanders' steadfast forcefulness on moral and spiritual issues made James envious. Sanders knew where he stood on biblical doctrine and never buckled to the liberal contingent at the Ministerium. Truth be told, James had wilted on some items of discussion in those meetings that he wished he hadn't. In so doing, he'd left Sanders standing alone. He didn't understand to this day what enabled Sanders to hold fast to his convictions, while James felt the necessity to give in and compromise. It left him feeling inferior, not a strong follower of Jesus Christ like this man consistently demonstrated.

The man's secretiveness made him wary. "What's going on, Bob?"

Sanders lowered his eyes. "I...I have to apologize to you."

That startled James. "What for?"

"Pride. It's gotten in my way. I know you believe much as I do, and we're the only ones opposing what the Ministerium is doing, but I've never taken the initiative to really partner with you."

"What's pride got to do with it?"

"It leads to arrogance. In my spirit I've felt that I'm better than you. That's wrong. Will you forgive me?"

James took a moment to consider Sanders' surprise confession. He fiddled with his glasses by removing them and rubbing the bridge of his nose. A speckled yellow leaf floated down from a nearby oak tree. The creek was low from the extended drought, but the flow of the creek was still fast enough to rush the leaf away as soon as it touched the water.

"Why are you saying this now?"

Sanders bit his lip. "Because of what I've learned."

"About the Ministerium?"

Sanders nodded. "That and more. There's...stuff going on, dangerous things I found out. I don't know what to do about it."

"You want my help?" This man was normally so self-assured that James didn't know what to make of it.

"Yes. I'm sorry, but I have to share this burden with someone else. I can't carry it alone."

With little encouragement, he told James what he'd seen and heard. It was worse than James could imagine.

Sanders set the stage by recounting a series of accidental, overheard conversations and extensive sleuth work. He related that he'd learned the Ministerium intended to fully embrace Islamic teaching and to meld it with their version of Christianity in their churches. Yet this was not a local or recent phenomenon.

"The Muslim group encouraging this," Sanders said, "and engaging in this infiltration is well known. They've been at it for years. You're aware of the Muslim Brotherhood, right?"

James nodded.

"The group encouraging Chrislam is connected with the Brotherhood. Their very DNA dictates the overthrow of western civilization. I'm probably not telling you anything new, but prominent members of the Brotherhood have been proclaiming their intent for decades. Not surprisingly, governmental leaders in the U.S. have ignored their activities—known as civilizational, or cultural, jihad—and the Church has been asleep."

The advocacy of this group promoted the melding of Islam and Christianity into Chrislam. It made participants feel good because it exuded tolerance and multiculturalism. Its politically correct nature appealed to many who disliked being called names such as racist, exclusive, and bigoted.

Sanders stopped talking for a several minutes while a couple of teenagers holding hands crossed the bridge. The girl giggled when her boyfriend threw something into the creek. Whatever it was swirled away, lost in the flash of water. The boy pulled the girl close and they continued down the path paralleling the creek. A moment later a drone buzzed by, hovering over them and shooting past after presumably completing its mission.

No one else was nearby. Sanders picked up where he'd left off. "Through the advance of Chrislam, the real powers of Islam have the tool to water down opposition and to bring more people into a state of dhimmitude. Dhimmitude, as you probably know, is a component of Sharia law in which non-Muslims are subservient and must obey the dictates of Sharia, which are the rules by which all Muslims are required to live. Over the years, Muslims in America have set Sharia up against U.S. law. It starts initially as a parallel justice system. Ultimately when Islam reigns, it becomes the only legal system. We're seeing that more and more in various jurisdictions around the country. It began first in Texas, believe it or not, and expanded from there."

That was only the tip of the proverbial iceberg according to Sanders. Illegal alien immigration had gone on for years since the Obama Administration officially sanctioned it with various executive orders. "Through this invasion, illegals were relocated throughout the United States, primarily to conservative areas of the country." Although many people knew of this, conversely it wasn't widely known.

"The media didn't publicize it. That meant the majority of people in the country remained completely ignorant of the fact and are to this day, even as it continues unabated."

"I've heard a little of this," James said, "but like everything else of this nature, I've thrown up my hands in disgust, helpless to do anything. Why do you think the government has continued with this program?"

"There's lots of speculation because there are so many moving parts. What do I think? We haven't seen the impact of all these illegals yet in our elections. This could be the one where all these people come out of the woodwork somehow and skew the results. Big time."

"And Chrislam?" James asked. "Why such acceptance of that by the Church?"

"Deception, pure and simple." Sanders snorted. "It's Scriptural warning happening right before our eyes. False teachers, false prophets, heresy, and apostasy in the Church."

James found it shocking that Christian leaders would willingly go down the Chrislam road, but as Sanders and he discussed the situation, it made all the sense in the world.

"Churches in America have fallen away from the doctrinal purity of Scripture. You've seen this, James, as it's played out in the words and actions of the Ministerium pastors. What they think and feel takes precedence over the truth of biblical revelation. The Word of God is just another source of information to whatever they decide is right. Without the anchor of Scripture, the whisperings of the imams, with whom they've associated, has taken root. The lie these ministers believe is that all roads lead to heaven. They're such fools. Even the Muslim imams believe no such thing."

"It's distressing this cultural jihad has come to our town," James said.

"It's not isolated to larger cities. Islam has an agenda. Its leaders want to infiltrate every town and every church in the country until their political-religious scheme gains ascendency. It's like the takeover that happened in Europe. The difference is that Christianity had long since disappeared over there. They had to use a different strategy here. Thus Chrislam."

Given the facts Sanders discovered, plus James' own knowledge of Islam, it appeared the possibility of an Islamic takeover wasn't far off.

"There's more," Sanders said.

James puffed out his cheeks and exhaled. "What else?"

"Within a couple weeks, the government—our government—will be 'resettling' a large group of illegals here in our city, right here in Lighthouse. Our already robust Muslim population will soon be teeming with new adherents of the faith."

"I thought the illegal aliens were mostly Hispanic from Mexico and Central America."

"Back when Obama began this travesty, yes, the predominant illegals were from there. There was some number of Muslims who infiltrated even under that radar, but that has changed drastically. You remember the mass exodus from Syria and Iraq to Europe back in the mid-teens?"

James nodded. "Real mess."

"Right. It was an opportunity Obama couldn't pass up. He began bringing hundreds of thousands of these refugees into the U.S. Naturally, it was hushed up after a few early headlines, but that's been proceeding ever since. The next president did nothing to stop it. Our current administration expanded it and folded it into their plans for the ruination of this country, and we're close to the tipping point."

"And you believe this is all planned? That the transformation of America that Obama boasted of is close to completion under President Parker?"

"It's obvious," Sanders said, "but there's more goodies in this grab bag. You know the old adage: Follow the money."

"Sure."

"That applies here. Want to guess who profits locally from the Muslim invasion of Lighthouse?"

Taking a minute to ponder the question, James thought about the entire scope of their conversation. It came together for him. "The Ministerium?"

Sanders pointed at him. "Bingo. Although it's the Ministerium churches that have bought into this. The churches have social services arms that the Parker Administration is paying hundreds of millions of dollars to in order to resettle the illegals. Our good friends, Reverend Phyllis, Deacon Jones, and Pastor Tom Hall, along with other fellow travelers in the Ministerium, all benefit hugely."

"You're certain of this?"

"I've seen the official correspondence. You want to see where all these people will be housed?"

"You said this is happening soon?"

"Couple weeks."

"What's there to see? When do you want to show me this?"

"How about right now? We can take a little field trip, and you can see the preparations with your own eyes."

James hadn't expected this, but it made sense for him to personally confirm what Sanders had told him. "Why not? Let's go."

They crossed back over the bridge and walked rapidly to the parking lot. "We can take my truck." Sanders clicked his key fob, and the lights flashed on a black Ford F-150. "I got this used last year with pretty decent mileage, but I had to go to Illinois for it. It seems like used trucks in Michigan all have high mileage, along with a higher price. Hard to believe, but I saved a bundle by going to Chicago, even with their higher taxes."

It didn't take long to reach their destination. James hadn't been to this part of town in several years; the changes this area of Lighthouse had undergone shocked him.

"I don't recall so many businesses owned by Muslims."

Most of the stores, gas stations, and shops sported signs in Arabic. If James didn't know better, he'd think he was traveling down a street in Baghdad. The isolated businesses with English signage appeared out of place. The women walking along the sidewalks mostly wore hijabs, the Muslim head covering; some women were completely covered in black burqas.

The sight disturbed James. "Whatever happened to assimilation? America as a melting pot?"

"This is just the beginning. We're simply following in Europe's footsteps. It gets worse from here."

Sanders waited at a traffic light, and at the next stop sign, turned right. Half a mile down the street he pulled over, waiting for James to take in the scene. Just ahead, stretching for as far as the eye could see on both sides of the street a series of newer buildings rose six stories tall. The aftermath of the construction project was evident with barriers, piles of sand, wheelbarrows, and torn-up sidewalks. Windows hadn't yet been installed in the nearest buildings.

"Those are apartment units?"

"Uh-huh." Sanders gestured toward them. "Each one has forty-eight units. My count is there are twenty such buildings. That's free housing for the illegals that the government is sending here. Figure at least six people per apartment, if not more. Muslims have large families and many of the men have multiple wives. The five thousand plus people who will live there is only the starting point. I've heard there are plans to build a similar project a mile from here. Everybody gets welfare payments and food stamps, along with their place to live gratis. There's no expectation for them to work or meld into our culture."

For several minutes James sat deep in thought. Finally he said, "Bob, you're a man of God, like I am. In fact, you've probably got greater faith than me. I know this because you've been so bold in proclaiming it. I think of myself, and how I shrunk back in those Ministerium meetings. You're such a strong believer."

"Whoa." Sanders held up his hands. "I'm nothing and no one without Jesus."

"I know, I know. It's that you act out your faith, whereas I've been reluctant to do so. What's your secret?"

Sanders rubbed his hands together. "I appreciate you thinking I'm some super pastor or something, but believe me, I'm not. I'm just a guy who's grateful for God's amazing work in my life. Jesus did it all for me. He paid the ultimate and highest price for my sins. He died for me. I rest in His grace. The free gift of salvation He gave me is more than I could ever ask, and I try each and every day to give back to Him the little I can. That means, among other things, standing boldly and proclaiming His Truth."

As they were talking, a couple of men appeared and began walking down the street toward them. James noticed their swagger, and a niggling question of why they weren't on the sidewalk ate at the back of his mind. He ignored it in order to ask his next question.

"We know how bad this is for our country, yet we have an obligation to God. How do we hate all this that's being done to destroy America and still love on these people with the Gospel of Jesus Christ?"

The approaching men grew closer, walking right toward their vehicle. Sanders shifted in his seat and rested his hand on the gear lever. "That's the issue we have to wrestle with. In one sense, our friend Deacon Jones has it right. We have to evangelize out of relationships. Muslims generally are very family oriented. They're much more accepting of the Gospel once we've established a connection, shared a meal together, even questioned and explored their faith."

"The problem I see is with those who harbor ill intent."

One of the rough-looking men produced a hammer, the other a knife. Within feet of the truck, their ill intent was obvious.

"That's an issue." Sanders jerked the shifter into drive and floored it. The men yelled and cursed, jumping out of the way as the vehicle almost knocked them down.

James heard a screeching, scratching sound along the door on his side as the truck careened away. A clunk thudded behind him and the hammer skittered on the bed of the pickup, the thrown tool having missed the rear glass.

"It won't be long before this whole area becomes a no-go zone, a closed enclave too dangerous for people like us to enter." Sanders maneuvered around a corner, sped up, took several more turns, and eventually emerged out of the Muslim area, witnessed by the majority of signs reading in English.

The men rode in silence back to the park and the lot that held James' car. He stopped at the driver's window of Sanders' truck. "Thanks for opening my eyes to what's going on. Where do we go from here?"

"That's why I came to you. I haven't a clue. However, the one thing we can do is pray. If we can come before the Lord together, there's a lot of power in that."

"Yeah, that's good. When?"

"Let's take a minute right now."

How often had James said, "I'll pray for you," in a situation with someone in need and forgotten that promise?

He liked the idea of praying immediately as the need arose, rather than putting it off.

At the wheel of his pickup truck, Sanders bowed his head. "Lord, we come before You with nothing other than ourselves, our very lives. We give them to You right now and ask for wisdom and guidance. Show us how we can be a blessing in the midst of these troubled times."

After James added additional supplications, he turned to go, then stopped and held up a finger for Sanders to wait a moment.

"Just wanted to say to your earlier question that yes, I forgive you."

Sanders nodded solemnly. "Thank you." He stepped on the gas and pulled away.

Chapter 23

Virginia

It wasn't so long ago that General McCormick Wylie—"Mac" to his friends—anticipated coming home each evening. In those days he'd cherished marriage to his long-time sweetheart, Josie. He truly believed she had loved and respected him. To this day he couldn't accurately trace what had gone wrong, but it had. Now the evenings that had been so full of joy from simply being in each other's presence had disintegrated into blurs of booze and self-loathing.

He shut the front door after himself and faced the empty house. What he wouldn't give for those early years. His career had been on the rise, and Josie loved him with abandon; he thought it would last forever. That was a time when the world had its head screwed on right. Lately it seemed like society needed *The Exorcist* to help it like he'd helped Linda Blair in that old movie. Just like she'd been possessed and needed deliverance, the very culture seemed to have imbibed Satan's potion. If the devil didn't have free rein to turn things upside down and change what was right to what was wrong, Mac would be surprised.

Assuming there was a devil. Mac didn't know. He believed in God, so there must be a devil—the old good versus evil conundrum. How either one worked, Mac couldn't say. He definitely wasn't on speaking terms with God. He hoped for the best with the devil.

He hung and straightened his jacket, examining the many medals and commendations. They'd meant a lot at the time. What were they worth now? His hat joined the jacket in the closet, and he made his way to the liquor cabinet. Glenlivet. Straight up. It would be the first of many such drinks if recent months held any example.

Sitting alone in the living room, drinking alone, his thoughts wandered aimlessly, but always came back to the two prominent issues that plagued him: his broken marriage and what the military had become. Since he'd already beaten himself up over Josie tonight, his quandary over the military's demise came next.

Mac knew history. The military of old demanded its officers know, revere, and learn from it. In the George W. Bush days and the Iraq War with its Shock and Awe campaign, despite severe congressional opposition, the armed forces had seen its greatest glory in decades. But the Obama Administration had no love for any branch of the service; Obama loved only himself and his soaring empty rhetoric. Was it any wonder he'd cut funding, turned each branch into a social experiment, and decimated the esprit de corps? The president following Obama had an uneventful term, but the same awful policies continued. Under President Parker, the cuts and transformation of the military had grown so much that America couldn't project any strength beyond its own hemisphere.

Parker wanted Mac Wylie to undercut the few good men remaining in his command. These were soldiers who didn't bow to political correctness. They didn't go along with the feminization of the men under their command and the foolish transgender experiments. They actually held solid, traditional, patriotic principles. In a word, they were conservative. They stood out like sunburned albinos. Couldn't miss them. And that meant they had to go.

Mac downed the rest of his whiskey and went for a refill. Funny how early on one of these gave him a buzz; he'd noticed it now took three or four for the effects to hit in any meaningful way.

The "friendly fire" that decimated Mac was the presidential insistence that he order his men to shoot U.S. citizens should the need arise. To say he'd gone ballistic in that instant might be too tame. There'd have to be a celestial freeze both in the heavens and the netherworld for him to accede to that demand. He'd made that clear. Which had led to his glacial encounter with Vice President Abu Saif on the Maryland Shore.

The rest of the liquid in his glass went down without a whimper. He rested his head on the back of his easy chair and closed his eyes.

Chapter 24

The man who had secreted himself in General Wylie's house prior to his return for the evening saw from the miniature camera he'd set up in the living room that his prey was well on his way to inebriation. With his military and Secret Service training, Ibrahim Sufyan had the patience to wait until the right moment to strike. As the vice president's personal bodyguard, Sufyan was trusted to carry out the most difficult of assignments. Abu Saif wanted this man's earthly existence terminated. Sufyan would comply because the task glorified Allah.

Wylie walked unsteadily after his fourth drink. Upon retrieving his fifth, Sufyan decided the time to strike had come. He unfolded himself from his place of hiding and crept down the stairs. Earlier he'd tested them to assure they didn't squeak and alert the target.

Sufyan's plan was to stage Wylie's death by hanging. He knew of the general's divorce and extreme melancholy.

Coupling that with his refusal to comply with presidential orders provided plenty of motive for suicide.

The chair Wylie sat in faced away from the stairs. Sufyan crept up behind Wylie with his garrote and thrust it forward around the man's neck. But even in his drunkenness Wylie reacted. As the wire slipped over his head he managed to protect his neck by inserting his fingers against the loop.

Strong and quick as Sufyan was, Wylie's move foiled the immediate strangulation. Sufyan yanked the garrote tight, but it only cut into finger tissue. The general struggled in his chair. He reached up with his other hand, grabbed Sufyan behind the head, and pulled him forward. The front of Sufyan's head butted against the back of Wylie's. Both men fell to the side. The Secret Service agent tightened his hold even as blood spurted from Wylie's fingers. With another yank the garrote severed the fingers and the thin wire bit into the man's neck.

His opponent was large and strong, but couldn't overcome the suffocating wire cutting off blood and oxygen. They rolled back and forth with Sufyan maintaining his dominant position. Through sheer force of will he kept up the pressure. Wylie's resistance weakened, his efforts lessened, and his body relaxed.

Puffing from the exertion, Sufyan assured that Wylie was dead. He looked at the aftermath of his botched murder and cursed. It wasn't supposed to go down this way. His plan to make it appear Wylie hung himself was now out the window. Blood had spattered on furniture and Wylie's clothing. His drink had spilled and the pungent odor of whiskey rose to irritate Sufyan's sensibilities.

Thankful Wylie had closed the blinds as part of his nighttime routine and all the mess was hidden from prying eyes outside the house, Ibrahim Sufyan thought of the consequences if he didn't make this right. The kill order gave him wide latitude. It didn't matter how Wylie died, as long as he did.

Suicide by hanging was now out. A self-inflicted bullet to the head certainly wouldn't work. The only feasible alternative seemed to be a violent robbery gone badly. Cursing again at his misfortune that Wylie's reflexes had been so fast, Sufyan began the task of turning this into an accidental murder scene. It wasn't perfect but he'd make it work. The important thing was that Wylie had gotten what he deserved, and one more obstacle in the military had been overcome.

Chapter 25

Western Michigan

James scanned the stacks of papers on his desk as he held the phone to his ear.

"You got a little time later today?"

"Guess I could fit something in. What's up, Bob?"

"There's someone I'd like you to meet. It should give you a little more perspective on what we're facing."

The meeting Bob Sanders proposed was as clandestine as their original one. As much as James hated the idea of such secrecy, he understood the necessity. Unfriendly forces were gathered in their midst.

He returned to his sermon preparation, and after completing his work for the following Sunday, headed home. For several days he'd considered the little surprise he planned for Janna. Ticking off the items he needed, he gathered them together and put them in the car, leaving the house with a smile.

At the hospital he took great care with his bundle, which he'd disguised in a laundry basket. Carrying the basket made him feel a trifle silly, but he imagined people had brought stranger things through those doors.

The volunteer at the front desk gave James his visitor badge. He took the elevator and walked down the hall past the nursing station, where he paused before entering Janna's room. Closing his eyes momentarily, he prayed, *Dear Jesus, please let me be a comfort for Janna. Help me to be a source of joy for her.* He peered inside. A nurse stood by Janna's bedside entering information into a portable computer on a mobile stand. James gave her a greeting and set the basket on the couch across from the bed. The nurse returned his hello, finished her typing, and left with a wave to the both of them. James followed her to the door and gently shut it.

As weak as Janna was, she gave James a radiant smile when he approached and kissed her. He couldn't think but how much he loved this woman and her fighting spirit.

"I have a surprise for you."

"I love surprises, as long as they're good ones."

"I hope it is." James picked up the white basket and set it near Janna's feet.

Janna gave him a quizzical expression and James held up his index finger to indicate "just wait a minute." He removed the light blanket that covered Pepper's travel carrier. Janna's eyes shone. She clapped her hands with excitement, seemingly forgetting the weakness that beset her.

James lifted out the cat's carrier and put it beside Janna. A pathetic meow came from inside the enclosure. Upon James' unzipping the opening, Pepper remained inside for a moment then crept on feeble legs to her mistress. Janna shifted and enclosed Pepper tenderly in her arms. "Oh, James, thank you. This is a lovely surprise."

He wiped away a tear and watched Janna enjoy the company of her beloved pet. Once she'd received all the attention she needed, Pepper curled up in the crook of

Janna's arm. Because of her age and fragility Pepper didn't purr much anymore, but James heard one soft, deep-throated sound of pleasure when she settled next to her favorite person.

They talked at some length, mostly James detailing the latest news, particularly his adventure with Bob Sanders and their next clandestine meeting that afternoon.

About an hour into their visit, Janna became visibly more tired, but also distressed. "What is it, honey?" James asked.

Lines creased her forehead. Beads of sweat popped out; her face became pale. She closed her eyes, her body stiffened; she voiced a tiny, "Oh."

James jumped up, his heartbeat racing. His throat felt dry as he forced the words from his lips. "Janna? Are you all right?"

"Yes." She began panting with a shortness of breath.

"I'm calling the nurse." He turned to run out of the room.

"No. Wait."

He turned, worry eating at him.

"I have a word for you."

Reluctantly, he returned to her bedside. Her eyelids fluttered open.

"I saw you standing in the brightness of the sun," Janna said. "The heat encapsulated you. You melted in its burning intensity. There was nothing left of you but a tiny drop of water that fell into this intense supernova. You disappeared, burned up. Quiet filled the universe. Not a creature or anything living stirred. Suddenly you emerged from these red-hot surroundings shining, new, and singing for joy." Finished, she fell back into exhaustion.

As she related this vision, James felt a powerful sensation of something pouring over and into his head. It traversed his entire body and left him trembling.

He sat down beside her. With a shaky hand he stroked the back of Pepper's neck. His fingers paused to linger on the soft fur and touched Janna's arm.

Tears welled up and a sob escaped him. "Oh, Janna."

Without looking Janna seemed to know that Pepper had died. She held her dear cat, as a tear trickled down her cheek and dropped on Pepper's ear. The animal didn't twitch or move. "It was her time. She lived a good life."

James couldn't see or talk. He fumbled for a tissue from the box on the nightstand, wiping angrily at his flooding eyes and blowing his suddenly running nose. "But why now? This was to be a good surprise for you. Just a happy visit. Why did she have to die?"

His stomach clenched, and he rubbed his face in his hands.

Janna reached for him and held his arm still. "It's okay. I wouldn't want it any other way. She died in my arms. She was at peace. What could be better?"

They spent the next several minutes in prayer. When they'd finished, James arranged the blanket in the laundry basket and lifted Pepper into it. "I'll give her a proper burial."

Janna sniffled. "I know." She visibly mustered the last of her meager energy. "There's one thing you must do: Horde cash at home. Do it today."

On the way out of the hospital James didn't feel foolish carrying the basket and Pepper's travel carrier; he only felt sad.

Chapter 26

James found a shady spot in their back yard and buried Pepper, wishing Janna could be with him to share their remembrances and sorrow. The bittersweet thought that stayed with him was Pepper's strong attachment to Janna and her utter indifference to James. The mystery of cats. Despite that, he'd loved the animal and missed her terribly. He sat for a while by the grave until it was time for him to go. With a last look back at the freshly turned earth, he trudged from the yard.

Pulling his car from the garage, James thought about Janna's car that had been sitting there unused for months. The realization that he'd have to soon sell it caused a fresh wave of sadness to wash over him. He squeezed the steering wheel a little harder and clamped down on his emotions. Remembering Janna's final warning, he ran the errands necessary to do as she had instructed.

Later, James met Bob Sanders in a prearranged location where they were soon joined by a woman James didn't know. With her mid-length, gray-streaked hair held back in a scrunchie, she was attractive with an angular face and wore a modest skirt and blouse. James introduced her as Carla. The men climbed in her car, Sanders in the front, and they drove to a small county park by Lake Michigan. The lake tempered the afternoon heat with a slight cooling breeze. They settled around a picnic table after Carla removed a briefcase from her trunk. The waves rolled gently onto the shore; the late afternoon sun reflecting off the water promised a clear evening.

Sanders gave Carla a fuller introduction, explaining that she taught in the Lighthouse public high school as an English teacher. "Carla's in my church and came to me with concerns as to what she's been told to teach in her classes."

"I've been aware of this kind of thing happening around the country," Carla said, "but somehow I never expected it here. Maybe I'm naïve, perhaps too hopeful we'd be insulated from this."

She opened her briefcase and took out some papers and books. "Our whole curriculum has been changed. It's almost completely geared toward the teaching of all things Islam."

Among the several books was a copy of the Qur'an and a much larger book called *Reliance of the Traveller*, which dealt in depth with Sharia law. James picked up *Reliance* and thumbed through it. He found a passage on jihad and said, "This is interesting. Section o9.10 says that Muslims can't kill women and children unless they're fighting against the Muslims, but quote: 'It is permissible to kill old men,' that is, someone older than forty. Since I've passed that milestone, I guess they can go after me in jihad. And here's a lovely passage, Section o9.13: 'When a child or woman is taken captive, they become slaves by the fact of capture, and the woman's previous marriage is immediately annulled.' Carla, how are you instructed to teach this book?"

"It's to be used all four years of high school, beginning with freshman English."

"That's pretty serious indoctrination." Sanders leaned forward. "What else are they requiring you to teach?"

Carla shuffled through the papers and extracted an official document. "I'm not supposed to have this, but it made its way into my possession. I imagine the school district would be unhappy with my having it." She handed it to Sanders who shared it with James.

The paper briefly outlined several tests the teachers were to administer in the current school year. Among the items the students must learn were the Five Pillars of Islam, the Seven Blessings of Martyrdom, and the Six Articles of Faith.

"Sounds like a catechism class." James finished perusing the document. "These Six Articles will help make the kids better citizens: 'There is one God—Allah, angels are spiritual creatures who serve Allah, the Qur'an is the most perfect of the books of Allah, there are many prophets of Allah but Muhammad is the most highly praised, there is a day of judgment in which the deeds of Allah's followers will be weighed, and Allah's will is supreme—all things are according to his will.'"

"Students aren't allowed to bring any of these materials home," Carla said. "We hand them out in class, work on them only there, as well as do the reading assignments in class. Obviously parents aren't supposed to see what their kids are doing."

A seagull squawked overhead. James followed its flight to the beach near the water where it joined a flock of its fellows. "What have your superiors said is the purpose of this teaching of all things Islam?"

"Another teacher—a friend of mine—asked that question. They told her 'diversity' and suggested she accept the direction the school district is going or quit. She pursued the issue—mind you, this is all in the first couple weeks since school began after Labor Day—and they sacked her, just like that, the other day. She took it to the union and was told in no uncertain terms that she was out of luck; the union declined to get involved in her defense."

"It appears the design is to turn the students into good little Muslims," Sanders said.

"Oh, I forgot." Carla snapped her fingers. "Some changes were made in the bathrooms over the summer."

James had an idea where this was going. "Don't tell us, they needed to accommodate the religious needs of certain students."

"Muslim students. With footbaths," Carla said.

"I hate to even ask this," Bob Sanders said, "What about Islamic prayer?"

"Right, that's one more thing," Carla said. "Muslim students are excused several times during the school day to a special, private room for their required prayers. They use the footbaths in the bathrooms to wash and prepare as part of their ritual ceremony."

"Surprised the school didn't build a separate bathing facility," Sanders muttered.

Carla gave a rueful smile. "I heard through the grapevine the administration considered that option, but discarded it as a too costly."

"This is all beyond the pale." The state of the nation confounded James. Would this crazy stuff never end?

"It's evident there's a larger agenda going on in this country," Sanders said. "We're being Islamicized from every angle. Remember cultural jihad, James? This is it, in spades."

"You men are pastors," Carla said. "Tell me if I'm wrong: isn't this spiritual warfare?"

"No doubt," Sanders said. "The darkness has been closing in for years. The enemy is doing his best to destroy and demoralize us. Thankfully, we know how the war ends. We have the Book and we've read it. Revelation clearly reveals that Satan and his minions will be destroyed. Our faith in Jesus isn't for naught. There may not be much we can do to fight the established earthly power and authorities, but we can petition Jesus to intercede with our Heavenly Father. He hears our prayers and will answer."

Chapter 27

Washington, D.C.

President Luisa Parker hated long mornings, and this one had been the worst. First thing, her National Security Advisor demanded she sit down with him for his assessment of the world situation. Claiming a headache, which she really did have for once, she waved the man off. Relations with her husband, Mary Ellen, had taken a turn for the worse. ME had been moaning and complaining of late, coming off like a typical female, whining that Parker never spent time with her any more—was always involved in late-night meetings and traveling all over the country leaving her at home to stew. How did ME know that Parker wasn't having clandestine liaisons with someone younger and prettier? Parker might as well bang her head against a wall as argue with that kind of hormonal logic.

As for the NSA, what difference did it make what went down in the rest of the world? Parker had her agenda to complete in these last couple of months before the election. The legacy of her eight years was on the line. Her plan always had been the completion of the fundamental transformation of America that Obama began. Only his efforts would pale to nothing compared to Parker's final thrust.

Promptly at nine a group of schoolchildren were paraded in. Parker's personal experiences at the age of these kids—twelve to fourteen—had been the worst of her life. The angst and intrigue those years had fostered weighed on Parker. She hated having to deal with teens. Their teachers and chaperones were appropriately respectful, but kids these days—no sense of respect or honor for the Office of the President. One boy shouted out a question, then a chorus of voices chimed in. Parker's head about exploded, but she gritted her teeth until the ten-minute visit concluded, then sat back with a sigh of relief. She fumbled with a bottle of aspirin, downed five, and mentally prepared for the next onslaught on her public relations calendar.

Several phone calls came next. Parker dispatched them before getting a call from her Chief of Staff. "Madame President, the Interim Prime Minister of Israel is calling. He says it's important he speak with you."

She'd been ignoring requests from him all week and wasn't about to take his call now.

"Tell him I'm terribly tied up and don't have the time. Let him know I'll give him a call in the next couple days." Which she had no intention of doing.

"Right," her Chief of Staff said. "He's pretty agitated."

"He'll have to wait."

Since the incident at the U.N., when Israel's Prime Minister met his unfortunate end, she'd washed her hands of any further interaction with that nation. Severing diplomatic ties meant just that. If they had problems of some kind, that was no skin off her nose.

Two hours later, the real work of her administration began. Vice President Abu Saif arrived promptly as he always did. While waiting for their guest, they chatted briefly about upcoming events on the presidential calendar.

One of the pleasures of Parker's job had been working with the Director of FEMA, Matthew Ryder. He appeared in the doorway just as Parker glanced up from her discussion with Saif, and she waved him in. Balding and rotund, Ryder was one man who had gotten with the program in Parker's estimation. He'd bought into her vision on day one and had worked hard to bring it to fruition. That he, being a homosexual man in his own marriage, had similar sentiments as she didn't hurt her sensibilities toward him.

Parker walked around her desk and gave Ryder a hug. "What good news do you have for me today?"

Saif greeted the man with a handshake and followed, as Parker led them to the conversational cluster of chairs in the corner of her office so they could be more comfortable talking. After Parker called for and received coffee for the three of them, Ryder said, "We have only a few remaining details to care for. Everything else is in place."

"Review it for me one more time."

"As you know, Luisa, it is a big project. Having the resources of the federal government at our disposal is critical for such an effort."

Ryder snapped open his attaché case and pulled out two maps. The first depicted the United States as it currently was configured. The second reflected a different arrangement.

"Naturally there are fifty states right now. Each state government is semi-autonomous from the federal government. All can generally determine how they wish to handle affairs within their own borders. Federally, we can determine laws that override state laws only within constitutional limits. It's those limits that the project you assigned to me is meant to address."

Ryder sipped his coffee. "This is excellent, by the way."

"I get only the best. That's one of the perks of this office." Parker toasted him and they gently clinked their china cups. "Go on."

"This second map shows what will be once you trigger the continuity of government initiative which I've so cleverly named CGI-28." Ryder smiled in a self-deprecating manner.

Parker laughed. "Very clever, indeed."

"It is good that we can enjoy our work," Saif said.

"CGI-28, to use a favorite term of my favorite president, fundamentally transforms the legislative nature of the country. Rather than fifty states, there will be five federal zones, each corresponding to a geographical area of the country. Zones are further broken down into subzones or legislative districts. We have trained appropriate personnel who will assume command of the zones and subzones. Because of the tight coordination we've achieved with the current configuration of executive agencies and the military, we have every eventuality covered. You name the alphabet soup agency, and it knows its role. IRS, DOE, EPA, Army, Air Force, what have you; all are on board and ready to roll when the time comes. The billions of rounds of ammunition each agency has purchased over the last two decades is stored and ready to use at a moment's notice.

"The camps?" Saif queried.

"They're in alignment with the federal zones. We have hundreds ready throughout the country to house those who won't cooperate with the program. They will adequately house the dissidents. The fewer people we have running around free who disagree and might push back against this initiative, the better. I believe, Mr. Vice President, that you're scheduled to review a number of them in the coming weeks?"

"That is correct." Saif set his coffee cup down. "I have assigned my most trusted aide to travel in my place due to my heavy schedule of campaign appearances. He will report back alerting us of any issues he foresees."

"We paid significant attention to getting these facilities right. I imagine he won't find much to criticize."

"I am happy to hear that. A well-designed and implemented program makes the heart glad."

"By the way, how is the campaign coming?"

"I am sure you've seen the polls. We have a large percentage of the country behind us. Naturally, we never want to take anything for granted, but all looks well. I should be elected the next president of the United States."

"That's wonderful news," Ryder said, clapping his hands. "I appreciate the solid working connection we have."

Abu Saif bowed his head in acknowledgment.

President Parker interjected, "What about the unions?"

"They've been terrific." Ryder's face lit up. "They're so excited that your administration considered them worthy of this level of involvement. They're armed and waiting for the word. The preparations the prior administrations made in purchasing firearms and ammo has made my work a breeze. The few people who followed conservative media at the time and heard about those purchases have forgotten all about them. They were stored securely awaiting this moment. I'm stoked!" He made a fist and pumped it.

"Nobody knows the overall plan, other than a trusted few, is that right?" Parker asked.

"Correct. This is a huge undertaking and the most senior individual of each group involved had to be brought into the fold. Prior to that, we vetted each person carefully. If there was any question as to their loyalty, we purged them and brought someone on whom we were absolutely certain we could control. Everyone else is essentially isolated in knowledge of the overall scheme. Just like in a spy network, you don't want one person able to spill the beans and expose the whole cell. We operated on the same principle."

"Let me know if there's anything you need from me before we go live. When we do, I'm sure there will be plenty of pushback. We need to rapidly respond to that."

"Our team is up to it, Luisa. We await your word."

"Soon, Matthew, soon. We must set the table. The DSS does that and more. Where does that stand?"

Ryder's enthusiasm showed in his face. "It's completely ready. We've worked incredibly hard with the major search firms and other large corporations to perfect it. I can proudly say that the Dissident Scoring System has been field tested for the last four years and, with minor tweaking, has produced flawless results. We have all the information available that we need, and it's being constantly updated. When you say go, we can move."

"I love it, Matthew. Well, gentlemen, speaking of setting the table, how about lunch?"

Chapter 28

Western Michigan

It was one of those typical government releases that came late on a Friday afternoon. The intent was to make the information official, yet to miss the news cycle of the day and make it extremely difficult for the Sunday shows to feature it. They'd already booked the guests, and nobody was prepared to discuss the ramifications, assuming they wanted to tackle the subject in the first place. James happened to be at his computer checking out various websites he frequented. He saw a blurb on his favorite conservative site and followed the link. What he read caused him to lean back in his chair and shake his head with cynical wonder.

The president had issued another executive order. Hard on the heels of Barack Obama's example, President Luisa Parker had followed the same template. The liberal media in its day had huffed and puffed about the Imperial Presidency of George W. Bush. Obama, then Parker after a four-year hiatus, had made that a liberal joke with the executive dictates issuing from the Oval Office. Parker had seen Obama's full house and raised the ante with her royal flush.

The article showed up on an obscure website. The blogger, posting his thoughts, referred to a sentence buried in a paragraph deep into the text of the EO that read: "Those who are identified as Christian or who self-identify as Christian are hereby dismissed from all federal, state, and local civil service."

Was it possible that Christians would be singled out so blatantly in this way? James had to read the entry several times to digest the import of the statement. If this were true, hundreds of thousands of people at all levels of government were being discriminated against. They would immediately lose their jobs. The decree would impact literally every community throughout the nation.

James wondered if Bob Sanders had seen the announcement. He picked up his phone and dialed Sanders' cell.

"You got a minute, Bob?"

"Sure, I'm in the car."

"You probably haven't seen this." James filled Sanders in. "Can you believe it?"

"Funny that this happens now, and you bring it up. I've been meaning to read the Dietrich Bonhoeffer biography by Eric Metaxas for a long time and finally got around to it. He details the rise of Hitler and his Nazi party in 1930s Germany and how the government co-opted the church. One of the actions that caused great consternation and led to resistance by Bonhoeffer and others was the issuance of what's known as the Aryan Paragraph. It was only the beginning of a succession of laws quickly enacted, but it started a severe downhill slide for the Jews. The Aryan Paragraph declared that Jews could no longer work in civil service. Looks like our friends in the Parker Administration have taken a page out of Hitler's playbook."

"I haven't read the Bonhoeffer book either, but if Parker intends to begin treating Christians like the Nazis treated Jews, we could be in for even more surprises."

"You're absolutely correct. It quickly got worse for the Jews. Things could deteriorate rapidly for Christians if history is any guide, and it usually is."

They touched on another couple of subjects and hung up. Worried, James left his office for the hospital. Janna needed him more than he needed to fret about a future he couldn't control.

Chapter 29

October

The following week, reports began filtering in that Christians around the nation were being fired from jobs that had a linkage to any level of government. Outrage in the conservative blogosphere and Christian media met little to no resistance. The news never made any mainstream media press reports, and the administration ignored the few calls that rose above the deafening silence. Affected church members began calling James. He knew he couldn't promise benevolence help for all that might appeal to him, but he said the church would do what it could to help. This kind of an action that affected many promised to bring great hardship, both to the families directly and to organizations that would normally provide aid.

James called an emergency board meeting to discuss how Lighthouse Christian Church could respond.

The six men met with James that evening. James had given Joe Bennett the highlights for the meeting, and the head deacon had assembled the remainder of the group. After James opened in prayer, he outlined in more detail the requests for help he'd already received. He presented the fact obtained from his secretary that about ten percent of the church had government-related jobs that were affected by the decree.

"If we in our small church have that sizable a population hurt by this," James said, "there's a good chance the rest of the town of Lighthouse will likewise have the same issue. How do we want to prepare to address the need within our congregation? Should we try to help others outside the church?"

"The budget is tight right now," Joe Bennett said. "If we increase our benevolence there's only two ways to do it. We've got to receive more offerings from the congregation earmarked for that or significantly reduce already committed funds."

That opened the spigot for opinions, arguments, and counterarguments that spilled onto the conference table from every angle. James sat back and let the men expound. When silence settled back into the room, James jumped in again. "It sounds like the consensus is that the majority of you don't believe our people are willing to give more than they currently do. I disagree with that. The early church in the Book of Acts acted with compassion and a sense of self-sacrifice, giving to their brothers and sisters in need, even selling property to do so. Don't you men think we can generate the same kind of empathy and heart for giving for those in need in our own congregation?"

"When you asked for greater self-sacrifice in giving to missions, what response did you get, Pastor?" Bennett asked with the hint of a smirk.

James saw the expression and ignored it. "It was disappointing."

"When a congregation isn't willing to go along with a pastor's requests," Bennett said, "does the pastor have any responsibility in that?"

Because of the recent history between James and the board, and the ultimatum they'd given for the healing of Janna, James hesitated to respond honestly. However, he wasn't much of a politician, and he'd never been good hedging the truth. "I'll admit, if something is on my heart that I don't communicate well, and the church body doesn't go for it, then I'm definitely responsible to a degree. But it's not all on my shoulders. The Holy Spirit has to convict. He hasn't convicted you men of the necessity of giving a hand to those in our very own church. Why is that? Where are your heads and hearts in this matter?"

Joe Bennett crossed his arms. "You're not going to put that on us. You want to know the truth, James? You're just not a very good pastor."

With that proclamation, the air went out of James. If Bennett had spoken the truth, he hadn't done it in love. No one rose to defend him, and James knew that whatever happened with Janna, his days at Lighthouse Christian were absolutely numbered.

After a silence that stretched significantly past the comfort level, Bennett had a suggestion. "If you truly want to free up funds for benevolence, we can reduce one expenditure."

Given the exchange already, James was wary. "What's that?"

"How much of a pay cut are you willing to take?"

The attitude of the board had shifted well into hostile territory. James had a choice. He could respond in kind with a harsh cutting word—certainly his fleshly inclination—or he could take the radical approach of Jesus. He knew that too many times he'd given in to hurts and feelings in the past and responded in a manner that later had caused him to repent.

He clamped his jaw shut, not letting his unruly tongue run roughshod. In that moment he thought he knew what God wanted him to say. It wasn't logical or natural for him, and it was more radical than he could have anticipated. When he opened his mouth to speak, it was certainly him talking, but he still wondered who really spoke. "Joe, I can't think of a better way for me to care more for my flock. I'll happily give up half of my salary to help the people in our body."

James gave Joe and the others a genuine, heart-felt smile, gathered his things, and left the men speechless.

Chapter 30

James wondered how many shoes the Parker Administration had to drop. The following Friday afternoon, another proclamation came forth.

For years churches had submitted in the culture wars. Many had become like the world, making friends with those having ungodly principles. This falling away from biblical doctrine had manifested itself within the Ministerium group that James had tolerated as long as he could in the interests of ecumenical unity. Finally, seeing how entrenched those ministers were in their beliefs, he'd quit, as had Bob Sanders. His new friend had continued with the Ministerium for different reasons than James. Sanders had explained that he'd stuck close to gather evidence of the decay and destruction of their community. James had remained because of a lingering hope these men and women, purportedly of God, would change. He saw now how foolish a thought that was.

The lure of government money was deceptive. For non-profit organizations, it could become a lifeline. They often got to the point that the threat of losing access to government funding caused them to compromise more and more. Couple sucking at the government teat along with moral concessions that veered from Scripture's truths, and churches would turn away from God every time. Churches everywhere similar to those in the Ministerium had for years gone down this winding, muddy road. They'd slipped and slid into the ditch of heresy with increasing rapidity.

The latest government declaration solidified the partnership these apostate churches had chosen to engage in, putting non-compliant churches into jeopardy. With the stroke of a pen, President Parker pronounced that all churches and denominations would henceforth be required to accept homosexual clergy and perform gay marriages, regardless of their bylaws. Any resistance would be met with the full force of government persuasion. The possibilities of how this might happen were left unstated.

That Sunday, James preached on the similarities between 1930s Nazi Germany and America circa 2028 almost one hundred years later. He mentioned the apathy in the church at that time, how doctrine had been compromised, and how many churches this day had likewise conceded their moral ground. The Confessing Church was the response of Bonhoeffer and other true men of God who stood firm against the encroachment of the government into church canon. James urged his congregation to resist the worldly influences and to stand in love against those who would tear down the church. "Will you do it? Will you stand? Your eternity rests on your decision."

Afterwards, James received a mixture of praise and outrage. Those who agreed with his message quietly thanked him. Those who didn't gave him an earful, questioning how dare he compare current times and the church to the Nazis. He expected the pushback from certain quarters of the congregation, but there was more than he anticipated, particularly in regards to homosexual issues. It told him the church was sliding downhill fast, and he seemed helpless to stop it.

Chapter 31

James sat in his office Monday morning praying and pondering. The Word of God lay open before him. There were times in his reading that he found himself staring at the words and not comprehending, seeing black ink on white paper but not an intelligible letter in the mess.

His ministry was in shambles, his church falling farther away from him each passing day. He didn't know what to do or how to fix it. Where had he gone wrong?

A commotion outside his window startled him. It began as a low murmur that he ignored in his reverie. Only when it ascended to a dull roar did he truly notice. By then, it was full-throated and malicious.

A large crowd moved down the street. Men and women marched with locked arms in a form of solidarity. They chanted different words and phrases so that the words rose up in a jumble that he couldn't quite make out. James ran to the door of the church to gain a better idea of what was going on.

The crowd moved in unison to the intersection where it turned toward a residential area. Frowning and concerned as he began to understand what they were saying, James brought up their rear, along with a number of others who were caught up in curiosity. He saw that the people comprising the faction carried something clutched in their hands. Like a one-celled amoeba the assembly propelled itself forward until the leaders stopped in front of a single-family house. With mounting horror he realized it was the home of Mark and Beth Nelson, the couple whose photography studio had recently burned to the ground.

Bile bubbled in the back of James' throat as several people screamed curses through bullhorns. Their shouts turned to demands. "Mark and Beth Nelson, you're both homophobic scumbags. You can't hide behind your Christian platitudes. Come out and face us, unless you want your house burned down like your business."

James couldn't believe this was happening in his hometown. He prayed his friends wouldn't respond, but feared the consequences either way.

When the Nelsons didn't appear as ordered, the leader nodded to several young men who approached the house with baseball bats. The sound of shattering glass rang out. In moments, the men cleared the shards and jumped through the broken windows.

James watched with open-mouthed despair. He fumbled in his pocket for his cell phone to call 911 but discovered he must have left it back in the office. He agonized over what to do. He wanted to intervene to stop this madness, yet couldn't force himself to act. *What can one man do?* His sense of helplessness spilled over into guilt. *Where is my courage?* If Bob Sanders were here, would he step into the middle of this nightmare? *He just might.* But James also had to consider his responsibility to Janna. *Does that make me a coward?*

Within moments the front door opened with Mark and Beth emerging, shoved by the young men who'd forced their way into the house. Their arms were handcuffed behind them. When they resisted, the youths manhandled them and dragged them along, finally standing them up to face their accusers. James saw the fear on their faces. He felt it, too. What did this rabble intend? It became all too clear.

Using his bullhorn, one of the leaders addressed the Nelsons point blank, his voice echoing off the pavement. James saw the couple cringe at the volume directly in their ears. He smelled the hate of the crowd. Its odor hovered like a haze.

Sweat beaded on the leader's forehead. He wiped his free hand on his pants and pulled out a sheet of paper that shook a moment before determination steadied his hand. A smug smile tugged at his lips.

"Mark and Beth Nelson, we the people hereby charge you with propagating hate under the guise of your Christian religion. We've tolerated your disrespect of the LGBTQ community for more than a decade. You've spoken out against human persons of sexual diversity: gays, lesbians, bisexuals, and the transgender community, and we've been more than patient with how you've disenfranchised us. You've stirred up conflict between our people and Muslims of good will, even blaspheming the religion of Islam. Enough is enough! You've fomented discord, hurt, and pain among sensitive individuals, and it stops right here, now, today. You are guilty of the charge of oppressing every person gathered here and those who support our cause.

"How can you condemn us without a trial?" Mark cried out.

"You're Christians. You've flaunted your Christian propaganda on your studio walls for years. You've humiliated us, pretending you're better than us. No more, I say! Not one more day!"

Spit dribbled down his chin as he screamed the words while pumping his fist in the air. The throng responded to his chant, repeating it in a rising crescendo. "Not one more day! Not one more day!"

When the uproar died down, Beth responded in a low tone. "We live for our Savior, Jesus Christ. If you indict us, you indict Him too."

"Jesus lived thousands of years ago and was nothing but a common criminal," shouted a woman. "How can you follow someone like that?"

"Your sins are consuming you," Mark said. "Repent of them, trust in Jesus, and be saved."

"Who are you to call me a sinner?" a man yelled. "You're both hypocritical fools."

"You're right." Beth stood taller. "We're fools for Christ."

"We won't tolerate you Christian fools any longer." The leader raised his voice even more through his bullhorn. "You have one opportunity here. Renounce your religion. Spit on this Jesus you cling to. If you do that, we'll leave in peace."

Mark and Beth clamped their lips together and shook their heads. Mark sidled closer to Beth. "Jesus died for our sins and yours. We have only one life to live. We live it for Christ."

"You refuse to renounce Him?"

The couple looked resolutely at each other and Mark responded, "We refuse."

The leader looked to his right and to his left. Men and women took the cue and formed a semi-circle around the Nelsons. The young men at their sides forced them to their knees. James inhaled sharply as he spotted the movement of the stones in each person's hands, gleaming dully in the morning light.

Without a further thought he shouldered his way through the crowd. James grabbed the arm of the leader and spun him around. "You can't do this! This is the United States of America. We don't practice mob justice here. You'll regret it if you hurt them."

He shrugged James off and held up a hand. "I know you. You're a preacher."

The set of his face and the dull malevolence of his eyes chilled James. "Yes, I pastor the church they attend. I believe in Jesus Christ. You can't achieve peace through violence like this. You'll bring guilt and condemnation. You're going to bring the wrath of God upon your own heads."

The man snorted in laughter. "God. If there is a God, He certainly has better things to do than worry about us. You Christians say He created us with free will. Well, here it is. We *choose* to help Him run this little piece of the universe by making it a better place without these two people. As for you, we'll deal with you another time. We've got business to attend to." He gestured to one of the young men who'd retrieved Beth and Mark. "Get him out of the way."

Several of their companions jumped to help. They grabbed James' arms and pressed them behind his back. Cold steel bit into his wrists with the snap of handcuffs. They hustled him to the side and positioned him so he couldn't look away from the horrible scene unfolding just feet from him.

A rare hush fell over the people facing the Nelsons. The leader tossed a baseball-sized rock up and down in his hand. He addressed the couple. "For your crimes, you deserve to die. Before this jury of your peers, you've been found guilty."

He half-turned. It almost looked like he was going to walk away. Instead, he whirled back with cocked arm and let his rock fly. It struck Mark in the throat. A painful gasp gurgled past his lips. More rocks flew. Some missed, but the men and women pressed in and began hitting their targets.

James wanted to turn away, but he couldn't. Before his very eyes two people he loved were being martyred for their faith. He'd read incidents of martyrdom for many years. Through his prayers, he'd gained great appreciation for suffering Christians because of the boldness with which they stood.

It was horrible. Rocks rained upon them. Blood gushed from their wounds, forming a dark stain on the pavement. They lay on the ground, their bodies twitching in the agonies of death. Aside from that initial sound Mark had uttered, neither said a word.

Then it was over. James despaired over their lifeless bodies. What cruelty! What waste! What evil!

Around him people melted away. They moved in different directions as they dispersed. Soon he was left alone standing before the gruesome scene. James couldn't do a thing with his hands still cuffed behind him other than kneel by the battered flesh of his friends.

A police car pulled up, its light bar flashing. An officer got out and strolled over to James while surveying the chaos of death. He saw it was the chief of police.

"Guess we'll have to get you out of those restraints."

Flabbergasted, James almost couldn't get the words out. "That's all you have to say?"

"An ambulance will be here soon."

"You were part of this."

"Sometimes certain emotions have to be allowed to play out. Choices have to be made. It's a new day. Different times call for different measures. Better let it go. You've already got a target painted on you for being a preacher. No sense in calling more attention to yourself."

"After the attack on the police a couple weeks ago, when so many of your fellow officers died, how can you justify doing nothing now? This is anarchy. Didn't you take an oath to uphold the law?"

"We've been under attack for a long time, accused of being racist, homophobes, what-have-you. We respond by trying to keep the peace, and when one of the bad guys acts up and we have to use force, we're the ones who get labeled as the evil perpetrators. We've had enough."

"Why don't you and every officer who feels that way quit? How can you continue to wear that uniform and not do your duty?"

"Most of us worry about collecting our pensions. Might as well serve out our time by not making waves."

James shook his head. For years the race hustlers had been making cops the bad guys. They had now succumbed in Lighthouse like in so many cities around the country. And without a meaningful police presence, violence would only increase.

The chief unlocked the handcuffs, and James rubbed his wrists. The ambulance drove silently up the street toward them. The chief headed back to his car. Before he got back in he turned around and said, "One more thing, Reverend. You'll have to declare where your church stands. The hammer is coming down."

Chapter 32

It would have been amusing if the circumstances had been different. In recent days an Islamic terrorist had destroyed a Messianic church. Numerous policemen and civilians were killed in the attack. A devout Christian couple died at the hands of a mob that disagreed with their stand on the moral issue of homosexuality. Two strident agendas that under normal circumstances would be in opposition had the same focus and their actions had the same result: death. They intended to destroy the people and the underpinnings of Christianity. There was no give or take in the matter. The First Amendment and freedom of religion meant nothing. The shredding of the Constitution by the Executive Branch had opened the floodgates for outrage and lawlessness. After all this, the Ministerium decided the time was ripe to celebrate further its partnership with the homosexual movement and the Muslim community.

James could only shake his head when he heard of the Ministerium's plans. With much fanfare the announcement circulated around town, in flyers, via newspaper ads, on the Internet, through video postings, at the churches of the sponsoring Ministerium pastors, in mosques, and in gay bars. If anyone wasn't aware of the event he'd been sleeping the last week.

The Ministerium's "Rally United Together" acquired the unfortunate acronym RUT that held the promise of saying much about the event. Amused whisperings in some quarters about the RUT in the Park pointed out the applicability to the homosexual side of the party, while a shocked few expressed astonishment that Muslims would associate with people of this ilk. If nothing else, the dynamics and interplay between the two groups had the potential for an entertaining Saturday morning.

Amusement at the concept of the event didn't cause people to stay away. Just the contrary. The country did, after all, have a decidedly lesbian president and a Muslim vice president. While the inevitable drones circled overhead, people gathered, first in twos and threes, then in a swarm. James came because of his fascination with the two groups, knowing their joint hostility toward Christianity, yet their traditional animus toward each other. It didn't escape him that Islamic law held little regard for homosexuals, in fact, it dictated their death. It wasn't unusual to read about a mob of Muslims in other countries attacking a gay blogger and throwing him off the roof of a ten-story building. Admittedly though, James had also seen their common cause in recent years against Christians. He wondered if it was really possible for the two disparate groups to truly make nice with each other in the long term.

There was plenty of room around the band shell, and that was the focal point of the rally. As people came, it didn't surprise James in the least that they congregated with others of their kind. The intent of the Ministerium was to celebrate unity through diversity, but the Muslims and those sympathetic to Islam gathered on the right while homosexuals and their supporters flocked together on the left. A clear delineation of space kept the two groups separated.

If James was running the event he figured he wouldn't have had Reverend Phyllis welcome everyone, especially since her so-called marriage partner stood beside her beaming with pride. That might have gone over fine if the rally were strictly for LGBT causes, but with half the people there being Muslims, it seemed to James that might be dabbing a little too much chlorine in their eyes. If they didn't see red after that, maybe the two groups could actually live together.

The Reverend Doctor Tom Hall came next and spoke eloquently of the many strides they'd made in the past year. He reminded the assembled of the unity achieved at the big event at his church and the meaning of that. The Christian Church and the Muslim community could worship in peace. On the other side of the equation, the church had long ago gratefully accepted the gifts of homosexuals among them. Because of the love and acceptance within ecclesiastical gatherings, many homosexuals had become ministers and priests. "All people are welcome in the house of Christ! Not only that, but the churches represented at this rally are compliant with all government requirements. You can rest assured we are working closely with the authorities to meet our every obligation. We are a safe place for all!"

Several other speakers came onstage to rouse the large crowd into an excited frenzy. They cracked jokes, sang, and exhorted everyone to love one another. Despite the disparity of interests, the vast majority responded positively in the spirit of the event.

James estimated the total number of people at ten thousand, split roughly in half between the two factions, an astonishing figure. The weather, though the temperature had moderated, continued to hold with no rain in the forecast. To go this late into the year without a drop of moisture made a lot of folks nervous. The grass in the park was brown, seemingly seared black at the tips in some places. Most farmers had lost their crops unless they had extensive irrigation systems. Forest management types spoke about the tinderbox effect and how dangerous that was. Local gardeners complained about the dearth of vegetables to can, unless they'd watered religiously during the drought; if so, they bragged about the size and quantity of their tomatoes. But the crowd gathered at the RUT in the Park couldn't have enjoyed the weather more.

Deacon Jones climbed the podium. He looked out hard on the gathering in silence for a full two minutes. As the quiet continued, uncomfortable stillness gripped the assembled. James recognized the technique and appreciated it for what it was. Extended silence either makes people nervous or heightens anticipation—often both. Being the pastor and showman that he was, Deacon Jones was well versed in crowd manipulation.

Suddenly, he shouted, "What are we here for?" His amplified voice boomed around the park.

A few people responded, but Jones shook his head and raised his voice. "I ask you again: What are we here for?"

This time someone replied, "Say it. You the man!"

A big grin showed Jones' white teeth against his black skin. "I'll tell you why we're here. It's about POWER! I tell you brothers and sisters, we have the power! Ain't no one got it more than us. Look around you. What do you see? White men, black women, Muslim, gay and straight, Christians. Do you get it! Do you? We got diversity. In diversity there is unity. In unity there is power. Let's hear it. Give yourselves a big hand!"

The crowd erupted in yells, cheers, and clapping. The drummer behind Jones pounded a throbbing beat. Jones shouted and encouraged. The drumbeat rose in tempo. Slowly a frenzy built. The deacon continued egging on the crowd. James saw the faces around him grow red in their intensity. Nearly everyone participated. Individuals melded into the greater whole, into a sea of humanity whose one purpose was to rise in the spirit of the day and the shared concepts of unity and power.

Ten minutes later the amoeba—the single cell that the crowd had become—paused. In that moment Deacon Jones called out. "I'm a Christian man, but there are some who call themselves Christian who don't believe as we do. These heretics hate you. They hate gays, they hate Muslims, they hate us true Christians who want to bring peace and harmony to you who are gathered here today. We are all one. There is no room in this town or this nation for haters!"

Jones pointed toward the sun. "There is a greater power at work in this universe. This power demands that we eliminate those who won't get along. You came here today thinking the rally would bring unity and encouragement, and you're right. But this rally is intended to do more. You are part of a movement. You have a say in how we will shape our society in the years ahead. It begins now.

"There is a church at the end of that street." He thrust his arm toward the east. With a lurch James realized the deacon pointed at the church where Bob Sanders was pastor. "That church is the center—the hub—of great apostasy. It brims with heretical teachings. It overflows with hate toward all of you. If it continues to stand it intends to destroy you."

James felt the rise in antagonism around him. Emotion flared at the injustice the man described. Deacon Jones had just personalized the inanimate church. The church itself had become the congregation. Its people had become faceless and nameless. The church had become the focus of evil incarnate.

"The question is what are you going to do about that church? Are you going to let it spew its hatred and attempt to destroy you? Will you stand for that?"

One voice rose above the murmur. "No!"

Another, then two, and three more joined in the frenzy until a cascade of voices ascended into the dry air and the cloudless sky: "No! No! No!"

A shout broke through the clamor. "What can we do?"

Jones turned the question back. "What do you think you can do?"

The voice of a woman set off an explosion: "Destroy the church!"

It was like steam blowing off the lid off a pressure cooker. The gas of indignation propelled the crowd eastward. It was no longer comprised of man, woman, youth, gender dysfunctional, or highly religious. Disparate had turned homogenous. From blob, it became mob.

As one, it ran toward the church. In moments the first person reached the front doors. They were unlocked and a horde entered. Some in the crowd headed for their vehicles where they found sledge hammers or pry bars. An old man revved up his ancient pickup truck, raced past the stragglers, and rammed the side of the building under a stained-glass window. The window shattered as the brick crumbled. The vehicle's horn blared from the pressure of the man's head on the steering wheel where he lay slumped from the impact.

James felt a sense of déjà vu from the last mob scene he'd witnessed not even a week ago. In that one his friends had perished. Now it was only a church building. He spotted Bob Sanders looking on helplessly. Of course, it was Sanders that Deacon Jones and the Ministerium wished to hurt, apparently vicariously this time. He had been the stalwart conservative, the doctrinally pure voice at all the meetings. Never once had he wavered. It was payback time.

Sanders saw James staring at him and gave a helpless shrug. James joined him, and the two watched in silence as the mob demolished the inside of the church and broke every window. It had been a beautiful structure, a long-time fixture in town. Its stained-glass windows were the envy of every other church for their rich colors and depiction of biblical scenes. No price had ever been put on them, but their worth was priceless. All gone at the whim of hostile emotion.

The men stood together in hopeless solidarity. After a time James spotted the chief of police observing the carnage. He saluted them and watched, making no effort to call other officers or to arrest the perpetrators. Like he'd previously told James, there was only grief in it for them, so why bother? At the end of several hours, the church resembled a building from a war scene. Devastated inside and out, it was a useless shell.

Tears stained Sanders' cheeks. James gave him a hug and trudged home. He noticed a drone high above him, a dark spot against the brilliant noonday sun.

Chapter 33

A number of envelopes cluttered the mailbox. James grabbed them and made his way inside, throwing the bundle into a scattered pile on the kitchen table. He yanked a frying pan from the cupboard, knocking another clattering to the floor in his agitation. It took several frustrating tries to shove it back in its place.

He snatched a chunk of cheese from the fridge and chopped slices of it off with a vengeance. Fumbling with a package of flour tortilla shells, he sandwiched the cheese between two of them to make a quesadilla and threw the concoction into the pan. He turned on the flame and walked away to stare out the window. The smell of burning food got his attention, and he ran back to the kitchen. One side of his lunch was smoking and blackened. With contained anger he cooked the flip side on lower heat. After quartering it he sat down to eat, making a face at the burnt part he'd placed downward on the plate. If he could get through lunch in one piece, he planned to visit Janna after he finished.

A hard knocking at the front door interrupted his forced prayer of thanks for his meal. Getting up, he went to see who it was. Again, an insistent knock before he got there.

"I'm coming. Hold on."

Three men in business suits plus a police officer stood outside, one of the three poised with his hand raised to knock once more. "James Glazier?"

"Yes, what can I do for you?"

"We're with the IRS. You were ordered to respond to our correspondence with an exact accounting of every firearm you own. You failed to do that. The president has ordered that anyone not in compliance with these demands immediately have all their weapons confiscated." The man was lean with an angular face, a hard glint in his eyes.

"This is the United States of America," James said. "Neither the president nor you have any right to confiscate any firearms I might or might not possess. Do you have a warrant? Are you arresting me? Who do you think you are?" The more he considered it, the more indignant James became. He crossed his arms and stood in the open doorway. He had the fleeting notion that he no longer had to worry about Pepper running out the door. In that instant, the thought of their deceased cat saddened him even in the midst of this crisis.

"We're not asking, Mr. Glazier. This isn't optional. We're here today responding to orders from our superiors. You can make it easy or difficult; it doesn't matter to us. What'll it be?"

"Let me see your badges."

Each of the men reached inside his coat pocket and flashed his credentials. Focusing only on the leader, James saw that it appeared authentic. The man's name was Carter.

"Do you have a search warrant?"

With a smirk Agent Carter produced a set of papers that James scanned. Jaw clenched and eyes blazing, he stepped aside. The three suited men pushed past him while the uniformed officer remained outside.

"You going to get the guns or tell us where they are?" Agent Carter's no-nonsense, impatient demeanor raised the hackles on the back of James' neck. Through all this, he knew he somehow needed to maintain a Christian witness, but he had no intention of being a limp noodle.

Before he could say anything, Carter stated, "We know you have four handguns and a shotgun. That would be two Glock 26s, a Sig P224, an S&W 637, and a Mossberg 500 pump action. We also know how many rounds of ammo you have for each gun. We want that, too. You gonna mess with us or do we tear your house apart?"

James sank onto the couch. They knew exactly what he and Janna owned. For all the talk about the FBI instant background check data being destroyed, it appeared that wasn't the case. He'd been right in his assumption. The government had an accurate database, and if this visit by the IRS was any indication, all other gun owners in the country were going to lose their weapons just like him. The implications were staggering.

"I'm getting impatient." Carter crossed his arms and tapped his foot.

Holding his tongue, James shook his head in disgust, and got up slowly. "I'll get them. You wait here."

"Agent Harris will accompany you."

The man had a round face and thinning hair. He nodded at James. "Let's go."

"You guys are a piece of work. You think I'm going to come out with guns blazing?"

"Numerous studies have shown that gun owners are unstable and prone to violence." It sounded like Carter was repeating something he'd been told time and again. "We're not putting ourselves in jeopardy with people like you."

Agent Harris lightly gripped James' upper arm. James shook him off. "I can do this without your help."

Agent Harris followed close behind as James led the way. In order to provide the home security they desired, James and Janna had stashed the guns in strategic locations around the house. Each weapon he picked up and handed to Harris caused James to fume even more. Upon rounding up all five of the firearms and every box of ammunition they owned, they returned to the living room.

By now Agent Carter had produced a large canvas bag. The agents ejected the magazines of the pistols, checked all the chambers, and dumped everything into the bag after counting the rounds of ammo. James blocked their way to the front door as they moved to depart. "I'd like a receipt."

Carter reached around James to the door handle. "This isn't a retail transaction, *Mr. Glazier*. There's no quid pro quo. Maybe you're not getting this yet. We're confiscating your guns. You won't be getting them back. Oh, by the way, one more thing. Because you didn't cooperate with our initial request, we've frozen all your bank and investment accounts. Don't mess with the IRS. Have a good day."

The three agents climbed into their black SUV while the police officer drove off in his squad car. Speechless, James watched them leave. It took several minutes for him to be able to close his mouth that was hanging open in frustrated astonishment.

Chapter 34

James trekked into the hospital. It felt like he was slogging through muck so thick that he couldn't lift his feet. The mire sucked at him, making his legs heavy and without life.

He stopped at the entrance to Janna's room and tried to pull himself together. He did a couple of deep knee bends to release some of his anxiety and forced a smile. Seeing her eyes pierce his as soon as he entered, he knew she'd also penetrate his defenses to learn of his lousy day. The last thing he wanted was to upset her, but he'd never been able to hide anything from her.

She clutched his hand and moaned as she shifted position in the bed. Without waiting for a word from him, she said, "Tell me about it. No matter what, I'm always here for you."

"You know everything about me, don't you?" He shook his head, marveling at her discernment. Tears welled up in his eyes as he leaned over to kiss her. He needed her so desperately, especially at times like these.

He closed his eyes and told her about the morning rally and the burning of Bob Sanders' church. "What 's with these people? How can they justify this—sponsoring it, egging on a crowd like that? Especially people who are supposed to be ministers of the Gospel. It's pure evil."

Janna shivered and pulled up her blanket, tucking it under her chin. "What did you pray after that?"

What a question! Leave it to Janna to get to the heart of the matter. James hung his head and mumbled, "Not sure I prayed anything."

Her hand came free from under the covers and stroked his arm. "It's okay." After a moment, she asked, "Is that all that happened this morning?"

He scratched his head and gave her a rueful smile. "Not exactly. After I got home and almost burned the house down making lunch, the IRS practically knocked down our front door. They demanded I hand over all our guns under the pretense of my not complying with a law that forces disclosure of weapons to doctors."

"Did you?"

"Did I what?"

"Provide the information to who—Dr. Mason?—that they required?"

James shrugged. "No. There was no way I was going to capitulate to that intrusion in the doctor's office that negated the Second Amendment."

"So the IRS followed through on its threat?"

"It took all my God-given strength not to go ballistic and end up in jail for assaulting Federal agents. I gave them the guns. They even knew how much ammunition we had and wanted every bullet."

She squeezed his hand. "That must have been difficult for you."

They were both silent for a minute until Janna probed again. "That wasn't the end of it, was it?"

"You know, I've never liked the concept of soul mates. There's nothing in the Bible I've ever found that spoke of the idea. God leads people in certain ways to accomplish His purposes, such as with the mating of certain individuals like Jacob and Rachel. God also shows us how we can be dear friends with one another, like David and King Saul's son, Jonathan. But Janna, the way you understand me and what's going on in my head is uncanny. We may not be soul mates, but God certainly has something going on between us."

Her delighted laugh was a balm to his spirit. "Let me get the rest of this out." He told her of the final, chilling statement by the IRS agent regarding their financial accounts. "When they left, I checked, and he was right on."

He'd immediately gone online to his bank and brokerage, only to find that neither financial website would allow him to even login. Because it was Saturday, the recording at the contact numbers for his particular issue said to call during the workweek. "I threw up my hands and almost swore. Instead I said, 'Okay, Lord, I don't know why You're allowing this to happen. I don't like it and I can't do anything about it. It's all Yours.'" Truthfully, though, he didn't feel like he'd truly given it to God, and a germ of resentment remained in his heart.

"Are you ready to kill that germ so it doesn't kill you?"

It was like she'd read his mind. How well she knew him! He forced a smile. "You won't let me out of here until I do, will you?"

"Not a chance."

He held her hand while praying it out and repenting of any animosity he harbored in his current situation. In his prayer he voiced his confusion. "Why, God? Why am I resentful of what You're doing with Janna and me? My 'whys' are piling up and I'm having difficulty processing them. Help me to understand so I don't grow a root of bitterness that consumes me."

When he finished, she gave him a weak smile that stabbed at his heart. One more of those from her, and he felt he'd die of despair. He had to strain to hear the next words she said because her voice was fading.

"Honey, I know my illness has been tough on you. On top of that you've got so many things going on that impact your life. But don't give up; don't give up on God. He'll see you through. I promise. Give your questions and your heavy yoke to Him. He has so much in store for you. Allow Him to work in and through you. Don't fight Him."

How James wished he could embrace her words. They rang of truth. They spoke of light in the darkness of the collapsed mineshaft; hope that would lead him to fresh air and freedom. But a sense of abandonment had begun suffocating him. He hated the lie, but it was all he could say, "I'm okay with God."

Her heartbreaking awareness penetrated him. His spiritual helplessness mirrored her physical vulnerability. She had to rest and could no longer speak. He barely heard her faint words as an exhalation: "I'll keep praying for you."

Chapter 35

Washington, D.C.

Strolling the grounds of the U.S. Naval Observatory, the two men walked near one of the rounded domes housing an advanced telescope that provided a window to the universe. One of the men had an appreciation for a god of creation and served him, the other had no use for any such being. Despite their vast differences in spiritual orientation they both believed in and used the power of government to achieve their aims.

Arnold Rickards had joined Abu Saif at the vice president's home for lunch to discuss the latest successful initiative they had long planned. After their fine meal of a tasty arugula salad, jumbo crab legs, and tiramisu for dessert, they'd removed their suit jackets and begun a leisurely walk in the continued warmth of the season.

"It is impressive indeed how successful we have been in a week," Abu Saif said.

"All it takes is money and brains, my friend." Arnold Rickards tapped his temple twice to make the point. "Speaking of which, your share in our little scam of the airlines is safely in your Swiss account."

"Yes, that was so very clever on your part. You have a gift for turning opportunity into money."

"My people worked extremely hard to make the day a success. I particularly enjoyed the aftermath of the hacking scandal." Rickards' gaze took on the long-distance characteristic of one deep in thought and far from his present location. "The airlines were sure they would have to keep their planes grounded because of their systems being so severely compromised. But then they learned that their computers weren't infiltrated after all. We completely deceived them with our ghost programs. But it was enough that they made the major public announcement and their stocks went down significantly at the threat.

"The beauty was that we made our money on the short with the stocks falling and timed our buys back into the market to coincide with the announcement that everything was okay—no hacking, no problems—and we made money on the upside as well. Yes, it was a good day."

"Perfect, perfect," Saif said. "It's good to profit from uncertainty. Your DSS has provided you another means to do that."

"The Dissident Scoring System! How I love that program. I always fantasized using my company, as provider of the largest Internet search engine in the world, as a means of accomplishing another dream of mine, namely to rid this nation of its guns. Now it is no longer a fantasy. I have always hated the fixation so many have for their firearms. They are phallic substitutes for little men who have no testosterone. To be able to work with you and Luisa on the realization of this vision, and to accomplish it, the world simply gets better and better."

"Tell me, for I am very curious, how does the DSS work?"

"Come, let us sit for a moment." Rickards grabbed the back of a bench along the path and settled into the seat. Saif joined him. Before them the Queen Anne residence of the vice president rose in its splendor. "Lovely house," Rickards remarked.

"The DSS?" Saif prompted.

"We dubbed the program Jezebel. There seemed to be a rightness to our ability to compromise and infiltrate so many different sources of information, to in essence, fornicate with them. I'm sure that you, as a Muslim knowledgeable about the Christian's Bible, can appreciate that."

Saif rocked back with a laugh. "How appropriate. I love the story of Jezebel. She hated the Jews and led them into idolatry, sorcery, and every kind of sexual immorality. It drove their God crazy and He punished them for their wickedness against Him."

Rickards nodded. "Our Jezebel doesn't quite accomplish all that, but it penetrates that which is supposed to be sacrosanct. It makes data that is supposed to be pure and virginal a bloody mess. We gather it all, massage it, and use it for our purposes. In this case, for the government's purposes, which dovetail with mine. We collected and collated data from all pertinent government agencies, such as the IRS, FBI, BATFE, and many more; then illicitly gathered data from every large retailer in the country, Walmart, Target, you name it, even independent gun stores. Once we put all that data together the collection was massive, but Jezebel handled it with ease. We correlated every bit of information that could point us to people who owned any kind of firearm and the results speak for themselves. We knew exactly who had how many, when they acquired them, and the ammunition they bought."

"And the information proved priceless. It allowed us to commission the IRS and like-minded agencies to cover the country, to literally swoop down on every community in the nation and confiscate their guns. At this point there should be relatively few people who have firearms of any kind. It's been amazing." Abu Saif couldn't help but admire Rickards. It glowed, exuding from him.

"The future is bright for those who have the power to control. You have allowed me to realize my dream and I am indebted to you and Luisa for that."

Abu Saif stood and slapped Rickards on the shoulder. "You are correct, Arnold. Many more changes are coming. Power will be consolidated even more. The fate of this nation will soon be completely in our hands."

Chapter 36

Western Michigan

In a deep funk, James sat in his office and pondered the situation. With his secretary at lunch, he had the church to himself. He got up and wandered into the sanctuary. The empty seats spoke of his empty heart. The pulpit in front of him looked forlorn; it would be the condition of his soul when Janna died, and the church dismissed him because of it. The cross of Christ stood farther back on the altar. Even it seemed to echo the depth of despair that welled up in his heart.

He felt his faith slipping away. How he'd worked at the ministry. Since being saved, he'd given his very life to it. He'd stood week after week proclaiming the Word of God. He'd labored, cried, and stood alongside his flock. And what did he have to show for it? An ungrateful church, a dying wife, and a faith that shimmered and shifted like a chimera. At times tangible, at others an illusion. What was faith? It certainly wasn't this false reality he seemed to be hanging onto. He whacked the back of a chair in frustration, then had to rub his hand to reduce the pain he'd caused.

Once, twice, he circled the perimeter of the sanctuary, trying to pray, trying to find what he'd lost. He so longed to hear the voice of God, the reassurance that he was doing something right, but nothing came except the echoing silence of the large room.

He sat and stared at the cross. After a while, he lowered his head to his hands. There seemed to be no point in any of this. Maybe he wasn't even saved. Perhaps he'd been fooling himself all these years. The blind leading the blind.

A Bible lay a couple of seats away, and he reached to pick it up. Were these living words, or was this simply a dead tome? Surely God would speak to him if the former were true. He leafed through the pages, hoping his eye would fall on some special verse of encouragement. What he got instead was Matthew 7:21. He read it out loud several times with a heavy heart. "Not everyone who says to me, 'Lord, Lord,' will enter the kingdom of heaven, but only the one who does the will of my Father who is in heaven."

"Well, Lord, if You're even there, I guess I know my fate. I obviously haven't done Your will. And my hope for seeing Your kingdom? Hah! Doesn't look like that's happening. Oh, God, I'm so sorry I haven't been faithful. I'm so confused. I just don't know what to do."

"Sounds like you have a problem, my friend."

The voice right behind him startled James so much he yelped and jumped to his feet, his heart beating so crazily he thought it'd leap right out of his chest.

"Gadi!" he exclaimed. "Oh, my gosh. I about died." James shook his head, his hand on his chest, and the realization came to him: "What are you doing here? Didn't you leave? Didn't you lose your visa? Why haven't they thrown you out of the country like they promised? And what are you doing in a church? You're a Jew. You don't even believe in God."

"Whoa, whoa, my friend." Gadi Benjamin motioned with his hands for James to slow down. "One question at a time."

"Sure, no problem. I'm just so shocked to see you."

"Given your prayers, I imagine I am the last person you would have expected."

James felt his face redden. "Well, yes. I've been doing some soul searching."

"More than that. It sounds like a very deep search for God." Gadi placed his hand on James's shoulder and applied a little downward pressure. "Please sit. I am probably not the one to help you find God again given my agnosticism, but I can at least let you know what I decided to do—why I am here."

Gadi sat in the adjoining seat and looked around. "You know, I have never been in a church before." He chuckled. "With my background it is certainly implausible."

"Yet, here you are. There must be a story behind this."

"There is, and it is perhaps as disturbing for me as your spiritual quandary is for you."

"Disturbing?"

"Have you ever had a dream you believed came from God?"

"I haven't, but my wife Janna is quite prophetic. She's had a number of dreams and visions over the years. In specific instances she's also been given a Word of Knowledge so as to speak into someone's life to give them guidance or encouragement." James spoke wistfully, thinking of his beloved wife and how their long relationship was soon to end. He blinked away a tear and said, "From my experience with Janna, I know God speaks to us."

"Yet, you question His existence and whether He has anything to do with you?"

"Messed up, isn't it?"

"Perhaps no more so than those of us who struggle to find the true meaning of a God."

"What's changed? You've had a dream you think may have come from Him?"

Gadi shifted in his seat. He leaned back and interlaced his fingers behind his head. "In a word, yes. If it had not been so vivid, so real, so immediate, I would have dismissed it out of hand. But it was more than a simple dream. It impressed me so much that I have remained surreptitiously here in the States rather than go back to Israel."

"Something in the dream told you to stay?"

"More than something." Gadi compressed his lips and breathed deeply. "Someone."

"Tell me more."

"I was walking in an open field on a cloudless, sunny day with the blue sky so intense it made me ache. The beauty of the green grasses and the flowers all around me of every color and hue created this sorrowful void within me. I loved all that I saw and experienced, but it was not enough. I was empty despite the fullness of creation surrounding me.

"I was about to say, 'How I need more…,' but the words never left my tongue. In that instant a blinding light encompassed me, and a figure entered the aura of this light. It was a man. He held out His hands to me and I saw holes in them. His eyes flashed with such a passionate love that I began to weep. I fell to my knees, and He spoke to me."

As Gadi recounted his dream, an intense warmth rose from James's core. It ascended from his belly to the top of his head.

Gadi continued. "He told me to stand up. He said, 'You will bow your knee to Me. First, you have work to do.' I wanted to worship Him, but He said I have to help you. Then my time will come."

"Help me? What does that mean?" James couldn't fathom the message and its implications. "I'm nothing, nobody. What's to help?"

"I have no idea. I only know that regardless of my lack of faith, there is definitely Someone greater than I have been aware of, and He wants me to remain here, not to go back to Israel."

"Sure sounds like Jesus to me."

"Maybe. The one thing I can say is that my spiritual boundaries have been enlarged."

"But you're not yet a follower of Jesus Christ?"

"If He had called me to follow Him right then, I probably would have. What He meant by it not being my time yet, I have no idea."

"Sure sounds like you've changed your outlook. You're about as ready as anybody I've known who came to Christ."

"Ah, but I am a Jew. It may be that I have to work through some more issues regarding my bias against Christians in general before I can fully surrender."

"You're not biased against me."

"No. You are a good man, James. You have heard this phrase before no doubt: 'It is complicated.' There is the meme about Hitler being Christian and punishing my people. There is garbage in our past going back to the Crusades. I have a whole litany of negatives that I have absorbed being a Jew, and I have not totally dealt with them."

"In our talks I thought I'd done a good job of debunking those myths."

"You did. Give me time. It may be that your God has put a stirring in my soul for Him to also be my God. Perhaps the work He has for me will purge me completely so that will happen."

"What are you going to do until that work becomes clear?"

Gadi grinned. "I will be around, just not in plain sight. I was effectively instructed to remain underground, and to remain ready, watching for when I am needed."

Chapter 37

The IRS agent had told him exactly what to expect. Actually experiencing it left James without recourse. Agent Carter told him that his bank and investment accounts were frozen. The reality made him wonder how he'd manage.

James went online again to try accessing his accounts. When that failed he drove to the branch office of his bank. Inside he waited for a personal banker. After a short wait, a young man came to where James sat looking out the window and introduced himself as Alex.

They walked to Alex's nearby desk. After a few pleasantries James explained that he was having trouble accessing his account without mentioning the reason.

Alex tapped on his keyboard, waited, and frowned. He entered more information, shook his head. "Sorry, Mr. Glazier, I can't find any record of your bank accounts here."

A heavy weight settled in the pit of James' stomach. "Maybe you spelled my name wrong. Let me give you my account number."

He fumbled in his wallet and came up with a slip of paper, which he read to Alex. The result was no different. "I'm really sorry. That's an account number like we use, but there's nothing here showing you as a client. In fact, I tried the number twice."

Frustrated, James said, "What am I supposed to do? How can I not have an account when I know I do? I have direct deposits going in there; I've got automatic payments out of the account. What am I supposed to live on? This is crazy."

In a sympathetic and helpless gesture Alex turned up his hands. "I don't know what to tell you. If you can find more information, I'd be glad to check further for you. As it is now, there's nothing I can do."

James left mumbling to himself. Outside the sun had hidden behind a cloud, lending to his gloomy feeling. With a glance up James uttered a short prayer, "I need Your help, Lord," but by this time he wasn't expecting much in return. The continued absence of rain worried many, James included, yet an outpouring of beseeching prayers for farmers and others had yielded no relief. It didn't matter the sphere of prayer, God had apparently decided to ignore every need.

Turning his car's ignition key, James realized that without access to his bank account his life would soon drastically change. How would he fill his gas tank? Where would the money come from to buy food? He hadn't tested his ATM card, but if his bank account had disappeared through the machinations of the IRS, then he certainly wouldn't have access to money through their cash dispensers. How would he pay his home mortgage, or basic utilities like gas, electric, and water?

Panic squeezed at his heart. He quickly drove from the bank's parking lot heading for his broker's office. Maybe the IRS hadn't yet cut off access to his investment money. As he worried, his mind strayed from the road. The next instant a man appeared immediately in front of him.

Chapter 38

James slammed on the car's brakes. His heart pounded at the relief of missing him. He shook his head to clear it, settled his glasses back on his nose, and saw the man was Bob Sanders.

Coming to James' passenger-side open window Sanders said, "That was close."

"I'm so sorry. I'm really distracted. Are you okay?"

"Not a dent or crease on me, thank God. What's going on with you?"

"Got a problem with the IRS. Can I drop you off somewhere?"

"As a matter of fact, I wanted to talk with you." Sanders got in the car and strapped himself in. "I've heard of others having issues with the IRS this week."

James let that sit for a minute as he resumed down the street, then sighed. "I refused to provide information to my doctor that the government required. I didn't believe it would lead to actual problems, but it did." He proceeded to detail what had ensued with the IRS.

"My dad had guns, so it was natural for me to own them, too," Sanders said. "He taught me about gun safety, how to shoot, enrolled me in some NRA classes, and taught me how important the Second Amendment is to preserve our freedom in this country. We're seeing that all slip away. He'd have a fit if he were alive. Guess I'm lucky in one respect. For now, the powers that be have ignored me. I've gotten three or four calls from people in my congregation that they've experienced exactly what you did. Agents effectively invaded their homes. Their bank accounts disappeared. As you can imagine, they're freaking out."

"Like me. I'm not sure what to do." James signaled and turned at the next intersection. "Do you mind my checking with my broker? Should only take a couple minutes if my experience at the bank is any indication."

Sanders told him he had plenty of time. "I'll stay in the car," he said, when they reached the broker's office building.

Inside, James went through the same routine as he had earlier at the bank. He and Janna had been frugal over the years. This had allowed them to save both inside and outside tax-deferred savings plans. Thankfully, the health plan they belonged to had protected them during Janna's long and expensive illness, leaving only minimal medical bills to pay—a miracle in itself given the mess the government had made of health insurance over the prior fifteen years.

The amount they had stashed away at the brokerage was substantial, but now, the representative echoed the bank's story. "I'm sorry, Mr. Glazier, there's nothing I can find. If you had an account with our company, it's been closed or something. Well, not even that. A closed account would show up as just that. Assuming you had an account here, it's as if you never did in the first place. I don't know what to tell you."

Feeling more than defeated, James slowly walked back to the car. He sat in silence, hands on the steering wheel as Sanders patiently waited.

"This is terrible." Even as James stewed about his predicament, he felt his cheeks grow warm. He dipped his head in embarrassment as he remembered that Sanders also had difficult issues. "Bob, I was so caught up in my problems I forgot all about you. How have you been since they destroyed your church? What's happening with your congregation?"

"It's been tough," he admitted. "I wanted to scream and yell and go hit someone right after it happened. I wake up at night sweating at the thought that I have to completely forgive these people who did this. I know that God forgave me when I didn't deserve it. I know that. But making that real, changing it from an intellectual understanding to a living, breathing forgiveness is so much harder than I anticipated. So, yeah, I struggle with it. In the meantime, we're meeting in people's homes, going house to house like in the Book of Acts. There's something to that, my friend, something deep and special. I know the Church will survive. I just pray God gives me the grace to live out my commitment to Him through mercy to others who I...can't stand right now."

Sanders' eyes hardened for a moment before softening again. James could only imagine the anger he held back. "What you're dealing with," James said, "makes me see that my problems aren't isolated. I guess we tend to blow up what's in front of us and make it all-consuming so that we forget there are others who face issues of their own. That doesn't negate how hard it is for me, but it gives me an appreciation of the need to not be so self-centered."

Sanders grew somber. "It's going to get worse. This chaos, confusion, violence: there's a purpose in it all. More and more, day-by-day, I see God's hand in this. That is, the withdrawal of His hand. We were never perfect as a nation. We committed more than our share of sins, but we were founded by Godly men with Godly intent, and enough of us over the years held true and fast to that ideal. Our churches sent missionaries to the world in response to the Great Commission; many churches and their people held to the

Word of God and walked in it to the best of their ability. Probably most important, we, as a nation, blessed Israel. We've drastically fallen away from these virtues. And our greatest national sin may be the cursing of Israel. The Bible says that's a death knell, and we've sounded it.

"Speaking of which, would you care to see the next step down into the morass for our fair city?"

"There's more?" James thought they must have reached the bottom by now.

"No doubt even beyond what we'll see today if you wish to join me."

James shrugged and let Bob Sanders direct him. Their destination shortly became clear—the shops with their Arabic signs, the women with head coverings. From the pit of his stomach James felt a twisting and turning that caused a bitterness to rise in his throat. He remembered their last visit to this part of town when the two men attacked them.

As they drew nearer, the difference from then to now—only weeks later—blared forth. Today was a celebration. Balloons and streamers draped the sparse bushes around the apartment buildings. Welcome signs had been erected. Children's bouncy houses littered the street ahead. As they drove closer, numerous yellow school buses parked one behind the other along one side of the street.

James took all this in with astonishment. "What in the world?"

"You'll see," Sanders' replied.

The found a spot to park amidst the buses and walked toward the large gathering of children and adults a couple of blocks away. Great excitement animated the boys and girls. Many held hand-drawn welcome signs mirroring the larger ones around them.

A figure up ahead looked familiar. James pointed and said, "Is that...?"

Sanders nodded. "Carla."

James recalled the clandestine conversation Bob and he'd had with the woman, a schoolteacher concerned about the infiltration of Islam in the schools. She caught sight of the two men, spoke a quick word to the children around her, and came over to them.

"Gentlemen, welcome to the logical conclusion of the indoctrination of our kids."

James glanced around in confusion. "What is all this, Carla?"

"This...," she acknowledged with a tilt of her head, "is our welcome committee for the illegal aliens we are gladly settling in our community. They will be arriving imminently. The school district, along with numerous other functionaries from our fair city, will extend to them our warmest wishes for a happy and prosperous life. And why wouldn't they be thrilled with free housing, food, medical care, transportation on the city's dime, and a generous monthly cash stipend?"

Sanders rubbed his forehead. "Don't be surprised if they soon turn dissatisfied and want more. Such as having mosques built with taxpayer dollars, along with seats of power in our city government."

A cluster of men and women passed by the three of them. Although the month of October was well along, the general warmth of the season continued, primarily because of the dry weather conditions. The news had been full of reports lately as to how severe drought plagued much of the country. The prophets of climate change clamored about global warming. They disclaimed any other source and proclaimed the persistent heat as a harbinger of greater weather-related calamities to come. The group passing by James and his friends talked with great animation and snatches of their conversation dealt with the ongoing crisis of climate catastrophe.

Yet that wasn't the important point. The people in this larger grouping were self-absorbed and blind to others around them. James had no such issue. Among the august individuals were Reverend Phyllis, Deacon Jones, and Pastor Tom Hall. James indicated one of the other men. "Isn't that the imam?"

"It certainly is," Sanders affirmed.

"I don't know who the other two men are," Carla said. They were darker skinned and walked with an air of authority.

"Not to worry," Sanders said. "They're just the two top honchos in the Muslim Brotherhood in our region.

Carla's face revealed her shock. "Oh, my. I can only imagine why they're here."

"Guess we'll find out," Sanders said.

A thought came to James. "Carla, I wanted to ask you: Did the government decree affecting Christians working for the government impact you as a teacher in any way?"

"Not as yet," she said. "Friends of mine working at different levels of government were fired for "walking while Christian," but it hasn't touched teachers in my school so far, although I do hear rumblings of worse to come."

"What does *that* mean?" Bob Sanders asked.

"Wish I knew," Carla said, "but I'm afraid it won't be good."

The Christian ministers and their Muslim compatriots came together in a tight knot, having summoned over a couple of men in white shirts and ties and a woman in a pants suit.

Carla pointed discreetly. "The woman is our school district superintendent."

"And certainly, James, you recognize our mayor and his assistant," Sanders said.

"This is quite a celebratory event," James said.

One of the Brotherhood men answered his cell phone, spoke a moment, and informed the others of something. Within a matter of minutes a silver bus turned on the street heading toward them from the other direction. Other buses followed.

"I have to get back to the children. We were told we had to be a part of this today. All I can do is try to subtly lessen the damage to these little ones and counter the indoctrination they're constantly fed. See you later." Carla hurried back to where another teacher stood with a multitude of kids around her.

The first bus stopped. James saw how full it was. As bus after bus came up and stopped, every one bristled with heads behind the tinted windows.

The ministers, the Muslims, and the city and school officials stood in a semi-circle holding hands. The teachers, upon instruction, arranged the many children behind these leaders. As the first of the occupants of the buses emerged, the men, women, and children burst forth into song. Although the tune was familiar to James he couldn't place it. He did hear the lyrics and could only shake his head.

"Oh, Allah, to you we bring praise.
Peace be upon your prophet.
We worship you as the one revealed by
Muhammad,
And we lift up your name in reverent fear.
Might we submit all to you,
Bringing your rule over all the earth.
We kill and we die for you,
Showing your mercy and justice."

"Did our," James wiggled his fingers to show air quotes around the next word, "*Christian* friends really just sing that?" He couldn't fathom it.

"Rather sad, isn't it?" Sanders said.

The men watched in silence as the buses emptied. By the time they'd finished, hundreds of people had flooded the area, talking, gesticulating, some bumping and jostling those around them.

"What little I read, indicated these *refugees*," James rolled his eyes at the word, "were mainly women and children fleeing intolerable conditions. From what I actually see, the majority of these people are young men. They look restless."

"They'll fit right in with the bunch that's already here, like those guys that attacked us last time."

"As pastors, shouldn't we be thinking of how to evangelize them?"

"I'm sure those opportunities will come. And, yes, I fervently pray we can bring the Message of Jesus Christ into some of their lives. Unfortunately, the welcoming committee is comprised of those who want to compromise the Gospel. Whatever Reverend Phyllis and the others accomplish will be severely deficient when it comes to the true Word of God. They're in bed with the Brotherhood; they're Marxists; they've watered down Christianity to make it palatable to Muslims—don't forget the Chrislam sermons we heard our fellow Christian leaders preach. There may come a time—I'm sure God will provide those kairos moments, those God-appointed moments—but I haven't seen anything as yet to indicate this is one of them."

The two Muslim Brotherhood men shouted instructions. More local helpers appeared, and they began escorting the new arrivals in fours and eights to the various apartment buildings—their new homes courtesy of the generosity of U.S. taxpayers.

To James, it had the all the makings of a time bomb.

Chapter 39

Camp Grayling – Central Michigan

The personal Secret Service bodyguard of the vice president of the United States, Ibrahim Sufyan, carried the mantle of authority of the man most likely to succeed the current president in the nation's highest office. Over the years, his boss had dispatched him on various clandestine assignments outside the normal run of duties that Secret Service personnel might be expected to perform. His previous task had been to assassinate General Wylie who had dared to disagree with the direction the Executive Branch was taking the military. Today's commission brought him to the Midwest to inspect the readiness of the various FEMA camps run under the auspices of the Michigan National Guard.

Camp Grayling was the third facility Sufyan had visited today, having already been to Kincheloe Correctional Facility—formerly Kincheloe Air Force Base—and Sawyer

AFB both in the Upper Peninsula. The remaining camp on his itinerary for the day was Raco Field, a so-called inactive World War II Army base. Each of the camps was unique, but their common denominator was the secrecy that surrounded each one in its local community. Most resided under the heavy cover of dense forest. Aside from the civilians employed in various aspects of construction, few people knew about them. Their superiors had ordered the local employees not to divulge any information about the bases to anyone under the threat of significant unpleasant consequences. Few dared cross their superiors in this regard.

Colonel Trask, who'd been part of the project since the Obama years, accompanied Sufyan on his tour. Trask had overseen much of the building of the special requirements that had been handed down and displayed evident pride in the outcome. His pleasure at Sufyan's visit and being able to share his work shone through as they walked the inner perimeter.

"We built the double fences ten feet high and added barbed razor wire embedded with shards of glass. Each guard tower covers less than the standard requirements providing greater coverage over smaller areas. This allows each guard to maintain complete surveillance of his assigned territory to a much higher degree." Trask pointed to the railroad tracks in the distance. "These assure we have complete access to the movement of necessary equipment, supplies, and people who will enter the facility. Naturally you're aware of the landing field nearby that you flew into. We have great access. We're a little smaller than Kincheloe. I believe they can hold about five thousand prisoners; excuse me, guests." Both men laughed. We can do thirty-five hundred. It's a good solid number."

Sufyan had seen enough of these camps that after their moment of mirth he tuned out Colonel Trask, who continued extolling the virtues of his oversight and all that had been done to create a more secure environment for detainees. The agent wasn't privy to the complete extent of the plans that had been set in motion, but he knew enough to please him greatly.

Some eight hundred camps around the country had been constructed in recent years. He'd seen the maps showing the placement of each one and marveled at the grand vision that had brought them to fruition. As a devout Muslim, who read the Qur'an daily and revered the prophet Muhammad, he couldn't help but chuckle. He thought about the kafir, the infidels, these camps would soon detain. They were excrement, a perfect description—unbelievers worthy of nothing but to be buried with the filthy flies they attracted. He had waited all his adult life for this moment.

"Did you say something?" Trask asked, interrupting his reverie.

"No, just thinking how pleased the president will be with the completion of all these camps."

The two men examined the housing, medical experimentation, and punishment areas with Colonel Trask practically glowing while describing how many could simultaneously be dealt with in a punitive manner. The medical experimentation lab was of particular interest to Sufyan. Its gleaming, stainless-steel interior contained specially built beds and reclining chairs. According to Trask, three highly-trained doctors were ready to work as soon as they were needed. Sufyan wished he could be here when the camp became populated. He knew he would enjoy watching the doctors ply their trade.

"Do you have any idea, Agent Sufyan, when the flow of prisoners will begin?"

"That's classified, Colonel Trask. The important thing is that you and your team are ready to accept them."

"With assurance, sir, I can say that we are."

Ibrahim Sufyan surveyed the facility one final time, his gaze stopping at different points as he looked. "That is good, Colonel. The president and vice president will be quite pleased."

Chapter 40

The result of the IRS action left James in a precarious situation. Because of the prior actions of the government against Christian employees and James' empathy for members of his church who'd lost their jobs due to unprecedented persecution against people of faith, James' salary had been halved. He'd given up money due him for the benevolence of those in greater need. In the wake of the IRS seizing his accounts, he realized he'd made that decision in the heat of the moment in the board meeting with his deacons and hadn't prayed about it beforehand. He leaned his head against the back of the chair. Closing his eyes, he shook his head in dismay at how presumptuous he'd been. His intent had been mercy, but was it really what God wanted him to do? If he'd stopped to ask God for guidance, would this have been His answer?

Beyond his quandary, he had to do two things. First he needed to stop his direct deposit so that his subsequent salary payments wouldn't disappear into the vapors of the Internet. In so doing, he'd have to hope and pray the IRS wouldn't seek him out for further punishment for his transgressions against its anti-gun agenda.

The more difficult task before him was to meet once more with Joe Bennett and the other deacons to ask for relief from his earlier commitment. Without access to his bank accounts, his paltry salary wouldn't cover his monthly obligations. He snorted at the irony that he was now a benevolence case himself.

James knew his relationship with the board was tenuous at best. The evolution of that relationship saddened him. He'd originally come in and gotten along well with these overseers of the church. He'd hoped for a long, healthy relationship. To his dismay their connection had frayed. The love of Christ had been lost, replaced with harsh words and dirty looks. When James looked back, he saw his responsibility in the breakdown. Yet, just like in a marriage, one party was never solely at fault. The board members had been guilty of hardening their hearts on any number of issues and finally against James himself. He never suspected, however, that they'd actually refuse to meet with him during this tumultuous time.

His phone conversation with Joe Bennett didn't go well. "Why should we bother, *Pastor* Glazier? One way or the other you're out of here."

"One way or the other? Joe, what does that mean? I get it that some might think Janna's still sick because of my lack of faith, which, by the way, is utterly ridiculous." James squeezed the phone so tight his hand turned numb. "Tell me, what other crimes have I committed?"

"We want nothing to do with somebody like you. You can whine about us being heartless until the cows come home, but we won't put up with immoral, sexual behavior."

Shocked and speechless at the accusation, James couldn't even formulate a reply. He had no clue what Bennett meant. Feeling like a fish gasping for air, he tried opening and closing his mouth several times. No sound came out, not an objection, not a denial. Nothing.

Bennett grunted. "Like I said, there's no point in our meeting to hash over your troubles. You've brought them all upon yourself. You of all people should know that God says he'll judge those who disobey Him in this way, that He'll throw them in the Lake of Fire along with liars and murderers. Maybe you should pick up your Bible once in a while *Reverend*. Seems like you've misplaced it during your extracurricular activities. I have to go."

James stood dumbly looking at his phone after the line went dead. What *way* was he talking about? He recalled Watchman Nee, a great man of God in China during the mid 1900s. Accusations flew about certain aspects of his life and ministry causing many of his friends and supporters to fall away. Watchman never said a word in return, emulating Jesus and His silence when facing His accusers. He believed that God would vindicate him in His own time. Was the speechlessness that James experienced God shutting his mouth from replying? That seemed a stretch. Still, his inability to talk in that moment was puzzling.

Regardless of God's plans, James still had a life to live and issues to face. What better place than at Janna's side? Within twenty minutes he was at the hospital.

Entering Janna's room, he encountered several doctors and nurses gathered around her bed plus a man in a business suit. One of the nurses who knew him looked up and saw the confusion on his face. "Good timing, Mr. Glazier. We were just discussing the release of your wife."

James had no idea what she meant. "You're sending her back to the nursing home?"

The man in the suit straightened. "You're Janna Glazier's husband?"

James nodded.

The man squared his shoulders. "I'm Todd Burton, Executive Vice President of the hospital. We've discussed your wife's situation extensively in our offices today. It seems your health insurance is no longer valid, and we're obligated to release her immediately. Since you have no coverage, we can't send her to a skilled care facility. We have no choice but to send her home."

"What do you mean we don't have insurance? Of course we do."

"We were notified this morning. It didn't seem right, so we double-checked. Something about the IRS."

"Oh, no!" It felt like he'd been sucker punched in the gut. "What about her care? This is so sudden. Isn't this illegal?" He panted, searching for air, desperately trying to make sense of it all.

"I can't tell you, Mr. Glazier. Your wife's doctors are obviously concerned, but there's no alternative. We have to do what we have to do."

The IRS connection sickened James. With difficulty he pulled himself together to argue their case. "You appear to be under some pressure, Mr. Burton. In the normal course of events there can often be exceptions made. Are you telling me that's not possible?"

"I'm afraid so."

"This means you're effectively going to dump a dying woman into the streets. Do I have that right?"

A light sheen of sweat appeared on Burton's forehead. "She cannot remain here, sir. I've ordered the doctors to discharge her within the hour."

"Was anyone planning to let me know? You were just going to put her on the street? The IRS must have really put down the hammer on you guys. This is disgusting." He turned to his wife. "Who's going to help me get Janna ready to leave?"

Burning inside, James did his best to not say anything more. For some reason he was acutely conscious of his Christian witness in this moment and knew how easy it would be to bring shame to Christ through his words. The odd thing for him was the contradiction between this sensitivity to Christ and his severe questioning of where God was in this mess—of where He was in all that was happening.

Maybe He was on vacation and forgot to leave His angels a note to check up on James and Janna in His absence.

The room cleared following a final few actions and discussions by the doctors and nurses. A single nurse remained who helped him prepare Janna to leave. For her part, Janna said little, accepting the situation with a wan smile.

Janna could barely sit up in the wheelchair, which added to James' sense of injustice. The nurse stayed with Janna near the hospital entrance while James brought the car around. Before closing the car door and going back inside, the nurse offered an apology that wasn't hers to give. "I'm so sorry for all this. Good luck."

In the brief ride home, James tried to reassure Janna. "Everything'll be all right, honey."

She inched her hand onto his leg and squeezed, offering a brief reply. "Of course it will. It's all in God's hands."

Tears came to James' eyes. How many times had he cried at the plight of his beloved wife? How could God do this? The injustice of man was nothing compared to that of God. He wiped the tears with his sleeve and tried to focus on the road.

At home, he managed to maneuver Janna inside and into their bed. He wasn't at all prepared. How was he to handle this? Although his position at the church was highly questionable, he was still the pastor and had duties and responsibilities. He had to add caregiver to his resume without the means to do the job. They had access to none of their money and only a meager income. James ran his fingers through his hair. It was hopeless.

Janna's strength was so slight that she slipped into sleep as soon as her head touched the pillow. James looked at her rhythmic breathing and knew she was out cold. Despite that, several mumbled words passed her lips, hard to understand, but definite. "Use what you put away."

"What?" She didn't stir. It had come from the depths of her sleep. It took several minutes of puzzling over the words for James to understand their meaning. He literally hit his forehead with the palm of his hand in comprehension. He ran from the room.

Five minutes later, at the place he'd hidden the money, he said a brief word of thanks, both to God and for Janna hearing His word and speaking it. Some weeks ago Janna had spoken a prophetic word to James. Following that, she'd told him to pull cash from their accounts. He'd completely forgotten it in the midst of their troubles.

It wasn't a fortune. On the other hand, the stash of cash would hold them for some time. He'd even made the effort to purchase some gold coins as further backup. This would keep them going for a while. The lights would stay on with Janna home. He could only give thanks to God despite his troubling unbelief.

Chapter 41

James sat next to Janna, holding her hand, wishing and praying that God would intervene to bring back the health of his wife. He hated seeing her so helpless. Her skin was cool to the touch. Her pulse barely registered when he took it. At one point she'd regained consciousness and told him the doctors had informed her they'd gotten the MRSA infection under control. That made him feel marginally better. He'd been given a prescription for IV-based pain medication, which he'd filled, and had set up a rack to hold the bag of liquid painkiller. Besides trying to feed her small amounts of mashed and blended food every couple of hours, there wasn't much he could do—only keep Janna comfortable.

The next several days became a blur of the same routine. Knowing she couldn't last much longer, James spent hour after hour sitting, stretching on the floor beside the bed, trying to read his Bible and closing it all too often in disgust. He knew his mind and heart weren't right with God, and Scripture seemed to mock him. All his long-held beliefs had seemingly gone up in smoke. The God of the Bible had forsaken all His promises. He had completely abandoned James and his beloved wife. He looked back over the years and wondered at the waste they'd been, serving this God who couldn't be bothered to answer in his desperate hour of need. At times, he paced the house in exasperation. If he hadn't been afraid of disturbing Janna , he would have shouted his discontent. As it was, he mumbled and hissed, cursing God, and upbraiding Him for His lack of faithfulness.

Janna lapsed in and out of consciousness. Sometimes her lucidity startled him. At others her lack of it caused him to weep. He had a church service coming up that he still had to preside over. What could he possibly say? Given the state of affairs with his alienation from the church, would anyone bother coming, knowing he would still take the pulpit? Regardless, his obligation remained, and he continued wanting to be known as a man of his word.

James didn't think life could get any worse. He was mistaken.

When the Nazis rose to power in Germany in the 1930s, one of their most deplorable acts was to identify and shame the Jews by forcing them to wear yellow stars. Not long after that humiliation, they suffered economic isolation. Hitler and his minions didn't stop there. They conceived a pogrom to purify Germany: round up all the Jews, send them by the trainload to concentration camps, and exterminate them in crematorium ovens. Following World War II, the nations of the world declared "Never again."

It seemed that nations had short memories. In the years that followed, many genocides took place around the globe: prominently in Sudan where the government killed its own people in the Darfur region, in Rwanda where the Hutu ethnic group slaughtered the Tutsi people, and in Iraq where the Islamic State terrorists massacred Yazidis and Christians in a horrifying spectacle.

The Executive Order directly from the President of the United States couldn't have been more appalling. It hit the media like a nuclear bomb, even in its late Friday afternoon announcement.

The president, in a solemn speech, declared that divisiveness in the country had reached an all-time high, and she could no longer countenance it. "There is one single group responsible for the tension and violence racking this country. If it weren't for these people, we would achieve harmony, peace throughout the nation, and the lessening of discord with other nations. This group is self-identified Christians." Christians, according to the president, opposed the tolerance that other religions espoused and harbored intense hatred for the growing homosexual population. "Neither of these conditions will be allowed henceforth."

Christians were to be given a one-week grace period in which they could denounce their religion. Failing that, the Oval Office by its decree was imposing the wearing of yellow crosses by every Christian throughout the country. The president made it clear that the government had the means to determine where everyone stood, Christian or not. Anyone not registering faced the severest of penalties. "Deny your faith if you have the slightest doubt. Otherwise the government renounces all responsibility for your safety."

The Sunday talk shows scrambled to rearrange their guests. Prominent politicians on both sides of the aisle weighed in after the firestorm of Internet commentary the preceding day. Republicans excoriated the president for this decree, which they described as beyond constitutional and an affront to the American people. Democrats praised the leader of their party as, ironically, having the wisdom of Solomon in finally coming to grips with the very source of all controversy since time immemorial. As the opposition party in Congress, Republicans vowed to fight this pronouncement to their very core.

Unfortunately their track record in following up against previous Executive Orders was abysmal. Even if they managed to pass a bill in the House and Senate, the president still had to sign it. The likelihood of achieving enough votes to make it veto-proof was miniscule. The alternate vow by

Republicans was to contest the order legally in the courts. That path had little chance of success. The composition of the Supreme Court had changed dramatically, tilting predominately in favor of liberal/progressive jurisprudence. The president in a brief follow-up speech went so far as to taunt the Republicans and dared them to reverse what she'd put in motion.

James saw his obligation: the necessity to morally stand against such atrocious thinking and governing. He was in a crisis of faith, but he knew right from wrong. He preached that Sunday on freedom, the freedom engendered by the Founding Fathers, and the freedom people had in Christ. Though the numbers were dwindling, James knew through his reading that many other pastors preached similar messages, all with the encouragement to pray without ceasing. The country was consuming itself, the Church was asleep, and the very foundations of the republic were in jeopardy. Could "we the people" reverse this course? Not without God, and much of the nation had rejected Him.

Few people attended the service. Little could have disappointed him more. In this period of lies and deception rampant in society, those who called themselves Christian needed to hear God's Word for their lives. Sadly, as James reflected on it, the rest of his congregation apparently didn't believe that he represented God anymore. Truth be told, he didn't know for himself whether or not he did. The inference Joe Bennett had made about sexual immorality had likely made the gossip rounds. What it was based on, James had no idea. From that Sunday's attendance it was obviously toxic.

He also had to consider that some—many?—were thinking about the faith they claimed in light of the government edict. Certainly a percentage of congregants in the church had made the decision to renounce the faith and the label so as not to declare it. Who knew the outcome of wearing a yellow cross?

James returned home puzzled and saddened. Although Janna slumbered, he unloaded all his cares and burdens to the air at her side. In a sense it didn't matter if she heard and comprehended. The fact of speaking his troubles allowed him to create the semblance of sharing the load with her as they'd always done.

Chapter 42

Washington, D.C.

"Two more weeks, Abu, and the American people will speak."

Abu Saif laughed at President Luisa Parker's joke. "Yes, they will speak, but the voting machines will not hear their voices."

"Many will be silenced because they don't deserve the privilege of voting." Parker picked up her heavily gold-plated Cross pen. "This little baby has proven quite powerful. I owe a lot to President Obama for his years in office and stellar example of appropriating power. He couldn't have done a better job of paving the way. He promised he'd get the job done through his pen and his phone. He didn't need Congress, and I haven't either. You should have an interesting time when you become president."

"I'm looking forward to it. By the way, I've received the first report on the Christian yellow cross initiative."

"Great. What's the news?"

"The beauty is that we got another two-for. With the very fine print of the document those Christians had to sign, they also signed away their gun rights. It was a brilliant strategy on your part."

Parker preened, throwing back her hair and stroking her head. "Thank you. Yes, it was absolutely brilliant."

"You're something else, Luisa." Saif couldn't help but show his approval with a wink. "Indeed, the brilliance of the plan is that we get two strikes against the Christians for the price of a single decree. By adding gun confiscation, we're going to round up a lot of those hostile to us."

"How are our deputies doing?"

"Well. They're very eager. When you presented this opportunity to the union heads, they jumped at it. They love having their people deputized, armed, and commissioned to carry out your executive orders. We promised them significant firepower and DHS delivered. With the billions of rounds of ammunition that Homeland Security has purchased over the years, we can keep our private army of union thugs well armed for a long time.

"In fact, I saw this old memo the other day. Did you ever calculate what it truly meant for our various departments to purchase so much ammo?"

Parker pondered for a moment. "What it meant? Can't say that I did."

"These are old numbers from an issue of Forbes Magazine about fourteen years ago, so we're well beyond them now. Naturally they haven't been updated. It said that during the fiercest fighting of the Iraq War, the Army used something less than six million rounds a month. At the time of the article, DHS had purchased one point six billion rounds of ammunition. That would have been enough to sustain an ongoing hot war for over twenty years. Think how many years we can keep down insurgents should that need arise. It's staggering."

Parker gazed into the distance before replying. "I never realized it was so much! That's crazy. We might have to invent situations for our union guys to start shooting."

Abu Saif examined Parker. "You're serious, aren't you?"

"There are far too many people living in this country who have no business having the rights they do. The sooner we create the conditions for a nation to run the way we want it to operate, the better off we'll all be.

"But, we've digressed," Parker said. "You were going to update me on our success in bringing Christians under our heel."

"Right; here are the numbers so far of those who now wear yellow crosses and from whom we've begun to take away their guns..."

Chapter 43

Western Michigan

Since becoming friends with James, Bob Sanders had seen Janna in the hospital a couple of times. After James had told him that Janna was now at home, he came over to visit. "I'm only going to stay for a short time. I don't want to tire your wife out too much."

In spending these brief periods with her, Sanders had come to believe there was something special God was going to do in her life. It was just a feeling. but a strong one.

James escorted him into the bedroom and stood nearby as Sanders prayed. At the "amen" the sound of angry voices reached them. James pushed aside the curtain and shrugged. "Hmm, I don't see anything." A moment later the sound of gunfire made him draw back in surprise. "What the...?"

"That was close." Sanders strode out of the bedroom toward the front door with James following on his heels.

Cautiously, Sanders cracked open the door and they peered out. Fresh shouts erupted several houses down the street. He spotted a small band of men appearing seemingly out of nowhere. Across the street another group materialized. Some of the men waved knives and baseball bats.

James said, "A bunch of them have guns."

"Whatever's going on, this doesn't look good," Sanders said.

The first group of men stormed up the walk toward one the neighbor's houses. A man with a bat pounded on the door. When no one responded, two of them kicked at it. It didn't take long before the jamb shattered, and the men rushed in.

On the other side of the street the other group performed a similar dance. Shouts arose in a foreign language. The one word Sanders made out was "Allah."

More young men came on the scene. There now had to be hundreds of them. The rumble from their screaming and cursing grew ever louder. The first group emerged victorious with an older man and woman in tow. "That's the Rogers!" James exclaimed. "They wouldn't hurt anyone."

He took a step toward going out to help them, but Sanders stopped him with a forceful arm. "You can't help them alone. Wait. Look!"

Another group of young thugs began breaking windshields of cars parked in the street and in driveways. They tossed incendiary devices through the windows, and the cars started burning.

From the other end of the street a different group showed up. Four men armed with rifles walked slowly toward the melee. One raised his rifle, aimed, and fired. A hundred yards away a dark-skinned youth yelled and dropped to the ground. He clutched at his leg, incomprehensible words spewing from his mouth.

His cohort turned as one toward the threat. The men with rifles advanced. Rage flickered across the faces of the ruffians. The sound of a pistol retort brought an answering volley from the riflemen. Two more of the brutes dropped to the ground.

Many of the young men turned from their other tasks and ran as a crazed mass toward their attackers. The horrible sound of unfettered frenzy echoed in the street. Rifle and pistol shots rose like the din of war.

By this time James and Sanders had shut the door. They crouched by the corner of a window, watching the battle in the street as it neared the front of the house.

Bodies, writhing in pain or laying still, littered the street. By now, only a single rifleman remained picking off the thugs from his position behind the fender of a car. The attackers pulled back briefly. More of them amassed from nowhere. They spread out in twos and threes and kept pressing their numerical advantage. The rifleman took down several more. In the end, too many men from too many angles converged on him. He fired a last shot killing one final opponent. A hail of bullets struck him, and he fell with outstretched arms.

The shattering of wood inside the house drew the attention of James and Sanders. "That's the back door!" James sprinted toward the rear of the house.

Sanders yelled, but James didn't stop. He threw a glance into the bedroom at Janna's still form and turned to follow James. Almost in the kitchen, he saw James draw up hard. A man of Middle-Eastern origin faced him sweating heavily. He held a knife in one hand and a pistol in the other, which he pointed at James. Sanders observed just out of sight. A slow grin turned the man's lips into an ugly sneer. "You got money? You give me."

James raised his hands. "I don't have anything. Go away."

"You rich, you white, you infidel. You do what I say."

"There's nothing here, I tell you. Get out of my house!"

The man fired at the floor near James' feet. The bullet pinged and ricocheted, the noise of the shot deafening in the enclosed space.

"All right, all right." James backed up. "I have to get my wallet."

Sanders moved to remain out of sight as James and the intruder came into the living room, the man gesturing for James to hurry. He pointed toward the bedroom where Janna lay. "What there? Who that?"

The one thing Sanders knew was that they couldn't—wouldn't—allow this man to enter that room. In that moment he admired James as he planted his feet and shook his head. "You're not going in there."

The man smirked. With the quickness of a cat he swung his gun and struck James in the temple. He went down in a heap.

With a deliberate effort he ground his foot on James' outstretched hand and stepped over him to stand at the door, surveying the helpless woman huddled under the covers.

Chapter 44

Something had told Sanders to wait and stay out of sight. He'd positioned himself so that as James backed up at the prompting of the man with the gun, he remained hidden. James hitting the floor, blood oozing from his scalp was the time for Sanders to act.

Bob Sanders seldom left home without his Glock 43 tucked into a small holster at his side that looked to some like a cell phone carrying case. He removed it and stepped out behind the intruder, both hands holding the pistol steady and aimed at the man's back.

In a commanding voice, he said, "You. Turn around."

The man froze. With slow and deliberate movement he faced Sanders. "You cannot hurt me. I soldier of Allah. Allahu Akbar!"

With no further warning he lunged at Sanders.

The training Sanders had taken over the years stressed the obligation to refrain from shooting whenever possible, but to not hesitate should the need arise. There were few second chances. The man covered the fifteen feet between them so quickly that Sanders almost couldn't react. The man closed the distance and was upon Sanders before he knew it. He pulled the trigger once—twice—three times at point blank range.

The 9mm bullets tore into the man's stomach. His hot breath whooshed at Sanders as the impact took root. He grabbed at Sanders with weakened fingers and slid to the ground. The feel of the man's touch tingled from Sanders' chest all the way to his feet where he lay huddled.

The horror of the moment left Sanders wide-eyed and gasping. Nausea came over him, and he stumbled for the bathroom. With no time to spare he vomited into the toilet, his gut wrenching from the trauma.

He panted, trying to regain a sense of control, and wiped his heavily perspiring face with his sleeve. Shaky legs took him to the sink where he splashed water over his head and rinsed out his mouth. He looked at his reflection in the mirror and saw how drawn and pale he was. The gun lay where he'd dropped it on the carpet by the door as he'd raced into the bathroom. He hesitated, then picked it up.

His Muslim attacker—what else could he be?—remained in a heap where he'd fallen, but was still alive. His labored gasping for air told Sanders the man had little time before he died.

At the thought of death, Sanders remembered his calling as a follower of Jesus Christ. God's desire was that no man should perish without knowing Him. Sanders' Christian obligation was to bring the Gospel of light and life to his enemy, even this one who had tried to kill him. If he died believing what he did as a Muslim, he was doomed to hell. Satan would claim one more life in his ongoing quest to rob God of souls who would spend eternity with Him. Instead, this man, like so many others deceived by the lies of the devil, would dwell forever in the Lake of Fire. No one deserved that.

Sanders knelt by the man. "Can you hear me?"

With much effort he nodded and uttered a raspy, "Yes."

"What is your name?"

"Bahar." He lay on his side, his hands clutching his stomach. Blood stained the carpet a bright crimson. Sanders tasted copper on his tongue. The smell of fear permeated the man.

"My name is Robert, Bahar. I believe in Jesus Christ as my Lord and Savior. Do you know where you're going when you die?"

His chin dropped slightly. "I no succeed killing you. Only by death of infidel in jihad is paradise possible."

"I can show you the way to heaven, Bahar, and it's not by anything you have to accomplish. You know that you're a sinner, don't you?"

"Yes, much work to erase sins."

"There's no work at all, Behar. From the Qur'an you know about Jesus. But He is much more than what you were taught. Jesus died for the sins of mankind. He died for my sins and for yours. You can trust Him with your life. He rose from the dead that you could know Him forever. All you have to do is believe, Behar, believe that He died for you."

Behar coughed. Blood spurted from his mouth. A thin spray of it flew onto the knee of Sanders' pants.

"Will you believe, Behar? Will you trust Jesus with your life?"

"There is no god but Allah." Life was draining out of him. The ability to speak was coming harder.

"You said yourself, Behar, that you have no assurance of everlasting life. Jesus gives you that and more. Please, turn to the One who can save you." Hopelessness flooded over Sanders and tears threatened to blind him. He so desperately wanted this man to accept Christ. Could he not see his position? How tenuous his life was? His destination without salvation?

Even with his little strength remaining, Behar hardened his voice. "There is no god but Allah." With a final gasp, the remaining air left his lungs.

Sanders rocked back on his heels and closed his eyes. "Oh God, here was one who needed You. How could you let him go?"

At once, Sanders heard a voice whisper inside his head: "I loved him to the very end, but he chose the broad road."

Had he thought that, or had it come from outside himself? God's voice was so subtle; it often seemed like a thought arising within. A wave of sensation that he recognized as the Holy Spirit washed over him. It left him feeling that indeed it was God who had spoken. He mouthed, "Thank you, Lord, for Your mercy," and with difficulty rose to his feet.

Across the room he saw that James was sitting on the floor, his fingers pressed against his head to stop the flow of blood where Behar had struck him.

Wincing as he shifted his position, James said, "You tried to save him."

"He was a lost soul."

James shook his head, his eyes questioning. "But why bother?"

Sanders went over to James and examined his wound. "Jesus would have done no less. How can I follow Him, yet not follow His example?"

Chapter 45

Washington, D.C.

The images on the screen displayed the stark violence of the encounters. Arnold Rickards absorbed it with a hunger that little could abate. As he'd grown older it had taken more money, more sex, and more violence to bring him any relief from the inner demons that drove him. Whatever relief he got from his excessive indulgences lasted only a short while. He soon needed to pursue other passions so as to have any temporary peace.

The President of the United States, Luisa Parker, and Vice President Abu Saif sat with Rickards in the Situation Room. Parker had summoned the others early that morning to the White House to view the encounters captured by overhead drone cameras. The three watched, jotted notes, and commented as the dramas unfolded.

It was all there. Saif had sent the word down his chain of command. Once it reached the street, it had been executed flawlessly. Because of the coordination and the players that had been set in place, not only did violence erupt in Lighthouse, Michigan, but also in seventeen other chosen locations around the U.S. In each instance men had been goaded to act on both sides. It was better than a puppet show. The White House pulled the strings, and the marionettes danced.

Rickards' vast amount of money had funneled through numerous front groups to fund the organizations that seeded the unrest. They had done it in such a way that the strife appeared to be organic. The lie had been whispered that poverty caused the instability that led to the only solution: armed uprising. The media, much of it under Rickards' multi-layered corporate camouflage, ginned up the story. Obedient fools that they were, the willing media lapdogs gobbled up the deceits handed them. Everyone wanted a paycheck, and so the almighty dollar won through the underlying greed in the heart of each enthusiastic participant in the charade.

Abu Saif looked up from the computer into which he'd been writing his observations. "The Brotherhood does good work. Our young Muslim friends that they manipulate are quite proficient in the execution of their duties, are they not?

"You've done a masterful job in pulling the various factions together." Luisa Parker sipped at the hot coffee that an aide had just freshened. "We do need to perform some minor graphic enhancements and decide exactly what video clips to release to the media. Other than that, we're good to go."

"I have my people standing by." Rickards steepled his hands, bringing his fingers to his lips. He paused before continuing. "We're almost there. We've marginalized the Christians successfully over many years and have turned up the heat dramatically in the last month. It's almost time to bring about their final destruction. It is a life-long dream that I'll soon realize."

"I'm sure each one of us is ready for their demise, Arnold. It'll be a glorious day when we accomplish that."

Parker turned to Saif. "Abu, did you happen to bring that file on the Muslim Brotherhood you mentioned to me?"

"Didn't think we needed it right now."

"I'd like to review it with you, if you don't mind. Could you get it so we can discuss a couple things?"

Abu Saif nodded and left the room.

Parker leaned toward Rickards and spoke in a low voice. "Arnold, I wanted to tell you that I've made a final decision."

"The subject that Saif does not know about?"

"Yes. He won't be a happy man, but such is power and politics."

"When?"

She gestured toward the screen where the video had been frozen with the riflemen lying dead as Muslim youth approached. "Before the election. As soon as this settles into the collective American conscience."

Chapter 46

Western Michigan

The day following the Muslim violence, all the major media shared a coordinated theme. Their headlines blared: "Armed Christians Attack Innocent Muslims." James turned away from the Internet news feeds and marveled, thinking, *This is crazy*. Out loud, he said, "How could they get it so wrong?"

Because the police still hadn't shown up after many hours, Bob Sanders had remained with the Glaziers until they came. He'd said, "I need to be here to take the brunt of this since I killed the man." They'd covered the body with a sheet and done their best to ignore him. Afterward they gave Sanders the spare bedroom and a toothbrush. Following this morning's breakfast they'd settled down to watch how the news played out.

In the wake of the attack and the death of the Muslim man in their house, Janna, against the odds, was having a decent day in which her pain was lessened, leaving her more awake and alert than she had been for some time. "You know the answer, James. They don't get it wrong by accident."

"Yeah, I suppose. I just keep hoping somebody, somewhere, will tell the truth for a change. I'm so tired of everything always being turned upside down with Christians inevitably taking the brunt of the charges." He paced the room in frustration wishing for something he knew in his heart was impossible in this day and age. Janna, lying on the sofa with a blanket over her, followed James with her eyes. On every turn they locked onto each other, making James realize how fortunate he was to have her as his wife.

James glanced again at the image on his computer that showed the four dead riflemen. He furrowed his brow. "That's not right. Bob, come take a look at this."

Sanders came over and peered at the screen along with James. The men lay with limbs akimbo, their lifeblood draining. Each held a different pose in death, but their one similarity was the splash of yellow on their clothing. "I never saw those yellow crosses on them yesterday." He lowered his head in further reflection. "No, none of them wore this Christian symbol. I'm sure of it."

Sanders stood up, hands on hips. "You're right."

Janna said, "Does that surprise you, darling? Whatever their inclination, Christian or simply patriotic, is it any surprise they'd be painted as Christian extremists?" The tone of her voice reflected the sadness of her words. "Blame has been heaped on Christians for centuries, going all the way back to Emperor Nero."

In the twenty-four hours since the Muslim rampage outside and their own personal ordeal, their house and lives had been turned upside down. The larger picture painted by the media declared that the four riflemen were Christian vigilantes who had purposely attacked a peaceful throng of Muslim young men out for a love-filled midday stroll.

Following in the wake of the incident, the usual calls for gun confiscation increased in crescendo with the president promising to heed the public demand for removing every last gun from private ownership. The fact that there was no public demand, only partisan anti-gun rhetoric from the left, didn't make the news. The media, walking promiscuously with the progressive-leftist elites, who had no desire to adhere to Constitutional principles, did whatever its lover demanded. The nation would be made to care. The priorities of those who demanded this paradigm would be executed. Guns would be completely eliminated once and for all.

The other template, the one that dominated, was the one the media also walked with in lockstep and sounded most vociferously: "Christians Bad – Muslims Good". As James saw it, the scary part was how this theme had been woven and shaped over the years. He had no doubt it was coming to a head. First, anyone with Christian bona fides, who had any connection to government, was to be ostracized. On the heels of this atrocity came the yellow cross fiasco with the specific threat: "We know who you are!" The comply-or-else warning left most people with little choice. Christians could deny their faith—renounce it—or register, receive a yellow cross, and become a target. James feared where this downhill slope led. The snowball was gathering momentum. More snow adhered to it by the day and the ball grew larger. Soon, very soon, it would crush everything in its path.

The personal devastation James and Janna experienced in their very home had left James exhausted in his effort to shield his wife in her delicate condition. He'd slept little last night because of all that had taken place. Following the shooting, Bob Sanders had called the police to report the incident. Once the excitement had calmed down outside and the police could respond, several hours had elapsed. They said they'd get there when they could. The man in their house was dead; they didn't need to come immediately, as there were other priorities to which they had to attend.

During their time together, James and Sanders talked about God and guns. "Because the feds confiscated my weapons, I couldn't have protected us. We're fortunate you were carrying."

"I've been a big Second Amendment advocate for a long time." Sanders gave James a wan smile. "I may be a pastor, but I know the value of protecting what's dear to me. Michigan's had concealed carry on the books for years, so I've taken advantage of it. I'll tell you this; it all happened so fast I was lucky to react like I did."

"Thank God." But one thing puzzled James. "How is that they haven't come after your guns?"

Sanders glanced at his pistol lying on a nearby side table. He'd told James it was best to leave it out in plain sight at this point. "I didn't have anything like the doctor's appointment that got them alerted to you. I don't know. After this, I suppose it might be a problem."

Darkness had settled over the town when the police rang the doorbell more than twenty-four hours after the incident. James let them in, and they surveyed the scene. "Where's the firearm that did this?" an officer by the name of Hallowell demanded.

Bob Sanders walked toward the table where he'd laid the gun. "Over here."

He reached for it, but the second officer, Mahoney, barked, "Don't touch it!"

Sanders jerked back and retracted his hand. Officer Mahoney used a cloth and dropped it into an evidence bag. In the meantime, Officer Hallowell called for a body wagon.

The policemen questioned Sanders and James, seeing how little Janna could add. Mahoney nodded at the description of how Behar turned and was upon Sanders before he knew it. "So you shot an unarmed man."

"Of course not. You see what he had." Sanders pointed to the pistol and knife lying on the floor where Behar had dropped them when shot.

Officer Mahoney picked up the thug's weapons and without worrying about fingerprint contamination unceremoniously dropped them into a plastic bag. "From what I can see this man was no threat to you."

Sanders' eyes blazed; his voice was calm, but indignant. "This is ludicrous. You know what went down outside. This man broke into this home and was a clear and present danger to everyone here. If I hadn't shot him, who knows what he would have done to Janna?"

Officer Hallowell glanced into the bedroom where Janna in her illness slumbered after being up with the two men much of the day. "Right. Why would he care about her?"

By this time, James had also worked up a head of steam. "These people think nothing of human life. They kill and rape without mercy. They don't place any value on the things we do. How can you side with them? Why can't you treat this incident with concern for law-abiding American citizens rather than for someone like this Muslim thug?"

"Careful, sir. There will be no slurs on these people. We have our orders. They will be treated with respect, dead or alive." The doorbell rang, and Mahoney answered it, letting in the morgue team.

Within minutes, they whisked away Behar's sheet-covered body. James was glad they'd finally removed the corpse. If it had been much longer it would have begun to smell. The door closed behind them, and Hallowell pulled out a pair of handcuffs. "We have to take you to the station for booking, Mr. Sanders."

"Are those really necessary? Am I truly some kind of threat to you guys?"

"Protocol, sir. Hold out your hands. I won't cuff you from behind." Hallowell snapped the handcuffs in place. He grabbed Bob Sanders by the arm and led him into the night.

Sanders yelled back to James, "Call my attorney." James barely caught the name, but quickly wrote it down.

Mahoney prepared to exit. James pointed to the bloodstains on the carpeting. "What about those?"

"Clean them up if you wish." The officer didn't give a backward glance before joining his partner in the squad car, Bob Sanders a prisoner in the rear.

Chapter 47

The hours after the police took away Bob Sanders had caused James to again question his faith. He couldn't sleep. That was out of the question. The last two days had left him so keyed up that he paced and mumbled to himself throughout the night. He avoided the patch of blood, going so far as to cordon it off and hide it with plastic sheeting.

He'd left a message for Sanders' attorney, received a call an hour later, and explained the situation. The attorney promised to work on getting Sanders bailed out first thing in the morning. As the night wore on, James had to deliberately keep from becoming vocal and disturbing Janna. His equilibrium and eroding faith roiled within him. He wished he could get a handle on his inner turmoil, but it evaded him. Periodically, he turned to prayer, knowing deep down that was the one thing he should be doing above all. But his emotional disturbance kept him from effectively reaching out to God for comfort and peace. He hated the feeling inside him. It left him sick of life and trembling.

As a result of all this, Janna's awakening a second morning in a row with the strength to sit up in bed and talk with James surprised and blessed him. To have his wife present in a way she hadn't been for some time gave him optimism amidst the chaos that surrounded him.

He fed Janna breakfast and basked in the good feeling of being able to interact as they'd done before her illness. In fact, her hearty appetite gave him hope that somehow she'd turned a corner and would recover.

They spent much time discussing the events of the prior couple of days with James filling Janna in on the direction of their country. She asked questions and took in his answers with the quiet reserve he'd always known in her.

Later, she freshened up and resumed her place in bed. "James, I had a dream last night. From your description of the decay in this country, it's a confirming dream of sorts, I think."

Despite their conversations this morning James had been unable to sit still for very long. Now he sat on the bed and worked at stilling the restlessness within him. "Tell me."

"You know the old parable about cooking a frog? The best way to do it is to place it in cold water and gradually turn up the heat. By the time the frog realizes its danger, it's already dead from being boiled alive. That was my dream, only America was the frog.

"Our nation has slowly had the heat turned up on it without knowing or caring. Well, that's not entirely true. There have been people who cared and who saw the nation's calamity coming, but nothing they said or did made any difference. When I was well and could pay attention to such things, I remember strong, clear voices calling out warnings. They came from certain segments of the secular right and from conservative Christian pulpits. But inertia had already set in. We, as a nation, were in reverse motion—the financial snowball of excessive debt spending, the willful obliviousness to the danger posed by the illegal alien invasion, the homosexual agenda with its offshoot transgender movement.

"Imagine someone in the 1950s and what they would think of the ludicrous state of our nation, one that passed federal laws requiring complete bathroom integration between the sexes. Could someone from that time ever conceive that we would dictate that young men and young women should use restrooms and showers together without any concern for privacy and the feelings of those being violated by these laws? Would it be possible for anyone to conjure up the notion that pedophilia should be allowed and celebrated? When legislation allowing adults to sexually pursue children was rammed down our throats under the guise that kids must be free to experiment and choose their own way in life, I knew it was over for this country.

"And, to put the proverbial nail in the coffin, we've set the stage for an Islamic takeover. So many people have entered this once-great nation without our having any idea who they are or what they stand for. What did you tell me earlier? Since we've left the borders effectively unprotected and invited in so-called refugees from around the world, we've let in millions of people in the intervening years since President Obama opened those floodgates. Millions in these last twenty years since 2008. And because we treat them like royalty and give away everything that prior generations of people had to work for—food, housing, medical care—we've basically come to the point of bankrupting ourselves."

"Dear God." James rubbed his face. "And we're on the verge of electing a Muslim president. I'm sure that'll turn out well."

"As with so many Muslims that have been elected to public office, no doubt he'll be sworn in on the Qur'an. In so doing, he'll commit to finally bringing the caliphate to America. He certainly won't give allegiance to the Constitution." Janna patted James gently on his hand. "I'm sorry I won't be here to stand with you against this tide of destruction.

A knot twisted in James' belly. "Oh, Janna, don't say that! I can't bear to face this without you." Tears that he didn't notice in his angst streamed down his cheeks. "Please don't leave me! I need you so much."

"You're going to have to face this, James. God has spoken, and I've told you the little He's revealed to me. There are mysteries here. He hasn't told me everything by any stretch of the imagination. You're not going to be fighting against flesh and blood. This is a spiritual war. The spiritual deception that has arisen is very strong. It's an antichrist spirit that will test you to your limits. Because this antichrist spirit manifests in the highest levels of government—I'm talking about the very office of the president of the United States—the battle will be more difficult than anything you can imagine. And yet, God has imparted to me that you won't fight alone."

With great tenderness and care, James wrapped his arms around his beloved. Janna stroked his forehead giving the tender love of a wife who would soon be with the Lord.

Chapter 48

Two days later, Bob Sanders remained in jail despite the best efforts of his attorney. James had been in constant contact with his office, and the best they could tell him was the attorney continued to work the situation. No hearing had been set, and no bail determined, so Sanders remained locked up.

Assuming that Sanders would be released imminently, James hadn't gone to the jail. He'd been relishing the renewal of Janna's energy and the quality time they were able to spend together. Finally, however, James determined that in the absence of Sanders' release he had to visit him.

Due to overcrowding conditions at the city jail, Sanders had been taken to the county facility. The guards processed James through, and one led him to Sanders' cell where he opened the door and let James inside.

The two men embraced. James stood back and surveyed his friend. "You look tired."

Sanders gave a wan smile. “A lot of human animal sounds during the night make sleep hard to come by. I’m supposed to get a new roommate later. Not sure if that’ll make it easier or harder to sleep.”

“How are you doing other than that?”

“Good, actually. I’ve been pretty busy. This has given me time to read my Bible and talk a lot with God. When they let us out for meals and exercise time I’ve had several opportunities to share the Gospel, so I can’t complain.” Sanders bit his lip. “That’s not completely true. I killed a man. There’s no doubt I had to do it, but that doesn’t lessen the horror and the continual replay in my mind.”

“I’ve never been in that situation. I have—well, had—guns. The purpose was to protect our home in case something like that happened. Thank God you were there, Bob. If that man had come sooner or after you left, we’d have been helpless. I know this doesn’t stop the mental images. I can’t imagine what you have to mentally endure, but without you being there I shudder to think of the harm he may have done to Janna. You may not know it, my friend, but you’re an angel in disguise.”

“That’s good to know.” Sanders stared into the distance at a place James couldn’t see. “It’ll be with me a long time.”

To change the conversation, James bounced up and down on the second bed in the cell. “Kind of hard.”

“Too soft and it would probably give me a backache.”

“Listen.” James wasn’t sure where to go with this. “From what I can tell and the little I’ve gotten out of your attorney, I don’t know what they’re doing with you. They’re not in any rush to let you go. It seems they might hold you indefinitely.”

“I was getting that sense. Just have to make the best of it.” Sanders leaned forward. “Truthfully? It’s given me time to think how I, as a devoted Christian, should respond to the lawlessness in our country.”

“What do you mean?”

"You're familiar with the Revolutionary War. You know that many pastors put aside their black robes and picked up muskets to fight the enemy—the Black-Robe Regiment."

"You're telling me you're thinking about armed rebellion?" James rubbed his neck in bewilderment. "What would that look like? How could you even begin to counter the might and power of the U.S. government? Doesn't God come into this picture? Would He countenance violence against duly elected authorities? My gosh, Bob, are you crazy?"

"The founders of this nation believed they had to take a military stand. No doubt they prayed fervently prior to making such a decision. What I don't know, which is the greatest quandary for me, is how they knew for sure it was the right thing to do. I struggle with this. Do I stay on the sidelines and pray my guts out? Or do I take up the fight against an unjust, unrighteous government? Can I simply sit by anymore? Look at what's happening. Christians are ostracized, told they can't work for the government any longer because of separation of church and state. We're singled out like the Jews in Germany, made to wear a sign of our faith that's meant to make it a symbol of shame. They're confiscating firearms; they're disarming us so that we can't fight back. A people without the means to defend themselves are helpless. We're standing before the ravenous wolf like sheep. The slaughter is coming soon. Mark my words."

Listening to Sanders, James knew he was right. He felt the same dilemma Sanders had vocalized. What was the true, Christian response against an overweening, oppressive government? The founders of the nation had fought—because they could. Many believers in Christ around the world had endured persecution over time because they had no means to retaliate. The Bible spoke of the virtue in suffering for Jesus. Did that make it the only option? James tried to find his way through the morass: "Scripture makes it clear that we aren't to submit to anything that would destroy our faith. Shadrach, Meshach, and Abednego wouldn't bow before the golden idol of King Nebuchadnezzar. Neither would Daniel stop his daily prayers just because King Darius commanded. But those are instances of civil disobedience. Where do we come off thinking we can take up armed resistance?"

"That's the question, isn't it?" Sanders began pacing the cell. "I feel sometimes like a caged lion walking round and round my cage. That's what makes it so tough. At one point Jesus told his disciples to make sure they had swords. Was He being facetious? Did He mean it, or was the order given to them just for effect, to make them think in other ways? I know I'm not the only pastor over the years to struggle with this. I wish God would make it definitively clear to me."

"He hasn't made much clear to me at all. You walk round in circles in this cell; I do the same thing in my head day after day."

James heard the clang of an iron door and looked up to see the guard returning.

"I'll keep praying for you, Bob. I guess when the Lord's time is right He'll release you from this place." He paused. "You know, let's pray right now." He placed a hand on Sanders' shoulder and implored God's wisdom and strength to pour out to enable his brother in Christ to endure this difficult trial. He finished by squeezing his shoulder and hugging him.

Sanders wiped away a tear. "My assurance is in Him. There's nothing I can do on my own right now. Spend more time with Janna. It's important."

Chapter 49

While running various errands throughout the week, James had observed who wore yellow crosses and who didn't. As the week wore on, he had to reach a final decision himself. Should he register as a Christian and pin the yellow cross on his chest? Based on his Sunday sermon, he knew what a hypocrite he'd be if he didn't. Finally, on Friday, he went to the city hall and queued up behind those who'd waited until the last minute as he had done. Strategically located at several spots around the room, police officers stood with narrowed eyes watching the people who came to declare their faith. James couldn't decide if they were there for the protection of the Christians or placed there under the assumption that those gathered posed a threat of some kind.

A moment later, a man James knew who attended Bob Sanders' church took his place in line right behind him. Their greeting included sardonic smiles. George shared the latest with their itinerant church since the bombing. "There's one good thing that comes out of this yellow cross debacle. For the most part, we won't have to guess anymore who's a true Christian and who isn't. I've been amazed at how my brothers and sisters in Christ have been strengthened by this ordeal. It's given me and many others a backbone we didn't know we had. I've got a much greater appreciation for persecuted believers in the Middle East when confronted by Islamic threats. In their case, die, convert, or pay the infidel tax, the jizya, separated the wheat from the chaff. This has much the same result."

"I've read that in many areas over there the people went underground with their faith, and the church has grown like crazy in the face of extreme persecution," James said. "Is that really possible?"

"I've got a sneaking suspicion we may see something similar here as persecution increases. And no doubt, it will get worse. This is only the beginning."

"From what we've seen with Christians who opposed celebrating gay marriage, and some of the politically-correct charges that have stuck against those who proclaim Christ as Savior in opposition to the tenets of Islam, I can't dispute what you're saying."

The line had barely budged, but it finally began moving. A lot of people had waited until this last day, perhaps under the erroneous hope the edict would be withdrawn. With nothing of the sort happening, it caused a flurry of activity as the deadline approached.

An hour passed with the line moving slowly. The two men chatted until it was James' turn to register. Three clerks were tasked with taking the appropriate information and handing out the yellow crosses. It immediately became evident to James how serious the effort was when the clerk processing him demanded his social security number. He hesitated momentarily, which prompted the clerk to demand, "Come on, give me your number. It's almost lunchtime. I want my scheduled break."

It took all of James' effort not to roll his eyes. Far be it from him to deprive this poor employee of her rightful meal. Immediately following his sarcastic thought, James chided himself. Once again he'd neglected the Christ-like attitude to which he was called. He humbly responded to the remainder of the questions and accepted the proffered yellow cross.

With jaw tightening as he pinned the cross on his jacket, he saw it was made well. It was constructed of solid metal with a sturdy pin attachment. These weren't made overnight. They'd taken time and thought. Much planning had gone into their production. He idly wondered what lucky company had been on the receiving end of such government largess. He smirked and thought, *Some crony of a favored Senator, no doubt.* Again he had to repent of his attitude, which he knew was far from Christ-like.

George finished with another clerk at about the same time as James. As they exited the building, George raised an eyebrow and said, "The president and her fellow travelers must have had a master plan from the beginning. So many incidents have occurred, so much discord and evil perpetrated upon this nation. Thankfully Pastor Bob taught us to look at this biblically. He reminded us that, as Proverbs 21 says: 'The king's heart is like channels of water in the hand of the Lord; He turns it whichever way He wishes.' God is in control. I'm so grateful I can say that, knowing its truth in the face of so much opposition."

James nodded, wishing he had the faith these days to trust in God as this man did. The two parted, James watching George wistfully as he walked away, head up, not cowed by the wearing of the yellow cross. He heard the slight whir above him and saw that one of the cursed drones hovered overhead.

Chapter 50

Once he'd gotten the yellow cross, James did exactly what Bob Sanders had urged from his jail cell. He spent the day with Janna. And what a wonderful time it was. Although she was rail-thin with little strength, she had a rejuvenation of sorts during this time. She spent time on her feet and sat in a chair. She laughed so much it reminded James of days past when they so often enjoyed life together, regardless of what it threw at them. They did a Bible devotional and even played Scrabble once, with Janna winning as she usually did. James couldn't have asked for anything that would have blessed him more. When Janna told him she planned to go to church on Sunday to hear him preach and offer her encouragement, his thankfulness overflowed.

Late in the day, he thought about Bob Sanders again. With regret he told Janna he needed to go to the jail to visit his friend.

"Yes, I'm sure he needs encouragement." Janna sat in her favorite rocking chair and for all the suffering she'd endured, looked fabulous to James. "Don't worry about me. I'll be fine."

She did look fine. They had no knowledge or confirmation that God had healed her, but James had begun to hope and pray that perhaps He had. He gave her a loving kiss and set out for the jail.

A few guards stood around talking when James arrived. Another lingered near a barred door. At the front desk, he asked to visit Sanders. The guard checked his computer and shrugged. "Nobody by that name's incarcerated here."

"That doesn't make any sense. Please check again. It's Sanders, first name Robert."

The guard raised his eyebrows and shook his head. He punched at the keyboard once more. "Sorry, buddy. Maybe he's at another facility. Sure you got the right county jail?"

Exasperated and confused, James assured him that he'd visited Sanders in this very jail only a few days ago. "Do you show him being transferred anywhere?"

"We'd have a record if he'd been here. We got nothing. Far as the computer system goes, he's not been a prisoner in this facility."

James stood there not sure what to say or do. The guard glanced at him, shrugged again, and resumed looking at the comic book in his lap.

What could they possibly have done with Sanders? Bewildered at this turn of events, he sat down in one of the metal chairs provided for those waiting to be cleared for visitation. Deep in thought, it startled him when a guard passing by muttered, "See me outside in ten minutes."

The guard continued past him without a glance and exited the heavy glass doors. James sat back and thought about the events that had brought him here. Sanders had protected Janna and him. It wasn't surprising they'd arrest him for killing the man who'd invaded their home. From what James had heard, that was normal procedure. In the eyes of the law, Sanders had used deadly force. Until it was proven otherwise that it was in self-defense, he was the guilty one as far as the police were concerned. Sanders disappearing, however, from this jail where they'd held him, with no information about that whatsoever, was another matter entirely.

A clock on the wall indicated the passing of the necessary ten minutes. James rose with a sigh and left the building. Outside, the warmth that had stayed with them throughout the fall pressed like a dry brush against his cheek. The heat and lack of rain had been a nationwide phenomenon. Many called it a drought of epic proportions. For the entire country to be affected was unheard of. Normally if one part suffered from drought—which had been California's fate many times over the last decade—then another section of the country experienced torrential rains and flooding. The east coast had seen this far too many times lately. It was another puzzle that few could assemble.

There was no sign of the guard. Thinking he'd just wasted ten minutes, James walked toward his car. As he was about to open the door, another vehicle sounded a short beep on his horn. A car pulled up, and the driver motioned for James to get in. "Hurry! Now get down. I can't be seen with you."

He wanted to protest, but the urgency of the man caused him to do as he said. James crouched on the seat and made himself as small as possible in the foot well. The driver accelerated, turned, drove for several minutes, turned again, and parked. "Okay, you can get up. Sorry for the intrigue."

Rising up, James saw they were in a wooded area with several other parking spaces but no other vehicles.

"I come here for lunch a lot. Gives me a chance to get away and think. Besides, not many of the other guards want much to do with me. Oh, my name is Blake, Jack Blake."

He had graying hair and an expanding midsection. Blake reached out his hand, which James shook. "Why are we doing this?"

For answer, Blake turned slightly so that James could see the yellow cross on his chest. "We have a common problem."

Hesitantly, James fingered his own yellow cross. "I guess we do."

"I've been straight with my fellow guards for years. They know where I stand. Every day for as long as I've been in this job, I've witnessed to the new guys in the lockup each morning. A lot of them have come to know Jesus Christ because I've been faithful. It's been a great blessing. But I've also had my share of grief. I'm the only guard I know of who professes his faith. The others mock me, and I've had supervisors try to fire me. Each time the Lord has intervened and kept me safe in my position. I've lost a few of those supervisors, though; turned out they got transferred or let go for inexplicable reasons. It's made the other guards regard me with a combination of awe and suspicion.

"My opportunities to testify and speak boldly for the Lord have dwindled lately. There's so much resistance among the prisoners. I've also been shuffled around to different positions making it difficult to make my way to the lockup without abandoning my post. More importantly, pressure has come down from the upper echelons of the system making it clear that people of faith have no rights where we work. You're aware of the decree that said Christians can't work for the government?"

James nodded.

"For some reason that hadn't affected me till now. My boss told me this morning tomorrow is my last day."

"Simply for being a follower of Jesus Christ?" James closed his eyes. "A number of people in my church were also fired. We tried to help them, but..." He had no desire to rehash his issues with the board, so he turned the conversation. "What do you want with me?"

Blake gripped the steering wheel and stared through the windshield at the trees as dusk overtook them. "God may have kept me in place until today so that I could tell you what I know about your friend."

"You know what happened to Bob Sanders?"

"A little. You certainly weren't wrong. He was there. But he may have been among the first to be affected by another clandestine government program."

"There's been way too many of them."

"Yeah. Even though I'm an outcast I still hear things. I learned he was taken in the middle of the night because of his yellow cross. I heard the government has a special place for people like him. Which means it'll eventually be for people like you and me. He's been disappeared, and it's going to happen to a lot more of us very soon."

At a loss for words at this revelation, James joined Blake in studying the nearby trees. He saw a black squirrel dash across the concrete lot and scramble up a large oak.

Finally, his lungs began working again. "That's scary. Sanders was more up on the political landscape than me. I wonder what it all means?"

Blake started the engine and put the car into drive. "Whatever's going down, it doesn't bode well for Christians."

Chapter 51

Camp Grayling – Central Michigan

The gentle rocking brought Bob Sanders in his dreams back to his days as a boy traveling in the backseat of his parents' car. He would curl up with a pillow and light blanket in the big green Pontiac. Pretty soon the steady motion of the vehicle as it cruised at turnpike speeds would send young Bob into dreamland. This movement beneath him was like that sensation back then. The only problem was that a dark undercurrent wanted to snatch him from his slumber because something wasn't right.

An ear-wrenching screech rose from beneath his bed and jarred him to wakefulness. Only it wasn't a bed at all. He lay on a rough wooden floor with bits of straw beneath him. And he wasn't alone. Around him he sensed a number of others, crowded with him in the darkness of an enclosed space.

A drugged grogginess made it hard to think. Colors flashed before his eyes. Nausea erupted in his stomach. He swallowed hard to keep down the vomit; the sour taste remained in his mouth.

As he gradually adjusted to the murk that threatened to suffocate him, he noticed others nearby were beginning to stir too. The carriage slowed even more. *Clank!* The motion halted completely, and he realized they must be on a railcar. *Where did they haul us off to? And why?*

The panic building up around him was palpable as different voices called out: "John!" "Angie!" "What is this place?" "Does anybody know what's happening?"

As his mind cleared, a throbbing headache remained. Sanders didn't want to think what he feared to be the case—what his gut told him, but his mind, no, his heart—told him was the truth. He huddled into himself, thankful for the lingering warmth well into this fall season.

They waited. The hubbub of voices reduced to a murmur as people next to each other intermittently said a few words and lapsed into silence. An aura of uncertainty gripped the inhabitants of the enclosure. At one point someone called out, "The Lord is my shepherd; I shall not want. He maketh me to lie down in green pastures;"

Another voice chimed in, "He leadeth me beside the still waters. He restoreth my soul; He leadeth me in the paths of righteousness for His Name's sake. Yea, though I walk through the valley of the shadow of death, I will fear no evil, for Thou art with me; Thy rod and Thy staff they comfort me. Thou preparest a table before me in the presence of mine enemies; Thou anointest my head with oil; my cup runneth over."

Two or three others helped complete the recitation, "Surely goodness and mercy shall follow me all the days of my life; And I will dwell in the house of the Lord for ever."

The words of the 23rd Psalm seemed to bring comfort and release. Bob Sanders felt it not only in his own spirit, but in the lightening of others' burdens as well.

Eventually the sounds of men moving about outside made Sanders anticipate the end of his present captivity. He couldn't help but wonder if what lay ahead would be even worse. He heard the click of a lock, and the chunk of a lever being moved. The heavy door cracked a slit then rolled open completely. Blinding sunlight streamed in.

Suddenly a man issued them orders: "You inside! Get out now! Let's go!"

People edged toward the light, still unable to see past the brilliance that blinded them.

"Get it going! Out, out, out! On the ground! Come on!"

The double crack of gunshots moved them along. Sanders and the others tumbled to the hard packed earth.

"Stand up! I won't tell you again, you useless swine!"

One older, heavyset man struggled to gain his feet, but couldn't. He tried to turn from his backside to his knees and had no luck. Sanders and a couple of other men tried to help him, but his weight made the task difficult. He panted, "I need something to lean on. I can't do this."

The man shouting orders charged over. "Get away from him." He waved his pistol at Sanders and his two helpers. Reluctantly, they backed off.

They were barely clear when he leveled his gun at the prisoner's chest. With no hesitation, he pulled the trigger once, twice. "Wummph!" The heavy man collapsed in a silent, lifeless heap. His blood draining to the ground chilled Sanders.

A woman screamed. The guard turned to her. "Shut up, unless you want to join him." She lapsed into a silence broken only by intermittent hiccups, as tears ran freely down her cheeks.

The killer faced the group. "My name is Lieutenant Clocker. This," he gestured behind him with his pistol, "is your new home. You will do as you are told, and you will do it immediately. Otherwise, you will join your friend, the fat man. There will be no questions because we will give you no answers. Now, follow Sergeant Fortis."

"Let's go. This way." The sergeant waved them over, and the group hustled behind him. Guards lined their perimeter, watching with rifles ready.

They made their way single file toward a cluster of low, squat buildings. The place had the feel of a converted army facility. In the near distance a double row of heavy-duty wire fencing, each topped with rolls of barbed wire gave the distinct impression of a high security prison. As Sanders observed his surroundings during their short march, he noticed one other thing. He fingered the yellow cross he wore on his chest. From what he could tell, each of his fellow travelers also sported one. The whole setup made him feel queasy again, but for another reason. This place gave him the distinct impression of emulating a historical precedent in Germany that hadn't ended well for the inhabitants of those camps.

In reaching the barracks Sergeant Fortis counted them off, separating the men and women. He directed the three men's groups to one set of buildings and the corresponding three women's groups to another set. Once inside, Sanders found himself among thirty men in a rustic facility with bunk beds, a single bathroom, and little else. The only positive in the place was that thirty men didn't come close to filling the available space. Sanders chose a top bunk near the middle of the room.

A trio of armed guards oversaw their settling into their quarters. Sergeant Fortis came in shortly. Seeming to read Sanders' mind, he announced, "Don't get too comfortable with all the legroom you have in here. You've got more roommates coming soon.

"You're to stay here until we order you where to go. We have little patience with disobedience. We might tell you something a second time, but never a third. If you don't like it here, there's always the alternative of your fat friend back by the train."

The door slammed behind the guards when all had left. The men inside looked at one another in disbelief. After a time the man in the bunk beside Sanders' hesitantly offered,

"This isn't looking good." Another chimed in, "Why would they do this? It doesn't make any sense."

Sanders pointed to his yellow cross. "Doesn't it?"

The eyes of each man swept the room, landing on the myriad yellow crosses pinned on the chest of every one of them. With that, it was almost if the individuality represented in each person deflated, like a huge balloon had been released and exhaled every bit of air inside it.

No one had much to do. None of them had any belongings other than what they wore. Most of the men settled on their beds immersed in thought. One man eventually sat up and clapped his hands. "Listen, all of you. Remember the woman back at the train who recited the 23rd Psalm? Who are we? Aren't we all disciples of Jesus Christ? Would we be here, all recipients of yellow crosses, if we hadn't made that declaration when the decree first came down? Don't we have a Savior who is bigger than all this?"

Excitement welled up in Bob Sanders. "Yes, he's right! This is no different than others who have been persecuted for proclaiming the Name of Jesus. Who knows what we're facing? What I do know is that we have the opportunity to partake in trials and tribulation for Jesus Christ and to grow deeper in our faith. We have a harvest field all around us. The guards are hard-hearted. They've been taught and conditioned, possibly brain-washed to do this to fellow citizens. Our job, as Christ-followers, is to show the kindness and love of Christ, regardless of what they do to us."

The first man jumped up. "I propose we make a pact, a pact for the One who redeemed us all. Let's consecrate this time in this place and make it holy. What do you think?"

A chorus of yeas resounded. The men gathered in a large circle like a football team surrounding its coach; only in this case the one they encircled was Jesus Christ.

They made the declaration and lifted up prayers. In the middle of a strange and violent place, the Spirit of the Lord dwelt among them.

Chapter 52

Western Michigan

The days James spent with Janna had been ones in which he'd neglected any and all church business. After Blake dropped him back off at his car in the jail parking lot, James decided to make a quick stop at the church to check up on mail and messages.

He didn't expect much was going on given his tenuous position as pastor and leader of the church, so it surprised him to see a small group of people milling around the locked door of his office.

His secretary appeared with a harried expression. It took James aback to see her so late on a Saturday. "What are you doing here?"

She ignored the question as though it wasn't worth answering. "They've been waiting for you. I told them you wouldn't be in so late today, but they keep coming back, hoping you'd show up. It's not right to leave me in the lurch like this."

James couldn't help but think that if she hadn't been there she wouldn't be in the lurch blaming him. He held up a hand. "I'll take care of it."

One of the women saw him. "Oh, Pastor, finally. We have terrible news and don't know what to do."

James unlocked his office and ushered them inside. "What's going on?"

There were two men and three women, all of them married, but none of them to each other. It crossed James' mind that these were several of the faithful remaining in the church, ones he knew were strong believers.

"They've taken our spouses." The same woman, Amanda Sexton, had given James and Janna a lovely vase for their anniversary from a recent trip to Italy two years before Janna's illness. In her fifties, she and her husband were among those to whom James could turn when volunteers were needed for church activities. They loved to give and to serve.

"They?"

"None of us know who they were." Amanda looked around for confirmation, and the others nodded. "It's much the same story with all of us. Armed men came in the middle of the night. They flashed official documents saying our spouses had to come with them. They took my Eric away, as well as the husbands and wives of each of the others here."

"They took men and women?"

"Yes, Pastor." Tom Ratliff was another of those whom he could count on in a crisis. He was tall and muscular, but losing his tone as age crept up on him. "I told them to take me if they had to take someone, but they said they had their orders. They let Nancy get dressed then hustled her out. They had their guns trained on me the entire time. I couldn't do a thing."

The others recounted similar incidents. Not a word had been spoken about their being Christians or about the yellow crosses, but James remembered Bob Sanders and his mysterious disappearance.

He saw no value in keeping the information about Sanders to himself, so he shared his discussion with the guard and the man's suspicions with the group. One thing after another had been happening that appeared to be drawing a noose tighter and tighter around the necks of those who believed in Christ. This roundup didn't seem anything other than random regarding who was taken. Perhaps that was the point. Create chaos without a pattern. Generate fear and uncertainty.

James had nothing to offer the ones who had come to him for help. "I confess, folks, I have no idea what we can do. The authorities have been extremely unhelpful. They either have marching orders or don't care because of the repercussions if they do try to actually do their job. We're on the outside looking in and don't have anywhere to turn that I can determine."

"I feel so helpless." Amanda Sexton dabbed at her tearing eyes with a tissue.

"I completely understand. Because of the circumstances that I've been facing, I haven't been much of a pastor to you, my flock. My first response should have been to pray, in fact, to gather the church for prayer. I didn't do that. I hope it's not too late, but let's take some time now."

James led the group into the sanctuary where they gathered in a small circle near the altar. He began, and when he'd had his say before God, each of the others beseeched the Lord Almighty to help them through this difficult time and to see their spouses safely home.

The time in prayer left James with a warm, glowing feeling. He knew the Holy Spirit had been present among them, and he hoped this might open a new season of faith and devotion for him.

Each of the people promised to let the others know if they heard anything that shed any light on the matter. James would be the hub and the others the spokes. All promised to keep on praying.

Chapter 53

Prayer lifted James' spirits. Why hadn't he been praying like that all along? It seemed like such a no-brainer as the pastor of the church that he should be bringing believers together and interceding for the needs of the church family, the community, region, and nation. He didn't know how long he had left at Lighthouse Church, but he vowed to make it count by encouraging the congregation to a deeper prayer life.

Arriving home in the dark and feeling good, James called out for Janna when he walked inside. Not hearing a response, he assumed she was sleeping. He peeked in the bedroom and through the dim light saw the outline of her small figure beneath the blanket. Emotion welled up in his throat and threatened to choke him. Tears came unbidden. He hung his head and sprawled on the couch. *If only I could understand the purpose in all this suffering, maybe I could bear it. This is just too much, and so senseless.* All of his energy drained out of him.

He realized he'd done nothing to prepare a Sunday sermon. With the coming together of those earlier who depended on him to bring the Word, he had to make sure he didn't let them down. He dragged himself off the sofa and into his study. For the next few hours he worked on his message.

The content didn't come easy, but he finally finished. The darkness outside pressed against the windows. James got up, stretched, and padded into the bedroom in his socks. He turned on a lamp to the dimmest of its three settings and saw that Janna hadn't moved. He didn't like to disturb her but knew she needed to eat something.

Gently he put a hand on her shoulder. "Janna? Janna? You need to eat some dinner."

She didn't stir. The previous couple of days must have really taken it out of her. He tried again. No response.

A chill came over him. He shivered and put his hand under her nose. No disturbance of the air. Nothing.

"Oh, dear Lord. Janna!" He pulled back the blanket to touch her face and neck. Cool to the touch, he pulled his hand away.

James began hyperventilating. "No. Janna, you were fine today. You said you'd be all right. You c...c...can't do this."

He tenderly moved her onto her back. She lay with her face pale and slack. James took a step back, shaking his head, his vision clouding, and his nose suddenly running.

His legs gave out, and he collapsed to the floor. A moan rising from deep within escaped his lips. He took one of her cool hands in his and buried his face in the blanket.

The thought that he should pray came to him, not for her or her soul; that was already a sure thing and would have no effect anyway. There was no doubt as to her destination upon death: straight into the loving arms of her Savior. No, he knew he should pray for his own strength in the Lord and courage to carry on. The few words he could utter seemed futile and pathetic. What was the point?

Janna had left him. God had seen fit to take away the only rock in his life. Was there anything to live for without her companionship, her counsel, her love?

It was well toward midnight before James reached the point that he could dial 911 to have someone take his beloved away.

Chapter 54

The next morning James clawed at the empty side of the bed, grabbed Janna's pillow, and hugged it in desperation. It didn't relieve the pain, nor did it bring her back. He dragged himself to the bathroom where a bloodshot, haggard expression stared back at him in the mirror. The emptiness he felt eclipsed anything he'd ever experienced. He felt hollow inside with a cavity of need that nothing could fill.

Because he didn't know what to do, he began crying again. It was pathetic, but he couldn't control his emotions. Today was Sunday. There was no way he could go before the church in this condition.

The last person he wanted to speak to was Deacon Joe Bennett, but he had to alert someone of his absence. He dialed Bennett's cell phone, and he answered on the second ring.

"Sorry to bother you this morning, Joe, but..." The pain welled up within him again. He couldn't speak. Emotion constricted his vocal cords. He just sat there with his phone in hand and waited for a semblance of composure to return.

"Hello? You there? Pastor James?"

"Y...yes. I...I'm here. I'm sorry. I...my wife...Janna...she died."

"Well, that's unfortunate. Will you be at church this morning?"

"No. That's why I'm calling. I...I won't make it."

"All right. Well. Sorry to hear about that. We'll try to carry on. Is that all, Pastor?"

"That's all." James disconnected. If anything, he felt worse after the call than before. The coldness and lack of empathy in the man couldn't have been more evident. Did Joe feel Christ's love? How could he even claim to be a Christian? Where had James gone wrong with this flock and its leadership?

The emptiness in the house took on a persona that hadn't been there when Janna was alive but residing in the hospital and nursing home. It spoke to him from the corners and alcoves. The dust balls he'd let go too long skittered before him as he paced the vacant rooms. His heart wanted to break. James wished it would, killing him in the process.

Because they'd had a full life, the lack of children in their marriage hadn't been something either James or Janna had ever regretted to any extent. Certainly they'd each had melancholy moments wondering what it would have been like to have a child. The fleeting thought of adoption had crossed their minds, but there had never been the drive on either of their parts to pursue it, first with the other, then through the adoption process.

Their barrenness wasn't attributed to Janna and didn't have a natural cause. At a young age, James had decided to have a vasectomy. Prior to coming to the Lord, James had lived as many do, apart from God through ignorance, both willful and inadvertent. God had never been something or Someone that he thought about or worried over. He'd lived in the world, and its culture had greatly influenced him as a youth.

Television, movies, and much of the reading material that he came across extolled the lifestyle that included sexual liaisons. Friendly hook-ups, no-fault sex, and sex as a way to spend an enjoyable hour or two were all on the table. There'd certainly been no condemnation by those around him for this way of life because everybody did it. It wasn't wrong since the moral authority for right and wrong rested within James, just as it did with his peers. Looking back, he wasn't sure if the word "fornication" had ever made its way into his vocabulary.

It was only after one of the girls, who was the object of his affections at the time, became pregnant that James considered the consequences of this free and easy lifestyle. They talked about the situation. It was a nuisance. With little thought they had the child aborted. The abortion clinic described what grew inside his girlfriend as simply a clump of cells, an embryo. What was wrong with eliminating that which got in the way of their pleasure? Not long afterward, he and the girl stopped seeing one another.

Following that, James figured the most responsible action he could take was to avoid any possibility of getting future girlfriends pregnant. To accomplish his objective, while still in his late teens, he lied about his age and convinced a doctor to give him a vasectomy. From then on it was all free and clear, until various circumstances led him to an encounter with the Lord. He turned his life around, met Janna, attended seminary, and began what had been his life for many years.

As his relationship initially deepened with his future wife, the Lord convicted him that he had to come clean as to the possibility of children between them. He confessed the vasectomy, and to his amazement, Janna told him children had never been high on her to-do list. They had lived, ministered, and loved all these years and never felt a void.

But now! With Janna gone, how he longed for children to share his loss and grief. But it wasn't to be. Actions, even long ago ones, had consequences. He was destined to mourn alone.

Chapter 55

Food had never been a comforter to James. He knew many who turned to eating as a means of cramming hurt and pain deep inside them, just as some people hit a bottle or swallowed pills. Of the numerous blessings James had received over the years that he could identify, not feeling the need to succumb to these particular temptations had been among his greatest. Today food held zero interest for him. In fact entering the kitchen reminded him of Janna, so he steered clear of it so as to minimize the sharpness of his ache.

At midafternoon the doorbell rang. He trudged to the front and was greeted by Joe Bennett. The man often wore a Detroit Tigers baseball cap. Today he wore it so low James could barely see his eyes. With one hand he held an attaché case, and in the other one, an envelope.

"Got a letter for you, James."

His grief didn't keep James from noticing the lack of the pastoral title in Bennett's greeting.

"Would you like to come in?"

"No, I gotta run. Just needed to drop this off for you."

James eyed the envelope in the deacon's outstretched hand. "What? It couldn't wait a day?"

"Well, you know, when things come to a head, you just gotta take care of them."

His lack of food that day didn't help with the general absence of energy James was experiencing. The possibility of what the letter held contributed to the heaviness in his body.

"Sure. What's in the letter?"

"As often happens, I get to be the bearer of bad news. The board has taken your situation under advisement. We asked the congregation to vote today, and by a strong majority you've been relieved of your duties. It's obvious that your lack of faith led to your affair and the inability for God to heal Janna."

Affair! The very thought that they'd accuse him of adultery offended James terribly. What could these people be thinking? He remembered the references to sexual immorality. He'd dismissed them at the time because of so many other worries. "I'm speechless, Joe, that you would treat me like this, especially at such a time. This is so callous it makes me ashamed to be called a Christian."

"You brought this on yourself, buddy. Don't blame me or the board. If you weren't fooling around on Janna, we might have had some patience with you. As it is, you don't deserve any mercy, doing what you did to that poor woman."

James stepped outside onto the front porch. "What are you talking about? I haven't done anything that demands this kind of behavior on your part."

Bennett opened the attaché he'd brought and fumbled inside. "These are copies." He handed James a set of photographs.

James took them with distaste, knowing that whatever the shots held there was something filthy about them. A set of voices rose from a neighbor's yard. Children played down the street. The continued pleasant, dry weather—despite the fact that the drought continued—kept people outside and taking advantage of it as much as possible.

The photos showed James' office at church. They captured a woman hanging all over him. Somehow they missed the tension in his body before he escaped her advances and the actual fact of his rebuffing her. They were taken with an agenda under a manufactured set of circumstances. They caught him "red-handed" in an act of passion.

Exercising a self-control that didn't come from within, James handed the pictures back to Bennett. "You showed these this morning before the vote?"

"Of course. You hung yourself. All the evidence had to be presented. Even blew them up and showed them on the big screen."

"Aren't you proud of yourself. Were you behind this setup, Joe? Because you know very well that's what it was. There's not an ounce of truth in these things."

Bennett tossed them back in the attaché and snapped it shut. "You got some chutzpah, *Pastor*. Aren't *you* ashamed of *yourself*?"

"I sure do appreciate your coming by, Joe, to express your condolences. Maybe it's time you get off my property before I call the police."

The deacon held up his hands defensively. "Hey, like I said, I'm just doing my job. You're the one who's gotta live with himself."

"The fact that this could come out your mouth says a lot more about you, Joe, than you'll ever know." James stepped back inside.

Before he shut the door completely, Bennett's final words filtered in to him. "You're not welcome to hold the funeral at the church. Find someplace else."

Chapter 56

The rest of the day didn't go quite so brutally, for which James was thankful. He did have a tough spot in which he spoke to the funeral home to arrange for their services later in the week. Just the concept of that devastated him. *Funeral services for Janna! This cannot be.* The thoughts repeated in an endless loop. He'd never experienced anything like this before in his life. He'd lost his parents years earlier and a couple of friends to tragedy, but none of those deaths had affected him like this. Janna had meant *everything* to him. Now she was gone.

The doorbell rang soon after he hung up with the funeral home. To his surprise, Gadi Benjamin stood outside.

"James, I heard about your loss. Might I come in for a couple minutes?"

"Of course. Word sure gets around. Thank you for being so thoughtful." James ushered Gadi inside and pointed him to a comfortable chair. "Anything I can get you to drink?

Tea? Soft drink?" Gadi declined and James took a seat. "How did you learn about...Janna?" Getting her name out in this context was hard.

"This is the strangest thing, James. If these kinds of things keep happening, I may have to believe in your God."

"What do you mean?"

"Nobody told me about her. I have not spoken to a soul. I woke this morning as usual and was reading like I often do in the early hours. My apartment was quiet. I love it that way. I had just set my book down to take a break when you flashed into my mind. I saw you crying and brokenhearted. It greatly disturbed me. I asked myself, 'Could what I saw be true? What has impacted James so much he would have such emotional distress?'

"I tried to go back to my reading but had no luck concentrating. Finally I gave up and went out for a walk. This sense of trouble you were in continued to hang over me. I simply could not shake it.

"The hours went by with no relief. You were always on my mind. I got to the point where I said, 'Okay, if there is some kind of God, You need to make this clear, because it is driving me nuts.' This was an hour ago.

"Suddenly another picture flashed into my mind. It was so vivid I knew it was true. You know I only met Janna one time, so I don't have a strong image of her. This picture I saw was of her—I immediately knew it was Janna—lying in a casket."

As soon as he said that, James laid his head on the back of the couch where he sat. A sob escaped from deep within him.

Gadi leaned forward. "I am so sorry, James. This must be extremely difficult. Shall I go on?"

James managed a nod.

In a hushed voice, Gadi continued. "I saw that image in my mind and had no doubt it was your Janna. She was dead. What was I supposed to do with that? I am not a Christian. I am not even a practicing Jew. God and I have never been on speaking terms. Here I have this—what can it be other than a supernatural message?—manifestation, revelation, whatever you want to call it. How does that work for somebody who barely believes in God? What do I do with it?

"The one thing I knew was that it was true. The only decent thing I could do was to bring you my condolences. The other thing I wanted to tell you is that I am having serious second thoughts about my lack of belief. Something or Somebody appears to be communicating with me. And it—He?—wanted me to bring encouragement to you by my presence. So here I am."

James had never been at a loss for words like this. He tried to express what Gadi's kindness meant to him, but failed. Following Gadi's recitation, the two men sat for the better part of an hour, mostly in silence, but that was all right. Having Gadi there did more to help James than he could have known.

So much had happened at his church that never should have. People's hearts had grown cold. Gossip, lies, and deception had stolen in under his watch. Being the shepherd of this flock, he had to take the responsibility. How he had failed in his duties as a pastor and leader! He had let the congregation down. Likely many had been hurt because of him. He had sown tares; those weeds had sprouted and choked out the few good stalks of wheat. Yes, several good ones remained. He'd experienced fellowship with them yesterday when they'd come to his office and prayed. But there were far too many thistles. It had come full circle, and the very church he'd originally come to lead into righteousness had hurt him.

Where did his comfort come from? Not from the church. Rather, from a man who didn't know God and could barely believe He existed. That was divine irony.

Hours later when Gadi left, the hurt in James' heart hadn't lessened any, but a peace that had been missing crept over him. A couple of folks from church called, including Sylvia the prayer-warrior. She prayed over him and asked the Lord to help James through this difficult time. "God, You never promised to deliver us *from* trials, but *through* them.

We know You want us to grow stronger in our faith. That only happens when we have to deal with life, not with You removing all our troubles from us."

When Sylvia finished, James confessed he wanted nothing more than the removal of his troubles. "But I understand the concept, as much as I hate it at this moment in my life." He wished Sylvia were there so he could give her a hug for her faithful support.

An idea came to James as he prepared for bed. He'd given so much of himself lately in ministering to Janna and the community—unfortunately not enough to his church—that he needed some special time doing one of his favorite activities. Janna and he had loved to hike. Her illness had eliminated that as something they could enjoy together.

He decided that first thing in the morning he would set out and hike for the day. It would be a time he could remember the sweetness of his life with Janna and physically work out the frustrations that encompassed him. Janna's funeral was several days away. He had no duties at church; in fact he no longer had a church, and the time was his. He lay his head on the pillow thinking of the pleasure of the trail.

Chapter 57

Washington, D.C.

President Luisa Parker rubbed her hands together. "This is the day, and it's certainly not the day the Lord has made. Ha! What hogwash those Christians believe. Arnold, I can't believe one of those yellow cross bearers actually shouted that at me yesterday."

With great effort Arnold Rickards matched Parker's long strides as they made their way to the Oval Office. He huffed, "You're really going to do it?"

She snorted. "What did you think? That I would make all these plans for nothing? That I would cross and double-cross my own vice president for the fun of it? No, Arnold, this is the day, and God has nothing to do with what's going down."

"I understand the first batch of Christians was delivered to the FEMA centers like clockwork, Luisa. I have to hand it to you. Your planning and operational implementation skills are shining through."

"If awards were given for the mutual admiration society, you and I would both be winners." Parker laughed with glee and swept into the historic office. She turned back to Rickards. "But seriously, without your brainpower behind all this and your covert funding of our many initiatives, I couldn't have done what's about to happen."

"It's indeed a momentous day."

"The Christians are the key to our success. In a couple minutes when we pull the trigger, we'll have a huge leg up because we've identified them and made them easy targets."

"You don't think they'll resist?" Rickards took a chair, sighed, and sat back. "How about coffee?"

Parker pressed a button and a male voice came through the speaker, "Yes, Madam President?"

"Two coffees with cream and sugar, Wesley. In fact, bring a pot. We may be here a while."

"Yes, ma'am, right away."

The president walked over to a chair by Rickards. "Power is intoxicating."

"I'm not sure which is better, power or money. It's good to have both, Luisa."

"I appreciate that you've shown me how to skim from the government coffers. My Swiss account has grown dramatically, thanks to the American taxpayer. And it's soon to increase substantially as our initiatives play out."

There was a knock at the door, and the Secret Service agent, Parker's personal butler, entered with a silver tray. He set it down between the president and her advisor, bowed, and waited expectantly.

"That'll be all, Wesley."

The agent bowed again and left the room.

Rickards sipped his coffee and grimaced. "Hot!" He set it down to let it cool a bit. "Let me ask you again about Abu Saif. You expect no trouble from him? After all, he's the one who basically gets shafted the most. You don't think that'll have repercussions?"

"I have a special place prepared for him. He won't be in any position to harm us or cause any difficulties." President Parker looked at her watch. She drank the hot coffee with no apparent distress while Rickards looked on in amazement. "Are you ready, Arnold?"

"I wait with anticipation and watch the master."

A big grin crossed Parker's face. "All right. Now is the time. Let's turn up the heat."

Chapter 58

Western Michigan

The myriad red clouds on the eastern horizon, in an otherwise cloudless expanse, made James think of the old saying: "Red sky at morning, sailor take warning." For hundreds of years men of the sea and laborers of the soil had taken the saying to heart. Atmospherically the red clouds often presaged rain. Because of the extensive drought over the land, James had little faith that would come about. There'd been too many other false positives over the months. He had little doubt that a rainstorm would interrupt his hike.

He thought of the words Jesus spoke to the Pharisees when they tested Him, as they often did, by demanding He show them a sign from heaven. "When evening comes, you say, 'It will be fair weather, for the sky is red,' and in the morning, 'Today it will be stormy, for the sky is red and overcast.' You know how to interpret the appearance of the sky, but you cannot interpret the signs of the times. A wicked and adulterous generation looks for a sign, but none will be given it except the sign of Jonah."

James smiled. They always tried to trip Jesus up. But how does that happen? Can someone fool the omniscient God of all creation? They wanted a miracle. Jesus gave them a dual response. He implied that what they saw in the skies was a miracle itself. They could interpret the weather but couldn't see what was before their very eyes. The sign they wanted was actually Jesus Himself. A miracle? How about the fact that He was God incarnate having been born from a virgin? He would rise from the dead as Jonah had been brought out of the belly of the whale. The grave and death would spit Him out, as the whale had vomited out Jonah. The world had appropriated the "red sky" saying and trivialized it, missing the deeper importance of what Jesus meant, as unbelievers inevitably did.

The thoughts had come easily, but James caught himself. Given the mess his life had become, he frankly wanted nothing to do with God. The response of Godly things was ingrained, given his years serving the Lord. Maybe, just maybe, he'd served Him long enough. Perhaps the time had come to step away from it all. God hadn't healed Janna. He hadn't intervened in the mess at church with its accusations and falling away into hard-heartedness. He'd let the world around Him disintegrate into moral and spiritual decay. What was the point of serving this God who never answered James' most desperate prayers? Even Bob Sanders had suffered, and look at him. He was the most devoted follower of Jesus Christ that James knew. The hike would be a good thing. The solitude would enable James to sort out his thoughts and his future. He threw his backpack into the car and took off for the hiking area he'd chosen.

Chapter 59

Central Michigan

The drive a couple of hours north and east took James to the forest preserve. These federal lands were new to him, ones he'd wanted to try for a long time. They happened to be remote and promised that only experienced hikers should enter the wilderness area. Just what he wanted. The more solitary the better as far as James was concerned.

He entered a long dirt road that took him to the trailhead marked on his map. Upon opening his car door, he gave an appreciative look at the towering trees and the sun shining a pale yellow in a sky streaked with cirrus clouds to the east. It was then that he heard the voice.

"Go to the great capital city and preach against it, because its wickedness has come up before Me."

James froze. He thought he was alone. Cautiously he got out and swiveled his eyes around at his surroundings. "Hello? Is anyone here? Did somebody just say something?"

A few birds sang. A cricket chirped. He noticed the woods were tinder dry. Without any rain and because of the continued warmth, the leaves on the trees had only just begun to turn. Normally at this point in late October the riot of color would be dying, and the leaves would be dropping. Not this year.

A drone zipped by overhead. Even out here. How he hated those things and the intrusive government they represented. Maybe the voice had somehow come from that. It passed out of sight, likely not before noting that he was here. James laughed. Well, maybe if he ran into trouble, they'd come and rescue him since they knew where he was.

Maybe he'd imagined the voice. After all, he'd been under significant stress lately and that could do strange things to people.

His foot crunched on the gravel and the sound gave him comfort. He needed this time on the trail. Without further delay, he approached the trailhead.

At his first step on the dirt of the trail the audible voice spoke to him again.

"Go to the great capital city and preach against it, because its wickedness has come up before Me."

The blood in James' veins felt chilled. The hair on the back of his neck raised in fear.

That wasn't the voice of anyone human. Instinctively he knew it was God's voice. How did he know? It wasn't condemning. Love seemed to flow from it. It was a command, but one given from a loving Source.

But James was having nothing to do with it. He spoke to the air around him. "I'm not interested, God. I don't even know if I believe in You anymore, although here I am talking to You. I don't care. I've had enough. I need this time alone, and I want peace and quiet without You in the middle of it. And about going and preaching somewhere? You can forget that, too. I'm a lousy, washed-up pastor. You want somebody on fire for you? Go find Bob Sanders. At least he believes in You more than I do."

He put his hands over his ears and stomped down the trail.

Chapter 60

United States: Various Communities

Allen Grayson noticed a police car in his rearview mirror. He checked his speed and saw the gauge hovering just under the limit. With a shrug, he turned his eyes back on the road ahead. A moment later, a short blast of the siren alerted him to the flashing light bar of the squad car. He looked around and saw nobody else who could be the objective of the cops' attentions. A glance at his dashboard clock showed he would have been on time to work if he didn't have to stop, but stop he must.

Being a law-abiding citizen, Allen was also a supporter of the police. During a period in the recent past when police had been the target of organized protests and legal action, Allen had inevitably sided with law enforcement. He knew the police had a difficult task that put their lives on the line every day, and that because of evil intent, one or more might not make it home some night. In the rare instance he'd been the object of a traffic stop for a speeding violation, he was always courteous.

As a Christian, he believed in taking responsibility for his actions and exercising self-control, one of the fruits of the Spirit. A pleasant demeanor had occasionally been enough for a policeman to let him off for excessive speed with a warning rather than a ticket. He wasn't perfect. He knew he shouldn't speed in the first place, but he was human. When he got a reprieve, he thanked God for His mercy and did his best to obey the law.

Today he couldn't for the life of him imagine why they were stopping him. He pulled to the side of the road and rolled down his window. When the cop approached, he greeted the officer and complied when he requested Allen's license.

After several minutes, the officer returned. "Please step out of the car, Mr. Grayson."

Mystified, Allen did as instructed. "May I ask what the trouble is, Officer?"

"I'd like your permission to search your vehicle." The man wasn't giving anything away.

Allen knew better than to allow police free reign in searching his car or house without a warrant, but he had nothing to hide. He shrugged. "Go ahead." The officer glanced back at his own car, and Allen followed his gaze. The person sitting in the front seat nodded, and the policeman proceeded to look inside Allen's car.

While in the process of searching, the officer commented, "I see you're wearing a yellow cross."

Immediately self-conscious because of the negative press all wearers had received, he touched the icon. It didn't keep him from proclaiming his faith. "Yes. I'm a follower of Jesus Christ."

The policeman found nothing to incriminate him, as Allen knew he wouldn't. The man closed the car doors, straightened, and removed his handcuffs from his belt. "You'll have to come with me. Hold out your hands."

Nothing could have shocked Allen more. "What do you mean? I wasn't speeding, and you didn't find anything illegal in my car. What's the charge?"

No expression crossed the officer's face. "You are illegal. My orders are to take in you because you're a Christian. You confessed. It's all recorded. You confirmed what the yellow cross declares."

Allen had heard rumors of other Christians who had disappeared recently. He never thought they'd come after him, despite the insanity and humiliation of wearing the yellow cross.

"What about my car?"

The officer motioned to the man in the passenger seat of the police cruiser. "We'll take care of it."

Having no option but to do as he was told, Allen stepped into the back of the squad car.

The ruddy-faced man in the passenger seat who got out and entered Allen's car wore plain clothes. He also sported a pistol that he openly carried in a holster on his belt.

***

Martha Simmons pulled into her driveway, back from dropping her two children off at school. She had a busy day planned and expected good things to come from it. In fact, she hoped this would be the beginning of many good things for her. In her prayers she'd fervently asked God for a breakthrough in her real estate career. For years she'd done adequately, adding to the household income, but by no means was she a top producer. With the kids now in school, she had the time and opportunity to do better. All she needed was a few breaks with more people deciding to use her services. She loved the technical aspects of the job but fell down when it came to marketing. Still, if she could work referrals better, everything could definitely fall into place.

Two men emerged from the car parked at the curb. Both were plainly dressed but clearly armed. Martha shrank away as they approached. Cell phone in hand, she began dialing 911. "I'm calling the police. Don't come any closer."

One reached into his pocket and withdrew a small brown leather case. He flipped it open. "We're duly charged deputies of Homeland Security."

She saw the flash of the badge. "Stay there! Throw your badge over here so I can see it." As a real estate professional, she'd read plenty of horror stories of women agents trapped by scammers in empty houses seeking to take advantage of them. It made her extremely cautious, regardless of the circumstances.

The man tossed the case toward her, and she scooped it up. It gave his name and indicated his deputized position with Homeland Security as he'd said. Slowly she cut off the 911 call and lowered her phone. "What do you want?"

He walked toward her and held out his hand for her to return his badge. He pointed at the yellow cross she'd been forced to wear. "What's that mean to you?"

At first she'd hated it, but lately she'd come to regard it as a badge of honor. Its shame put her in good company: with that of her Savior, Jesus Christ. He endured the shame of the cross for her; the least she could do was suffer the same humiliation. Martha lifted her jaw and stood her ground.

"Everything. It's my life and my eternal destiny. Jesus died to save my soul. All that I have is His."

"Right. You'll have to come with us."

"Whatever for?"

The man smirked. "People like you are a danger to society. The fewer of you on the streets, the safer this country will be."

"You don't have any right to arrest me for my faith. You people may have labeled us with yellow crosses, but we still have something called a Constitution with a First Amendment that gives us freedom of religion."

"Yeah, whatever." He produced a pair of handcuffs. "Let's go, lady."

The seriousness of the situation brought Martha into a state of panic. "Where are you taking me? How long are you keeping me? What about my children when school lets out?"

"Not our problem. It'll all work out." He cuffed her and pressed down on the top of her head to force her into their car.

She began to hyperventilate. It was all she could do not to pass out as they drove away from her house.

***

Timothy Rhodes put his phone down feeling extremely puzzled. His secretary had told him that two men from the FBI wanted to see him. Timothy ran his business with the moral conscience of the devoted Christian he'd become. There had been a day that Timothy would have stolen the socks from his own father if it meant he could sell them to buy more drugs. But those days were long past. He'd encountered Christ at, of all places, a marijuana drug deal gone bad.

When he testified to people how God had given him grace and mercy when he deserved nothing but judgment and jail time, all they could do was marvel and praise God. That was his intent. Timothy now lived his life for the Lord and conducted his affairs, including his business, accordingly.

The FBI coming to his company to see him could only mean that they wanted his advice or possibly some information for a case that had nothing to do with him. He greeted the men as his secretary showed them to chairs in front of his desk. "What can I do for you, gentlemen?"

Only one of the men was dressed in a suit; the other wore business casual with slacks and a sports shirt. The man in the suit extracted his wallet and flashed his badge. He named himself and introduced his colleague as someone on special assignment to the FBI.

"We're here on serious business, sir. It has to do with your faith."

Timothy touched the yellow cross pinned to his suit coat. "What business could the FBI have with me that has to do with what I believe?"

The FBI agent pursed his lips. "We've been ordered to take you people off the streets."

With a wave of his hand toward his office, Timothy made light of the agent's statement. "Well, as you can see, I'm definitely not on the streets. This is a reputable, Christian-run business. Neither this business nor I personally are threats to anyone. Truth be told, if more companies ran on the moral compass we do, there'd be a lot less corporate shenanigans."

"This is no joking matter, Mr. Rhodes." The agent lifted his arm to see his watch. "I'll give you the courtesy of letting your secretary know you're coming with us. Other than that, we need to go."

"Wait! What are you saying? That you're taking me into custody?" This was ludicrous. Timothy had read novels in which people were unfairly incarcerated, but it didn't happen to real people like him.

The men stood and handcuffs appeared. "Your hands please."

"You have no idea what you're doing. This isn't pleasing to God. For the sake of your own soul, I'm begging you, rethink this. Don't anger God by harming an innocent person."

"Last of my worries, buddy. We've got people up the food chain who'll take their anger out on us if we don't do what we've been ordered. God'll have to wait His turn."

On their way out the agent didn't do as he promised. He marched Timothy out the door without giving him a chance to speak with his secretary to inform her of his plight.

***

Jake Alcorn stood next to his SUV atop one of the rolling hills that graced his property. He owned hundreds of head of cattle and loved to get to a high place like this to observe how the Lord had blessed him. The thought inevitably came to mind that none of this, the abundant grasslands nor the many beasts that roamed and fed, were his. It all belonged to God. The verse of Scripture said it well: "For all the animals of the forest are mine, and I own the cattle on a thousand hills." Jake was simply God's caretaker in this little part of the world.

A cloud of dust on the horizon indicated a vehicle heading toward his house. Jake swung into the driver's seat and gunned the SUV to meet his visitors.

The two cars arrived within seconds of each other. Jake had an uneasy feeling and retrieved his pistol from the glove compartment before stepping from the car. He never looked for trouble, but liked to prepare for it in case it showed up. Two men exited their vehicle and moved toward Jake.

Both men wore lightweight Western shirts and mid-calf leather boots with fancy stitching. Jake took in their appearance and nodded. "What can I do for you gentlemen?"

The taller of the two produced a badge. "We're deputized by Border Patrol and commissioned to bring you in for questioning."

The rancher laughed. "What? You think I'm harboring illegals?"

"We could care less about that, Mr. Alcorn. Where's your yellow cross?"

Jake's eyes narrowed as he touched the spot on his chest that he would pin the cross if he chose to wear it. But that was the last thing he would do. Nobody was going to infringe on his rights as an American citizen and coerce him to wear an unconstitutional symbol like the Nazis had forced the Jews.

"How'd you know I don't wear it?"

"You're a prominent man in town, Alcorn. Known for his Christian views. We have eyes and ears everywhere. Your not wearing the cross came up before us. We can't allow someone to arbitrarily disobey our president's direct decrees."

"You ever hear of laws passed by duly-elected representatives of the people in Congress? Talk about arbitrary." Jake spat. His anger began rising. "Just because some lesbo president with a chip on her shoulder decides Christians are scum doesn't make it right or legal."

"We've heard enough." The taller one pulled a gun from his leather holster. "We're taking you in." He motioned for his partner to handcuff Jake.

The shorter man readied the restraints. "Hold out your hands."

Jake snorted. His mouth became a tight slit. He put both hands together and allowed the man to come close. At the last instant Jake kneed him in the groin and caught his lowering jaw in a huge uppercut. The man dropped as Jake grabbed his weapon from the waistband behind his back.

The tall man shouted at Jake, "Drop that gun!" Without any hesitation, he raised his own pistol and fired.

Jake had anticipated the move. He dove around the SUV. Bullets pinged off the metal, and Jake fired back. He didn't miss. The tall man dropped. His buddy, shaking off the punch, found his gun. Firing from the ground, he tried to take Jake out.

The rancher returned fire and hit the shorter man squarely. Suddenly, what had been noise and chaos became quiet. Jake's wife ran from their farmhouse. "Jake, Jake, what's happening?"

He hugged her. "They came looking for a fight."

Squeezing his wife's hand first, he went over to each body and examined it, shaking his head. "We're in a real fix, honey. If we alert the authorities, they'll take me away one way or the other. It grieves me, but I think we need to dispose of the bodies."

His wife put a hand to her mouth. "Oh, Jake, they'll know. And what about God? Is it right in His eyes?"

"I don't think we have a choice. Everybody's been talking about a 'new normal' for years. Well, we're living it. These are new and dangerous times. We might have to do some things that were unthinkable in the past. In the meantime, we'll seek the Lord for His counsel."

Jake gathered the men's weapons and glanced once more at their lifeless bodies. "What a waste. Come on, honey, we got work to do."

Chapter 61

Central Michigan

His many years of trail experience had given James fairly sure footing upon treacherous paths. He'd traversed rocky mountain tracks, needing to balance on skull-sized stones, and on slippery slopes where he'd made his way over loose gravel slick as mud. On forest trails he'd learned to anticipate hidden roots that could trip a hiker and spill him into the brush, and maneuver over, under, and around downed trees that blocked his way. Not much daunted him. Janna had often joked that his feet were as sure as a mountain goat.

Not today. He hadn't gone ten yards before a low branch jumped out at his feet. It caught his right ankle and down he went. Pushing himself up, he saw that a thorn bush had caught his shirt with a tenacity that caused it to rip in two places as he extricated himself. Ten yards on the trail and he was already sweating fiercely from his exertions.

James didn't mumble much, but there were times when things went wrong and he couldn't help it. This was supposed to be a day of release, and he'd already lost that vision.

He shook himself off, glanced back once at the place of his minor undoing, and resolved not to let it bother him. At least the voice of God, or Whomever, had stopped, so he didn't need to cover his ears any longer.

Up ahead he came to a creek that had a narrow wooden bridge crossing it. It had waist-high handrails and worn slats that looked to be connected into five sections. He started across and noticed how rickety it felt. The creek was only about ten feet wide. He'd gotten two yards from the end when his feet went out from under him. The section he was on disconnected from the support behind him, like a trapdoor opening beneath his feet. Seeing the last section remaining still tied to the end of the bridge, he lunged for it. There wasn't much water flowing in the creek, but he didn't relish starting out his hike with wet boots. He scrabbled up the declining section that partially rested in the water and only dipped the toe of one boot into the creek.

On the other side he rested a minute, sweating furiously. For a day that was supposed to calm him, things weren't panning out so great thus far.

He wiped the sweat from his forehead and was about to begin again when the voice spoke once more:

"I've loved you with an everlasting love, yet I tell you this: Give careful thought to your ways. You expected much, but see, it turned out to be little. What you brought home, I blew away. Why? Because of My house, which remains a ruin, while each of you is busy with his own house. I am with you, but give careful thought to your ways. Heed My Word. Follow My commands."

The voice was like the roar of mighty rivers, yet soft like a springtime breeze. It brought both a chill to James' bones and a warmth of emotional feeling—of love—that he hadn't known since he was a baby in his mother's arms. Only this was deeper and stronger, beyond knowing.

He couldn't deny it now. This was God, and He was speaking directly to James. It was the most wonderful thing—yet the most awful—he'd ever experienced. Wonderful because this was the voice of the speaking God whom he'd always read about. Awful because this God wanted him to do something—to convey a message that James didn't want to carry.

The rebellious side of him won out. "You've got the wrong man, Lord. I know You don't make mistakes, but somehow You did. Maybe You got me and Bob Sanders mixed up. I don't know, but I'm not the man for the job. I'm taking a hike, and You can take one, too." Thinking that a little harsh, he added, "Respectfully, Lord."

Determined to make the most of this day, James marched up the trail, eyes set on the path ahead, trying to drown out any more Godly voices by repetitively sing-songing the trite, "La, la, la," in his mind.

Chapter 62

When people think about the State of Michigan they picture the mitten. Asked where he lived, James, like most residents, would hold up the back of his left hand with closed fingers and point to his approximate location on the mitten. To his and Janna's surprise when they moved there, they discovered the state contained hills and mountains. Looking at elevations on a map, they saw in the north center of the state are elevations of up to fifteen hundred feet. These whet their appetite for outdoor adventure as they pictured themselves skiing in winter and hiking in warmer weather.

This was the area where James had headed this morning. It included a decent amount of high exertion hiking and was exactly what he desired. On the upside of a forested slope surrounded by towering trees, James worked hard at ascending the hill. It had been a while since he'd been on a trail, and he was out of hiking shape. He huffed and blew out air with each step, inhaling deeply to get the oxygen he needed.

At the crest of the ridge, he saw that the trail meandered along at the top for a while and followed where it led. He came to a spot where the trees cleared with a beautiful view overlooking a valley. With the sun high overhead and the dryness of the day, he needed a drink. He normally carried two water bottles and pulled one from its position on his backpack. The bottle felt damp and was lighter than he expected. To his disappointment, he realized it was empty. He examined the sturdy plastic container and saw the minute crack near its base. How had that happened?

He took off his backpack. The pocket that held the water bottle was wet. Apparently he'd hit a rock or tree with the backpack causing the bottle to crack inside its protective pocket. He took out the second bottle, relieved it held its full complement of water.

Squatting to rest and stretch his tired legs, he appreciated the glory of the view. Up until now he'd avoided two major streams of thought: Janna and God. Oddly, memories of Janna hadn't been intrusive this morning. The labor of the hike and the beauty of his surroundings had effectively blocked that avenue of contemplation. Keeping deliberation of God from his consciousness had taken greater effort, but he congratulated himself on the success he'd had. Despite God's attempts to intrude on this personal time, James had won the upper hand.

He gathered himself and continued on. Before he could take one stride, the voice returned:

"I have loved you, O man, with an everlasting love. I have drawn you with loving-kindness. Before you were born I set you apart; I appointed you as prophet to the nation.

"Surely the day is coming; it will burn like a furnace. All the arrogant and every evildoer will be stubble, and that day that is coming will set them on fire. See, I will send you before that great and dreadful day of the Lord comes. You will turn the hearts of the parents to their children, and the hearts of the children to their parents; or else I will come and strike the land with total destruction."

This time fear struck James to his core. He began to run along the ridgetop path. The last thing he wanted was to be a prophet of God. It was unimaginable to him. His scream trailed after him: "Nooooo!"

He rounded a bend and began heading on the downward track, heedless of his safety. The brush got thicker and trees denser as he whizzed by them. "I will not, God! I can't! I won't! Leave me alone!"

James ran until he couldn't take another step, his lungs bursting. As he pulled to a stop, he didn't see the stone. He stepped on it and twisted his ankle. With a cry he fell to the ground grabbing at his leg. He sat on his rear grimacing and doing his best not to curse. He still knew better than to do that.

With tentative fingers he gingerly probed his ankle. From what he could tell, it wasn't broken, just badly sprained. Good, but not good.

He was hours from his car over rough, uneven terrain. Pulling out his cell phone he saw he had no signal. Somehow he'd have to make it back on his own.

At that instant he smelled smoke.

Chapter 63

United States – One Community

The roundup of some Christians wasn't quite as pleasant as it was for others. Whereas a goodly number had polite visits from agents representing various governmental authorities, a distinct few didn't fare so well. In every case where a semblance of manners was portrayed when the subject was taken into custody, the primary agent was an official state employee while the accompanying "agent" was inevitably a deputized union enforcer. This was someone who'd shown his loyalty to the cause of progressive politics and could usually be counted on to restrain himself from acting out of hand.

In the many other cases that didn't feature a true agent of the state, that is one employed by Homeland Security, the IRS, the FBI, or any of the myriad agencies that had been weaponized and selected to bring Christians to heel, only union thugs were sent to apprehend the target. That created greater problems for those arrested by their overzealous government.

Max Beathard, like Jake Alcorn on his western ranch, was another recipient of the police state gone wild. Max, an auto mechanic, displayed a Christian charity that astounded many. He worked in his small one-man shop and inevitably had more business than he could handle. His fame, for the way he charged fair rates with exceptional quality work, spread throughout his community. His renown also included a significant amount of pro bono work for those who couldn't afford service on their already old and untrustworthy cars.

A single mother of five might come in with her vehicle needing a brake job. Among the items on his work checklist was a quick verification of her background and need. Max had his sources. He was a Christian who believed the words of Jesus, who said His disciples should be wise as serpents and innocent as doves. He wasn't a man who could generally be taken advantage of; he was a man who thoroughly gave of himself and his services when the need arose because he loved his Lord and tried to follow His commands. Among those was to have mercy on widows and orphans. Max would fix those brakes of the single mother and give her twenty dollars to feed her children.

Years of hard labor had hardened Max's body. Friends had told Max that to shake hands with him was to feel those big mitts close around yours and hope to God he wouldn't squeeze too hard. He had belonged to the NRA forever; he believed in his country and the freedoms that came because of the Second Amendment. When duly-appointed representatives of his government had come to take away his firearms, Max had resisted as long as he could, but in the end, they'd absconded with his guns. It had only been Max's Christian self-control that kept him from punching out the men who took his weapons and landing in jail as a result.

Max knew the men who showed up at his shop this particular day. They'd been involved in union politics for years. One had spent five years in prison for excessive enthusiasm when it came to property that wasn't his. He'd been part of a strike picket line when a scab tried to cross to work for the day. The poor man's car had suffered the loss of its windshield, and all four tires had been slit by the time this guy finished protecting his union territory. The other man had made his reputation as a union boss engaged in voter turnout schemes that were somehow never prosecuted.

When they entered the garage the trip alarm sounded, and Max slid out from under the car he was fixing. He recognized his visitors, but polite as always greeted them cordially. "What can I do for you gentlemen?"

"We come to take you in for practicing Christianity without a license, Max." The ex-con elbowed his friend. "Pretty good, huh? 'Practicing Christianity without a license.' I'll have to remember that."

His buddy, the vote schemer, rolled his eyes. "You're a regular comedian." He displayed the badge indicating his deputization. "We've got orders to take you in for questioning. Here's the warrant."

Max narrowed his eyes. "What's this about? What are you two talking about?"

Vote-Schemer slipped his wallet back in his pants' pocket. "There's been a rash of unexplained acts of violence lately. You Christians have been implicated. You'll have to come with us."

Max started for the black phone hanging on the wall of the shop. "I'm calling my attorney."

Ex-Con pulled out his pistol and waved it at Max. "You can call him when you're in custody. Not before."

At the sight of the gun Max stopped. He faced his adversaries and folded his arms across his chest just below the yellow cross. "For some reason, I don't believe you."

"You can believe us or not; it don't matter." Vote-Schemer snapped his fingers at Ex-Con. "Throw me the cuffs. Shoot him if he makes a stupid move." He edged closer toward Max. "Don't make it hard on yourself."

The man reached for Max's right hand with the handcuffs opened, ready to slap them on. With a lightning motion Max struck the metal ring and knocked the restraints to the ground. He remained loose, waiting, never taking his eyes off Vote-Schemer.

The man rubbed his fingers that had been twisted in the scuffle. He spoke with a tone of regret that almost sounded genuine. "I wish you hadn't done that, Max." Once more he snapped his fingers at Ex-Con.

"You think I'm a trained monkey?" he complained before pulling the trigger and shooting Max in the leg.

"Ugh!" Max went down hard, blood soaking his greasy coveralls.

Vote-Schemer picked up the handcuffs and snapped on one side. "I hate it when this happens." He yanked Max's other arm behind his back and the second ring clicked tight. "If he gets any blood on my car seat, I'll be really ticked off." He noticed a large oil-spotted rag and brought it over to Max, tying off his leg above the bullet wound. "All right. That's number three for the day; only four more to go to meet our quota."

The men dragged Max to Vote-Schemer's high-end Cadillac and dumped him in the back seat.

***

Marcy Warren had become a follower of Jesus Christ because of the stunning kindness and mercy of His disciple, Max Beathard. He had shown her there was a better way to live. The single mother of five children still struggled to make ends meet, but she had come to know the grace showered upon her by the sacrificial death of Jesus, the shedding of His blood that washed her clean of all her sins and made her presentable to the God and Creator of all things. It still astounded her that He would perform such a selfless act for her and inspire His followers to likewise do good in His Name.

She'd begun attending Max's church, and the blessings had multiplied. Women she hardly knew helped out by watching her children. One of the members offered her a job at a pay level much higher than she thought she deserved. She received blessing upon blessing.

Through the solid preaching of the pastor, Marcy had learned that becoming a Christian would likely attract the hostility of the world. She didn't understand that fully, but she remembered her pastor reciting the words of Jesus to His disciples: "If the world hates you, keep in mind that it hated me first. If you belonged to the world, it would love you as its own." It was something she had tucked in the back of her mind, even though as a new Christian she was riding high because of the love exhibited all around her by her new church family.

Today she was glad she didn't buy into the false teaching that Christianity offered her the best life now. The two men barged into her apartment with little fanfare. They accused her of being a Christian, confirming the yellow cross she'd been made to wear. At her mention of a warrant, they both laughed.

The one in charge looked Marcy up and down. "Yeah, we got one. Say, you're a pretty little thing. You really got five kids? I'd a never guessed the way you keep yourself. Not like some of the cows we've had to round up. What do you think, Mike? Before we bring her in, maybe we should have some fun with her."

Mike glanced at his watch. "I'm free for the afternoon."

In the hours that followed, Marcy suffered terribly, but had the revelation of experiencing, in some small measure, what her Savior had undergone for her. Jesus' words made complete sense to her, even as the men had their way. The world didn't love her. The hate she endured proved that. What she had to undergo was simply the hate these men had for God. Before she blacked out, she prayed the Lord would forgive them.

Chapter 64

Central Michigan

At first it was just the hint of smoke. A slight difference in the air quality, an irritation of his nostrils. He hadn't seen any indication of other hikers or campers, but it was possible someone had started a small fire for some unknown reason. Shrugging his shoulders, James decided it was more important to minister to his ankle.

In his backpack he always kept elastic tape for this very kind of situation where he needed to bind and stiffen an ankle or wrist after a minor incident. He and Janna had had their shares of spills and had dealt with them accordingly. Most of the time Janna had helped him or vice versa depending on who was injured. But today—for the rest of his life—he was alone. James gritted his teeth and got to work.

He took off his hiking boot and sock, wrapped the ankle well, and got the boot back on with difficulty. A nearby sapling gave him a way to help himself up. A little weight on the foot proved agonizing. If he could find a crutch of some kind it might enable him to put less stress on the injury. The only option in sight was that small sapling. He took out his hunting knife. After working at it a bit he cut the one-inch diameter tree down. In a couple more minutes he'd removed the top portion and had a serviceable aid.

It hadn't taken long, but the smell of smoke became stronger. A breeze out of the west had come up while he'd been doctoring himself. Naturally that was the way back to his car. Not sure what choice he had other than to hobble toward his ride out and hope for the best with any fire that might have begun, he started retracing his steps on the trail.

The injury made for slow going, but he soon left the top of the ridge, not having seen anything. He hated the idea of going toward the fire and began questioning how wise that was with the increasing pungency in the air. It would have been a three-hour hike on a healthy ankle. In his current condition, that time might be doubled.

He realized how unlucky he was in his timing. November was almost at hand. Days were much shorter. Once Daylight Savings Time came the next weekend, he would have had another full hour of daylight. The gain of that time could have been helpful. As it was, darkness would come on him quickly.

His path took a turn and opened to a field that gave him an elevated view down the side of the foothill. There he saw the fire for the first time. And it wasn't creeping up the hill, it was racing.

James saw the dry grasses in the field and the parched trees surrounding it. The fire was consuming everything at an enormous rate. His heart began beating at a rapid pace. He was in trouble.

Not able to go forward without walking right into the teeth of the fiercest blaze, he surveyed his location. A couple of hundred yards away, across the field and off the trail, he saw a rocky outcropping fronting a steep hill. He couldn't recall any place behind him that might provide shelter. The best he could hope for was an indentation between the rocks that he could burrow into and pray the flames would pass over him.

He took his first step off the trail. His ankle throbbing from the extra stress of the uneven ground, he leaned on the crutch and did what he must.

Chapter 65

The trek across the field using his makeshift crutch took longer than James expected. The uneven terrain caused him to misstep more than once and go crashing to the ground. He would cry out in pain, breathe heavily to mitigate his agony, and rise again to force himself to the possible shelter of the rocks.

The light breeze picked up to a steady wind. It fanned the flames of the fire to a raging monster that bore down on him. James felt the prickle of heat as it crested the rise and licked at the dry field of brown grass.

Sweat poured off his face. It soaked his shirt as though he'd run through a downpour. How he wished rain would come! The thought flashed through his mind about his ruminations that morning. He'd seen the red sky and scoffed at the idea of rain. There'd been no moisture for months, so a sign in the heavens indicating the possibility of wet weather would have meant little. Now it likely meant his only salvation. A glance upward crushed what little hope he had left. Billowing smoke darkened the sky. *I'm doomed. It's definitely not going to rain today.*

He limped along as quickly as he could. It was only a fifty-fifty bet that he'd reach the rocks before the flames caught him from behind. Even if he did make the rocks, he had no assurance of safety. It could be a blind alley. He might be wasting his efforts, simply delaying the inevitable.

The beast bore down from the west. A flood of uncertainty overtook him. *Am I sure of my salvation?* Did he truly know the God of the Bible? *Will Jesus immediately hold me in His loving arms?* Was his doubt too overwhelming? *Perhaps God, like my church, will reject me because of my lack of faith.* Could these qualms be indicative of a real hindrance to heaven? *Is Satan playing games with me?* The enemy took advantage of every opening to sow seeds of deceit. *Are my misgivings the result of the devil's evil ministrations?*

He had no choice but to run the final yards. Shuffling along with his crutch slowed him too much. He cast it aside. With the first unaided step he roared as pain shot up the nerves of his leg. It threw him forward on the dirt and gravel, skinning his palms as he tried to prevent himself from falling. He scrabbled along the ground to the nearest cluster of rocks. Nothing caught his eye. It crushed his hopes even as the blaze licked at his feet.

The heat seared him. He looked back as the threads of his pants ignited. With a jerk he pulled his feet up and rolled over the top of the nearest boulder into a gap between the rocks. A couple of feet away he spotted an indeterminate dark area. His strength waning, he pulled himself toward it. Closer up it looked like a narrow opening. With the last of his reserves he dove into the cavity even as the flames howled above him.

Chapter 66

The rush of hot air from the roaring, living inferno drove James through the narrow aperture like a mouse wriggling through a tunnel only big enough for its head. He pushed his backpack through first. Somehow the rest of his body followed. He felt burning on his pants legs. James squeezed into a larger space and began beating at the flames licking at his flesh. Once he'd extinguished them, he lay flat on his back panting like a wounded animal. He'd been burned; it hurt like crazy, but he couldn't see well enough in the enclosure to determine how badly he'd been injured.

Thinking of seeing, he reached up to adjust his glasses. He touched only the skin around his eyes. They weren't there. He must have lost them in the mad scramble to make it inside. Thankfully, he wouldn't need them here to any extent since it was too dark to see anyway. Once the fire passed and he could try to reach civilization, it might be another issue. He'd been wearing them for so long they'd become second nature to him. Because of his dependency on them, naturally his eyes had grown weaker. It would be another obstacle he'd have to overcome in his future quest to reach safety.

For now he was thankful—to God?—that he'd found this shelter from the fire. Yes, to God. James had been a pastor long enough to know that despite his crumbling faith, God had given him the provision of this cave. "All right, God," he admitted, "You got me here. I'm safe for the time being. Now what?"

In retrospect, it was a question he probably shouldn't have asked at that immediate time. The smell of smoke had followed him in because of his burning clothes. From what he could determine, nothing had abated outside. He wasn't sure what was feeding the fire, but it was going strong. It took some time for the smoky air to clear in the chamber. The darkness made seeing all but impossible, and he began to think about actually lighting a little fire for light. With that thought, another smell assaulted his nostrils.

He sniffed. The pungent odor of wild animal made him jerk back his head. He wasn't the only one who had found this hiding place. The question was whether or not he currently had company. In a way he didn't want to know the answer.

James felt around his immediate space for anything that could be used for fuel. Patting the ground in a circle around him, he came upon some small sticks of wood. Was it possible a past hiker had sought shelter here and made a fire?

He fumbled in his backpack and remembered his flashlight. He grabbed it and a fire-starting flint. He turned on the beam only briefly to save the battery. After positioning various items he worked by touch to shave some of the wood pieces with his knife. He set them in a heap and used his flint to spark a flame. The ironic thought came to him that all he needed to start a fire was to stick a branch outside his door. In a few minutes he succeeded in his task. He fed his little fire, and when it was adequately going, he turned his attention to his surroundings.

The area inside was much larger than he'd imagined. By the flickering light and his poor vision, he saw he could actually stand in here if he were able. The injured ankle throbbed unmercifully and needed rest. His gaze moved around. He had to shift his body to see toward his rear. The sight that presented itself caused him to freeze. He'd heard the phrase that someone's blood ran cold, but he'd never experienced the phenomenon until now. The trembling began in the core of his being and ran throughout his entire body with his blood pumping from a heart working overtime in its fright.

It was among the worst of possible nightmares. Not more than thirty feet away stood three gray wolves. Their malevolent, blue eyes were all fixed on James.

Chapter 67

The lead wolf took a hesitant step toward James. In the dim light, even with his blurry vision, James noticed drool dripping from the animal's mouth. The wolf snarled. It held its tail in a stiff, horizontal position. James thought frantically about what he knew regarding the body posture of wolves. Not much came to mind. He'd heard that when dogs assumed that position they were in a predatory, attack mode. Wolves certainly had similar traits. He was in big trouble.

James snatched one of the sticks from his little fire and held it before him. With a soothing voice that hopefully communicated more peace than he felt, he tried to calm the wolf. "You don't want to do that, boy. That's a good wolf. Why don't you lie down? We can all get together and be friendly until the fire outside lets us go our own ways."

It was stupid and useless. The animal took another wary step forward, its companions right behind it. He remembered Daniel in the lion's den. The king had thrown

Daniel in there for violating the command to worship him. Daniel's tribulation came because he refused to serve any king except the One Most High.

James couldn't plead any such dedication and obedience. What had he done? At the Word of God, he'd run. He'd wanted nothing to do with God's desire to put him to work. He didn't understand why God would call him in the first place. The fact that He had, and He wanted to send James out as a lamb among wolves, made no sense. For his refusal, he'd become wolf bait, very much the object of attention of angry, hungry wolves. He wasn't a lamb, but in that moment identified closely with one for all the defenses he had. Namely none.

Maybe, just maybe, it was time for James to swallow his pride. It was hard to see that emulating Jeremiah and calling out a warning to the church and the world could be any more dangerous than this situation. If he was going to be torn to pieces limb by limb, it might be less injurious to take the barbs of men. Otherwise, he was in for a very short life from this point forward.

He recalled how he'd cried out that he had no purpose in living without Janna. At that time, he'd wanted to die. Faced with certain death now, the survival instinct kicked in. He wanted to live.

It was surprising how easy the plea came. "Oh, God, help me. I've wronged You. Please, forgive me."

He'd barely uttered the words when the lead animal discovered an itch that it couldn't ignore. It sat down and swatted at its ear with one paw. The others watched it, their eyes off James for the moment. When the lead wolf finished scratching, it ignored James. It got up and returned to the original spot James had first seen them. Each wolf circled around, found just the right place, and curled into a ball. From what James could tell, they'd forgotten entirely that he'd invaded their space in the cave.

Chapter 68

James couldn't recall having seen a miracle before even though he'd preached them for years. He'd articulated the gifts of the Spirit in countless sermons. How often had he spoken of the gifts of healing and recounted the miracles that occurred in Third World countries? Why else had he and Janna prayed so diligently for her to recover? How else could the church justify threatening to fire him with such a miracle?

It didn't take a genius to know what James had experienced came from the very hand of God. A sense of kinship with Daniel overtook him. Those lions had no more known Daniel was among them than these wolves knew James was near. God had blinded their every sense. They couldn't see or smell him.

With a grimace James clambered to his knees. In that position he thanked God for His mercy, for giving him a second chance he didn't deserve. Truly, this was the undeserved mercy and grace of the Lord. Again, he thought how often he'd preached the message, but how little it had penetrated his heart. He had a lot of learning and growing to do despite his having spent so many years in the pulpit.

After a time, he crawled to the entrance of the mouse tunnel through which he'd entered. With some effort and a prayer that he not get stuck, he wriggled halfway into it. From there, he got a view to the outside. It didn't raise his spirits any.

Darkness had fallen, that much he could tell. The most disheartening fact was the continued raging of the fire outside the entrance to the cave. There wasn't much room for even a sigh in that space, but James managed it. He worked his way backward and resumed his place by his own fire. The meager light had another benefit. With it, he located more wood than he thought was available at first. It gave him comfort to keep an eye on his furry colleagues. He knew their absence of interest in him was God at work; still, seeing was believing.

The flames of his campfire mesmerized James. He watched the play of colors, the heating and cooling of the embers, the rise and fall of sparks with the snap and crackle of the flames. Scriptural scenes came unbidden into his mind. He thought of Jesus preaching the Sermon on the Mount with His recitation of the Beatitudes. How amazing it must have been to hear the Son of God speaking from human lips! Would James have understood, or would he have been like so many who listened but didn't have ears to hear? With his inner ear James heard Jesus say: "You are the salt of the earth. But if the salt loses its saltiness, how can it be made salty again? It is no longer good for anything, except to be thrown out and be trampled by men." How close James had come to losing his saltiness! Worth nothing but to be stepped on and discarded. He asked God to increase any saltiness he had left, to use him to bring flavor and preservation into the world.

More images invaded his mind. The sight of Jesus being lifted high on the cross as the guards shoved the upright post into a hole. The toll on His limbs. The tearing of his flesh by the nails. Jesus' agony as the cross struck the bottom of the hole.

He thought of the men who removed His naked, bleeding body; preparing it for burial; lovingly laying it in the newly-prepared tomb; rolling the massive stone to close it up. The grief of all who loved Him.

The firelight shone on the tears James wiped away as he contemplated with joy how the third day dawned and His disciples saw the empty tomb. What bewilderment. What soul searching. Only when He appeared to His disciples did they begin to understand the importance of His life and death.

A longing to know Jesus more intimately welled up in James' heart. He knew without a doubt that Janna had loved Jesus and known Him at a much deeper level than he ever had. In this cave, alone, except for the wolves that thankfully God had blinded, the desire to give more of himself to God grew stronger. Jesus had died for him. Why run from Him? Wasn't He worthy of all James had to give? Yes, but first, James had to die to himself. He had to surrender all.

He said the words, but rising in the empty space around him, they didn't make an impact. He didn't even believe them. Once again he prayed, "Lord Jesus, I want to serve You with all my heart, soul, mind, and strength. I surrender everything to You, my Lord. Take me and use me as You will."

This time a satisfied feeling accompanied his words. He knew he meant them. He also knew that God had accepted them.

A deep heaviness came over James. He continued to stare into the fire as more memories from Scripture flooded his thoughts. His eyes shut. In moments he was fast asleep.

Chapter 69

Washington, D.C.

The dawning of the new day energized Luisa Parker. She had spoken to Arnold Rickards about turning up the heat. The mass arrests of thousands of Christians yesterday had fueled the fire. She had given the word. Her hordes of union toadies had been unleashed. They'd been holding back, waiting impatiently, periodically overstepping their boundaries. With the order to *go!* they went out in tandem with government agency flunkies and on their own. The result was planned chaos at its best.

Many of these foolish God-fearers had been imprisoned, with a goodly number already in the process of being transported by rail to the FEMA camps around the country. Just as delicious was the immediate rise of armed militias throughout the day in every corner of the nation. Before evening came, there'd been news reports of numerous clashes between her law enforcement ranks and those opposed to the taking of family and friends because of their faith. The opposition had come out with their remaining guns ready.

Parker had done her best to remove the firepower of individuals and thus the militias to which many NRA members belonged. The fewer guns in the hands of people opposed to her vision of government, the better. Her agents had confiscated millions of guns in a very short time. However, many remained. All that did was lend credibility to her next move.

Chapter 70

Central Michigan

He jerked awake. The cold nose touching his reminded him how their cat, Pepper, in her youth, had walked all over him in the morning and continually touched her nose to his in order to rouse him to feed her breakfast.

In the dark of the cave, as consciousness returned, James was sure that Pepper hadn't come back from the dead. With that certainty he couldn't imagine what had startled him awake. He reached out a tentative hand and felt rough fur.

The realization almost stopped his heart. One of the wolves! He was dead. God had decided to loose them on him. He said a brief prayer, closed his eyes again, and prepared for the worst.

Nothing happened. Slowly he patted around for his flashlight. The fire had gone out. He had no idea what was going on around him.

Swallowing hard, he switched on the beam. Miraculously, the wolf had retreated to the other side of the cave. It looked directly at him and walked to a place on its right. James continued to shine the light at the creature. Near the wall, it bent its head toward the ground. The next sound astounded James. The animal was lapping at water.

Suddenly James realized how parched he was. He wasn't sure if it was a dream or real, but he remembered overnight taking out the water bottle he'd been preserving and drinking all that was in it because his thirst was so great. With a groan he looked next to his backpack, and sure enough, the empty bottle lay where he'd discarded it. He would die from lack of water. Except that the wolf had shown him a source.

The wolf finished, glanced at James, and meandered back to its resting place. Could James trust this provision? Did he have the courage to try? He didn't know what was going on outside the cave, but for the moment, he had to have a drink.

His ankle throbbed. James attempted to stand but with the rush of pain quickly sank down. He'd have to creep on hands and knees to where the wolf had drank.

Light in hand he made his way over the rough stone floor. He shined the flashlight in the direction he'd seen the wolf drink and couldn't believe his eyes. All within the space of a yard, water bubbled up from underground, flowed through a bowl-like area to a small aperture, and disappeared. Without a further thought James bent to the water and drank with abandon.

When he finished, he filled his water bottle and returned to his side of the cave, exceedingly grateful to God.

Chapter 71

Washington, D.C.

Her makeup artist finished the final preparations for President Luisa Parker. She examined herself in the mirror. Just the right touch. She had to convey the power of the office. Her face must appear stern and decisive because of the nature of the threat. Yet, a modicum of compassion—the flavor of a woman—had to show through to impress her viewers that it grieved her heart to take such action. She dressed in a modest dark skirt and jacket with a light pink blouse and a fuchsia scarf around her neck. Feminine power.

One of her public relations aides knocked at her dressing room door. "Five minutes, Ms. President."

Parker gave herself one final look-over and joined her aide walking back toward the Oval Office. The cameras were set and a handful of permitted journalists were waiting for her. She smiled all around and took her seat behind the ornate, Resolute desk, so-called because it was made from the timbers of the British ship *HMS Resolute* in 1880.

The countdown began as she settled into her seat looking presidential. One of her team held up his fingers. "Five, four, three, two, one." He pointed at Parker and gave the OK sign with his thumb and forefinger.

"Good morning, ladies and gentlemen, young and old, gender stable or gender fluid. I come to you this morning bearing a tragic turn of events for this great nation of which we're all a part.

"As many of you are aware, a threat to our national unity has arisen from within. It has been allowed to grow unchecked for far too many years. It is a threat that will consume and destroy us if we don't take immediate action.

"Violence and chaos have spread across the land. Your government has worked diligently to remove the worst elements, yet they persist. They are organized, they resist the duly-enacted laws of this nation, and they are well-armed.

"This cannot continue. It must not continue. As your president, I will not allow this cancer to eat any longer at the wellbeing and prosperity of our country. It is destroying all that we call good and incites hatred wherever it's planted.

"Yesterday, we undertook a nationwide initiative to take back what is ours from these evil forces that have taken root. As you all must know by now, I am speaking of the wickedness known as Christianity.

"To keep the peace we made the initial effort to identify these actors with yellow crosses. The hope was twofold. First, we wanted to protect those of us who don't identify with this pernicious religion. Second, we also had an obligation to protect these misguided individuals who follow this foolish faith.

"Unfortunately, our efforts led to the hardening of the hearts of these Christianist adherents. We saw what they became, and we had to act. Yesterday, we brought many of these individuals throughout the nation into protective custody. For their own good they will be held at secure facilities away from the general populace. Our sincerest desire is that this will eventually reestablish a peaceful existence for all of you who abide by our just laws.

"However, the unfortunate fact of the matter is that many of those whom we had hoped to peaceably bring together have rebelled. They have declared their outright disobedience to the wisdom of those you have entrusted with the governance of this land.

"We deliberated long and hard as to the best course of action. We thought that the final hours in our emergency meetings that lasted throughout all last night would yield some other result. It saddens me to say that we are forced to make a difficult decision.

"Beginning as of this moment, the nation of the United States of America is declared as being under martial law. We believe there is no other means for us to quell the violence that these Christianists have begun and have vowed to continue until this government is destroyed. That cannot—it will not—stand.

"Under martial law we have to take some precautionary actions. The most important provision that affects all citizens is that the upcoming election next week is postponed. The threat of Christianists making a mockery of our electoral process is severe. I will not allow it. And I'm sure none of you would want such chaos to reign should the Christianists have their way.

"To oversee this entire process, I will remain in office as your president. I will monitor the situation and act accordingly under the legal constraints associated with martial law.

"I give you this pledge: I will work without ceasing to destroy every element in this nation that seeks to undermine it. When the time is right, we will reinstitute our electoral process. In the meantime I ask all citizens to be vigilant. If someone is a Christian, they must be apprehended and brought into the safe zone we have prepared. Do your part. Resist this malicious enemy from within.

"Until next time… I bid you peace."

Chapter 72

Central Michigan

With great hope that the forest fire outside his communal dwelling had subsided, James slid once more through the narrow entry tunnel. Near the opening, his heart sank in dismay. It was clearly daylight, but for as far as he could see, the fire continued to rage. It made no sense to him that it continued unabated after all these hours. In resignation, he inched his way back.

He had wood but lacked the energy to build another fire. Moving a little to the side, he found the rocky wall of the cave and leaned back against it. In the excitement of last night he hadn't been hungry, but now his stomach began to growl. For the hike he'd brought some high-energy protein bars and a bag of nuts. He stuck his hand into the backpack where he kept them and found...nothing. For a moment he became confused and hunted in every possible pocket and cranny in the backpack. He gathered himself and thought back to his preparations. In his mind he saw the food items on the kitchen counter. Then he saw the picture of his walking out without them. With a groan, he bent his head in frustration and berated himself.

The moment passed. He thought, *How fortunate the wolf led me to water.* He had fasted before; he could fast again for some short period of time. With water he could last for weeks if that was necessary.

James settled back and revised his expectations. From the looks of the ongoing blaze outside his door, he'd be here a while longer. God had provided water. He had dulled the senses of the wolves so they didn't consider him a threat or food.

Maybe God had a purpose for his time here and was supernaturally fueling the fire. To discover what it might be required James to sit and listen, to rest in the presence of the Lord. "All right, Father, You have me where You want me. What is it You want to teach me?"

Chapter 73

Washington, D.C.

"What are you doing? Get your filthy hands off me!" Vice President Abu Saif knew the three men surrounding him. He was familiar with most of the Secret Service agents; although these were ones he'd only seen at a distance.

One had grabbed him, and Saif shook him off. They'd come to his residence at the Naval Observatory under the pretense of taking him to see the president for an emergency meeting. Having seen her televised remarks, Saif was furious and more than ready to meet with her. What did she think she was doing canceling the election? What about his candidacy? As soon as Saif was ready to leave, the one grasped his wrist and attempted to snap on handcuffs. The other two drew their service pistols and leveled them at him.

"You will come with us, sir. And you will come in these restraints."

"I demand to speak to President Parker. Get her right now on your cell phone."

"She's the one who ordered this, sir. Will you come peaceably, or must we use force?"

Saif almost didn't hear the last sentence the man said, so shocked was he by his initial statement. "What do you mean she ordered this? That doesn't make any sense."

"We're obeying orders. You've been deemed a national security risk." The agent advanced on him again with the handcuffs. "Sir?"

Clamping his teeth together so hard his jaw ached, Saif held out his hands.

"Behind your back, sir."

Burning with anger, Saif did as instructed. They left the house and hustled him to their waiting SUVs.

"Where is my personal agent? Where's Ibrahim Sufyan?"

"He's been likewise restrained. You'll have to be quiet now, sir, or we'll be forced to make you be quiet."

They ushered Saif into the back of one of the vehicles with the lead agent joining the driver in front. The other two men got into the second car. Alone behind a soundproof divider, Saif wondered in his rage what Luisa Parker could possibly be thinking. Whatever it was, she hadn't included him in her plan, and he was enraged. She would pay for this. Oh yes, in the name of Allah, she would pay.

Chapter 74

Central Michigan

The darkness of the cave closed in around James. Without his glasses it was difficult for him to read the hands of his watch. Each time he looked, only minutes had passed. Waiting for God wasn't an easy task. James wanted Him to speak. It made him impatient. Once he realized that none of this was in his timing, James again had to repent. He had to let God be God and let His plans and purposes unfold as He saw fit.

He heard the panting of the wolves and the slight noises they made as they changed positions. Other sounds became magnified as James rested and listened. The distant crackle of the fire outside his dwelling eating trees and brush continued. With the fire burning so long, he figured the dense forests of white cedar and aspen that he'd hiked through must be decimated. He hated to think what it would look like once he emerged from his hideaway.

The loss of Janna overwhelmed and consumed him at one point. They'd been together for so many years. He thought fondly of how they'd met in seminary. *She was so beautiful. But from such a broken home! She struggled with so much unworthiness because of her father. She didn't trust men—didn't trust me—until the Lord got hold of her. And when He did! God radically turned her life around. He truly gave her a new heart and a new longing to serve Him.* Not only that, but somehow she'd seen in James a man she could love and cherish.

Tears came unbidden, yet with a smile on his lips from the recollections of his dear wife, James slipped into a sound sleep.

Chapter 75

Washington, D.C.

It didn't take long for Ibrahim Sufyan to learn the fate of his boss, Vice President Abu Saif. With a day off from his extensive duties, he'd hoped to relax, but that wasn't to be.

He was a man with his ear to the ground, having informants in both high and low places. A member of the Muslim Brotherhood, as was Saif, he expected loyalty from fellow brothers. The Brotherhood had the long game in view. Since its founding in 1928 in Egypt, it had progressed steadily in its objective of worldwide domination through the Sunni caliphate. It had come to America in the early 1960s, creating various organizations with different purposes, yet all with the same goal. It would impose Sharia law on America. It would wage jihad, both cultural by working through all systems available to it: legal, political, social; and with violence against its enemies who resisted its peaceful means.

Since the Obama Administration, the Brotherhood had grown in influence in every area of government. It wasn't only dark-skinned Middle Easterners, nor Black Americans attracted to social justice teachings, nor primarily Black inmates at prisons across the country who practiced Islam under the Brotherhood's tutelage. Whites, Hispanics, women, and children throughout the nation, and particularly people entrenched in the bureaucracy of the nation's capital, had become practitioners, or at the least, fellow travelers. Because the newly-faithful converted under the radar and didn't publically proclaim their allegiance, few people outside their immediate circles knew where their loyalties lay. This included officials as high as directors in the National Security Agency, the CIA, and Homeland Security, the Secretary of State, and the Attorney General of the United States. Many ambitious, high-ranking military men in the upper echelons of the Pentagon had likewise chosen this path as the most likely to enhance their career path.

It wasn't five minutes from the time that Saif was taken into custody that Sufyan received a phone call alerting him to the situation. The caller warned that men were on their way to apprehend him and that he must flee, which is what Ibrahim Sufyan did immediately.

The only minute delay in his escaping his house was to grab his service pistol and plenty of ammunition. He already had an emergency escape route planned and utilized it to perfection. Even as he was entering his underground lair, he heard the doorbell ring. With the closing of his hatch, no one would find it unless a thorough search was made of his premises.

His caller didn't know the reason for Saif being taken into custody, but for now that mattered little to Sufyan. He could only assume the kafir president, Luisa Parker, had pulled a fast one. Many times he had warned Saif that an unbeliever like Parker posed a danger, but Saif believed that he'd see the warning signs and be able to counter effectively. That hadn't happened and the plans he, Saif, and their

Brotherhood advisors had labored over now required a reworking.

Saif located the unregistered vehicle he kept in a private parking garage and donned the hat and sunglasses that would keep him from being recognized. As he drove to his safe house, he began to form plans to reverse this current tide of events.

Chapter 76

Central Michigan

The roar of mighty waters startled James into wakefulness. At least he thought he was awake. His surroundings weren't what he remembered. Rather than lying in a dark cave, he stood in bright sunlight next to a massive waterfall. He'd seen pictures of Victoria Falls in the southern African country of Zambia. What he saw and heard was as close to that as he could imagine.

Water spray and an obscuring mist rose above towering cliffs that shielded the sky. The sound of the waters was so great he couldn't hear himself think. In the midst of this explosion of sound in these vast forces of nature, he heard a voice that cut through the riotous confusion vying for his attention.

"James! James!"

This was no ordinary voice. It sliced through every fiber of his being. In reverential fear he responded. "Yes, Lord. Here I am."

"This is holy ground where you are standing. Remove the coverings from your feet."

There was no question of obedience. James quickly complied and stood barefoot on the rocks. He trembled like he never had before. As he did, he noticed the water from the falls in the pools below begin to rise.

"I AM the Lord. I am coming down from My dwelling place. I am coming down to tread the high places of the earth. The mountains melt before Me. The valleys split apart like wax before the fire, like water rushing down a slope.

"Look to Me, My son. Listen to My voice. I love you with an everlasting love. I died so that you might live. I sacrificed Myself; I paid the ransom that you might be set free from the bondage of sin.

"Though you have doubted Me, I have chosen you. I have set you on the wall surrounding this nation to be a watchman. This nation is suffocating in its sin. I have heard the cries of My remnant, of those who are faithful and desire that this nation be saved.

"You, my son, must call to the lukewarm church, you must call to the nation. I have resolved to shake the foundations. Will I relent? Only if the people turn back to Me.

"The stench of the sin of Nineveh reached its fullness, but the people heard the voice of Jonah and repented. Because they fell before Me in sackcloth and ashes, I turned away My wrath for a time. Will the people of this land repent? Will they give Me cause to stay My wrath?

"You will be My voice. You, My son, will go as My ambassador to the highest echelons of power in this nation."

The waters around James cascaded in unending power. He looked down as he felt the rising waters lapping at his toes. He'd expected they'd be cold, but they were warm. The very concept that he would speak for God was impossible. "How can I who am nothing do such a thing, Lord?"

"I will be with you. You will have favor. The ears of many will listen to you. You will have power to pull down strongholds in My Name."

"Oh, Lord, I beseech You. Don't send me to this task alone. I'm so afraid. I know only You are God; that You are great and mighty; but man—this man—is nothing but a wisp of mist." James had nowhere to go. Rock cliffs hemmed him in. The waters now came to his knees. He'd never known water to feel so warmly embracing. It brought the image of his mother's womb.

"My Name will be glorified in all the earth. Will you continue to run from Me, my son? Have you not yet learned?"

In the moments it took James to respond, the waters reached first his waist, then his neck. "Lord! Help me, I'm drowning!"

"These are the waters of My love. You are drowning in the waters of My Holy Spirit."

Even as the waters closed over James' head he said, "I'm yours, Lord. Do with me what You will."

James exhaled, and water gushed into his lungs.

Chapter 77

November
Camp Grayling – Central Michigan

The fire raging to the west frightened Colonel Trask more than he would admit. He'd been in the military for many years and was battle hardened. Despite that, the one thing he feared most was fire. The thought that one so near might come roaring through the camp and devour it made him wish he'd resigned his commission last year like he'd originally intended.

Orders had come down that nothing—nothing!—was to disturb the sanctity of the camp. What was he? God? He prepared a fire brigade using every able body, particularly those interred under his charge. If they had to die protecting the integrity of this place, so be it.

While they waited for the fire to come upon them, Trask received an impossible order. A drone had followed a

Christian hiking in the forest. For reasons Trask couldn't comprehend, the hiker had been targeted as someone that must be taken into custody. *Must be.* Did the higher-ups think he could work miracles and walk through fire? He communicated that the conflagration had indisposed him for the time being, but he would comply as soon as humanly possible. The reply indicated their displeasure: "Do it quickly."

For two days he watched as C-130s flew overhead transporting water to fight the fire. His panic increased as it raced toward the camp. In a jaw-dropping, heart-wrenching change of direction he saw from an observation tower the flames separate at the last instant and surround the camp, then continue on their way east, but never touching a single fence or person within the compound. The fleeting thought came and went that most of the prisoners were Christians who were likely praying. He dismissed the idea as soon as it entered his mind. Prayer! How foolish.

With the breaking of the third day, Trask awoke to a sound he hadn't heard in months and months: the deep roll of thunder. He sprang from bed. Rain had begun to fall. Glorious rain! Lightning illuminated the dark storm clouds making the barbed wire fences of their camp stand out in stark relief. Rain began pouring from the sky.

Trask gave the downpour time to work. He knew that already the fire-fighting efforts had helped greatly. With the hard rain, he felt confident the fire had been extinguished.

He ordered a small contingent of men to accompany him to try to locate the troublesome Christian the drone had singled out. What a waste! He couldn't imagine the man had survived. Where would he go to be safe against the massive forest-killing inferno?

The last noted coordinates directed the men through smoldering, steaming charred husks of what had been magnificent forest growth. By now the rain had slowed to a trickle. Colonel Trask gloried in the damp fields, but the surreal landscape depressed him. How sad that nature had to periodically destroy itself.

They came to a large open field that was burnt and bare, blackened with smoke rising in moist wisps from the ground. Trask spotted something across the field he hadn't seen before in his previous wilderness hikes. A jumble of rocks lay at the base of a hill. Before he directed his men to take their first step toward the rocks, he noticed movement.

Suddenly, before their eyes, three gray wolves materialized. They paused, sniffed the air, and with a swiftness likely born of the still-heated earth beneath them, bounded off at a rapid pace at a right angle to Trask and his men.

The man they sought couldn't have survived being around the wolves. He would have made a tasty meal while they'd been holed up, if indeed he'd found their hideout. But Trask had to check.

Chapter 78

Central Michigan

James awoke with a start, realizing he was still alive. More than alive. He had drowned, but wasn't dead, because it was the love of God that he'd taken in. The breath of God had filled his lungs. The Father had spoken to him. He was not only a son of God, His child, but also called of God. The thought humbled him. He lifted up a prayer. "Holy Father, what am I? Nothing without You. Thank You for loving me. Now set my feet aright on the path You have chosen for me. I give You the glory You deserve. I pray this in Jesus' Name."

In the dark he heard the wolves stretch and move. A fragrance caught his attention that he hadn't smelled for many months. First, an earthy tang, then the fresh aroma of a world washed clean. Could it be rain?

The wolves brushed past him into the entryway tunnel and disappeared. It must be safe to finally leave. James used his flashlight to find his possessions and stuffed them into the backpack. He checked his watch, but it seemed to have stop working, leaving him no idea as to the day or time. Regardless, he was excited by all that had transpired. Without a further glance back, he made his way into the outdoors.

The rain must have been hard and steady as everything was drenched, but now the sun had come out. For a couple of minutes it blinded him, but he heard voices. Squinting to see, the brightness became manageable. Not fifty yards away a small group of men approached.

Standing outside the cave, James made another discovery. His ankle no longer gave him pain and discomfort. He could put weight on it and walk as if it had never been injured. It was one more thing for which he could praise God, and he did so in a quick prayer that rose unbidden when he exhaled.

The approaching men were still a ways off in the distance. Even from far away, he made out the military insignia of the lead man rapidly moving toward him. Frowning at the seeming anomaly of such clarity of vision, James felt for his glasses. Not there. Yet he saw more sharply than he previously had with them. He turned his head looking at the steaming, burnt landscape. He clearly saw details from across the field. A moth fluttered up from the ashes and he saw its fine markings with such clarity that he gasped. A chuckle followed.

"You there! Are you James Glazier?"

Torn from marveling at the return of perfect sight, James blinked. "Yes. Who are you? How do you know my name?"

"Were those wolves in there with you?" The incredulity in the man's voice made James want to laugh.

He didn't, because the fact they somehow knew his name disconcerted him. "They were. God protected me from them."

The man drew himself up and smirked. "Right. I'm Colonel Trask. You're to come with me."

Trask brooked no questions from James. He and his men, all hard-faced military, obviously had an assignment and intended to carry it out. Before they reached the end of the burnt and alien landscape of the field—very different from that which James had previously seen—his knees buckled. One of the soldiers caught him, but for the moment his legs didn't work.

"What's the problem, Glazier?" Trask had ordered them into a quick pace and had little patience.

"It's been a few days since I ate, Colonel."

"Give him a couple energy bars and some water. Snap to it."

James gratefully accepted the rations. Before he took his first bite, he paused to thank God for providing.

"What are you doing? Eat! We haven't got all day."

"I'm thanking God for this meal." Before his experience in the presence of God, James had been hit and miss with mealtime prayers. Now the boldness and gratitude rolled off his tongue.

"Christians!" Yet Trask backed off and allowed James the space he needed to pray and eat.

Blackened trees littered the landscape, many still smoldering and dripping water like heavy dew. So much of the forest had been lost. It made James think how many things had to die for new growth to occur. That was true with older growth forest; it was especially true with humans. The old life that one lived had to be completely eradicated so that a new life in Christ could be born and fully formed. James felt it. He knew a major transforming work had been done within him. It made him sense the freedom he now had. Before he had labored under a bondage of sin, not even realizing it shackled him. Without that burden, a new clarity was revealed. He could already sense his thinking renewed because his mind had been transformed along with his heart.

He thought of the book *Pilgrim's Progress*. The hero, Christian, made his journey with a heavy load. Only when he became a new creation, a true Christian, did the burden drop off. Christ now carried his yoke and gave him real freedom.

James couldn't wait to see how this new path God had placed him on would play out.

On the approach to their destination, James wondered at the concentration camp look and feel of the place. The double fencing. The barbed wire. He wondered what was going on, why such a facility existed in the United States.

They hustled him into the camp command offices where Colonel Trask made a phone call from across the room. James heard him protest briefly and slam the phone down in disgust.

He stomped over to where James stood surrounded by Trask's men. "I don't get it Glazier. You must have some influence. First they tell me to find you at all costs because you present a danger to society." He gestured back to the desk with the phone. "Then they say to get you back home posthaste." He glared at James, gave an order to two of his men and turned to walk away.

"What about my car, Colonel?"

He hardly stopped to reply. "It's probably burnt to a crisp. Collins, find his vehicle when you take him home."

The sergeant Trask had addressed as Collins saluted his assent, and they marched James out to a waiting Humvee. As James got in the car, he noticed a group of men working by the barracks some distance away. To his astonishment he recognized a familiar face. "Wait, what are those men doing over there?"

Sergeant Collins ignored him, started the Humvee, and prepared to drive off. James grabbed at the handle, but the door wouldn't open. He watched in frustration through the rear window, confirming that the man across the way was indeed Bob Sanders.

Chapter 79

Western Michigan

Little was left of his car other than a burnt-out shell. James had liked that car. How fortunate he hadn't yet sold Janna's vehicle. He settled back for the ride home and endured the silence of the men transporting him.

He thought of Bob Sanders but couldn't put the mystery together. Whatever the reason for his friend being there, James feared it had to do with the roundup of Christians he'd heard about. If that were true, why they would release James rather than retain him in that place was another puzzle. Perhaps the hand of God? James could only assume so given his assignment. With God, all things were possible.

The men dropped him off at his house and drove away without comment. Inside James noticed the emptiness without Janna, but for some reason it felt all right. God had a plan and purpose for him. It gave him an anticipation of an adventure ahead he could never have conceived of previously.

He checked the calendar on the wall. Thursday. Janna's wake at the funeral home was today! He'd made the arrangements and left it all behind in his hike, not giving a thought that he'd be delayed in returning. The shower he jumped into to clean up was long overdue.

At the funeral home he found the director whom he'd known for many years. Ted Westlake expressed his condolences once again and led James to the viewing room. Entering and seeing the open casket at the front, James paused. He closed his eyes to gather himself and proceeded with Westlake past the rows of chairs where mourners would sit to contemplate death, and later to hear James speak briefly to them.

Janna looked peaceful, but as pale as she'd become through her illness. Even flesh-colored makeup couldn't hide the whiteness of her face. She lay with eyes closed in a favorite peach-colored outfit, her hands folded over her midsection. James stood looking down at her while Westlake stood respectfully nearby. He thanked God she was finally pain-free and had no more cares or worries in the presence of the Lord. A bit of envy stole into him at that thought. Wouldn't that be nice? No more hardship, no more strife. That she was eternally in the loving arms of Jesus made a smile come to his lips. He nodded and turned toward Westlake. "She looks good."

The men chatted several minutes while they waited for friends and well-wishers to show up for the viewing. Much of their conversation centered on the long-awaited rain. It had come down from one end of the country to the other, breaking the nationwide drought. News reports referred to it as a mercy granted from Mother Nature. When the first several guests arrived, Westlake excused himself to attend to his duties.

It wasn't long before people filled the room. He knew many townspeople and those in the church who loved Janna, but the numbers astounded him. After standing in a long line to say their goodbyes to her at the casket, most waited to hear what James had to say. In the meantime he spoke with their friends and lamented with them the loss of his wife whom he'd loved so much.

People filled the seats in the large room and waited expectantly. Ted Westlake came up and opened the small service. One of the few remaining faithful friends from church played the piano and led several worship songs. Westlake then indicated for James to come forward.

In the adventure, boredom, excitement, and time with God these last few days, James hadn't prepared anything to speak, yet he knew it was the right thing to do. He wanted to acknowledge God's hand in all that happened in their lives and in the course of the nation as events would play out in the future. He also wanted to thank all who'd come to say their goodbyes to his beloved wife.

In the crowd he spotted several reporters and a photographer. These weren't friendlies; they were journalists with whom he'd been at odds over various social issues as they'd arisen over time based on what he'd said in his sermons. For the life of him, he couldn't imagine why they'd come. Perhaps to gloat over one who'd lost something dear?

He spotted Gadi Benjamin near the back. Their eyes locked in acknowledgment of each other, giving James a warm feeling about his friend.

A shock awaited him when his eyes passed over Pastor Tom Hall and Reverend Phyllis sitting together. Next to them sat Deacon Jones. Would surprises never end? What purpose could these have here who had traveled so far down the path of doctrinal error?

The last of his amazing discoveries was seeing a couple of the deacons from his church—rather his former church—Joe Bennett in particular. Wonders upon wonders.

James had to harness his cynicism at the sight of these whom he could effectively count as enemies: tares among the wheat. He stopped before another thought entered his head and prayed his forgiveness to these who had harmed him.

Who knew their intent and what might happen down the road in possible interactions with them? But James knew it was right and proper that he forgive every one of them.

With that, he began to speak, telling them a story. He wouldn't reveal it all, but he recounted a little of his last three days. "When Janna died, I was beside myself in grief. Hiking and enjoying the woods has always given me great pleasure, and I took off without much thought after having arranged this service with the funeral home. I wasn't prepared for what happened next. No doubt you're all aware of the forest fire northeast of here that ravaged thousands of acres. I was caught in that."

The eyebrows of those listening intently shot up. He no doubt had their attention now.

"During the early part of my hike, God was trying to get my attention with a couple of minor misfortunes that assailed me. One of them was a sprained ankle right before I became aware of the fire coming toward me. I had nowhere to go and no possible escape, particularly being hobbled by my ankle.

"Suddenly I noticed a hill far across the field with a jumble of rocks lying at its base. I could only hope they would somehow provide shelter from the fire raging toward me.

"With no time to spare, I made it to the rocks and noticed a small hole that turned out to be a very tight tunnel into a cave. God had provided my means of protection.

"It didn't take long for me to discover that I wasn't the only inhabitant in this hideaway. I was sharing it with three gray wolves."

Eyes grew large in the crowd and mouths dropped open.

"But a peculiar thing happened. The wolves had no interest in me. In fact, for most of my stay, they seemed to have no idea I was even there. The one time they did was when one came over to me, stuck his cold wet nose on mine, and went back to a spot in the cave where water bubbled up. It was about this time that I began to think that God's hand was orchestrating all this. For His own reasons, God was showering me with His grace."

Tom Hall turned to Reverend Phyllis at this point and whispered in her ear. She shook her head and laughed silently. Doubt clearly showed on her face.

"There was a point at which God brought me into a vision of mighty waters with His still, small voice speaking to me as crystal clear as anything I've ever heard. Among other things, he assured me that everything would be all right. He loved me and would be with me—in fact, right beside me—every step of my journey going forward. He also declared that all who believe in the Name of Jesus would always have Him by their sides whatever they did and wherever they went until the day He calls us home."

Smirks crossed the faces of the newspeople listening to him. One rolled his eyes.

James placed a hand on the casket. "My dear wife was a devout follower of Jesus Christ. I always wished I had her deep faith. Regardless of what transpired, she would turn to the Lord in prayer. She would praise Him and thank Him for the opportunity to exercise her faith through the challenges she faced. I couldn't do that. Truth be told, I didn't know God at the depth of intimacy that she did. Mine was more of a faith of the mind rather than of the heart."

A surge of feeling rose from the center of James' belly. More than feeling, it felt like a fire rising within him. At the same time, he began to weep. Words caught in his throat, and tears ran like a flood. He had to fumble with a tissue to gain some composure. "My time in the cave alone with God changed that. He changed me. He showed me His love, which is greater than anything we can imagine. That love is what transforms us when we allow God access to our hearts. I realized I have to choose Him. He won't force Himself on me. He provides the open door. I have to step through it."

He moved his hand over those of his wife's that were clasped together in her repose. Another great swelling of emotion came over him. His heart broke for his Janna. Not only for her. He knew his breaking heart was that of God's for every lost person in this room and for the entire world. More tears spilled down his face. He finally found words again. "I loved this woman so much. Yet God's love for us is a million times greater. He is giving us a final opportunity to accept His love and turn from the wickedness in each of our hearts. He wants us to know, love, and serve His Son, Jesus Christ. Is there anyone here who would make such a profession of faith? Who would repent of your sins and trust that Jesus will save you?"

The people before him sat in silence. Some knew the Lord, James had no doubt. Others he classified as lukewarm Christians whom he felt confident didn't have a personal relationship with Jesus. He'd always called them Chinos—*CH*ristian *I*n *N*ame *O*nly. A large number sitting here had various beliefs that had nothing to do with true Christianity. No one raised his hand or stood.

His voice broke as he pleaded with them. "God is calling you. Don't wait until it's too late."

At that moment, the fire in James' belly moved into his arms and down into his hands. Because of that, he couldn't be sure whether what he felt came from him or....

James' breathing stopped. The warmth in his hands was coming from Janna! Under the gentle pressure of his hand upon hers, he felt a slight movement. Color flushed Janna's face. What he saw and was experiencing wasn't possible! She had been embalmed. The preparations for her burial included the draining of her blood and the filling of her veins and arteries with a foreign fluid. But here she was growing warmer as though blood coursed from her heart through her body.

No one else saw or knew anything that was apparent to James. They weren't prepared for what happened next.

Janna opened her eyes, smiled directly at James, and sat bolt upright in the coffin.

Gasps and screams exploded from every throat. Not a person could help but exclaim in wonder, shock, or fear.

Janna's sudden movement to sit up rocked the casket. Before James could react, it tipped toward him. It fell toward the ground jarring Janna from her resting place. She tumbled from the enclosure.

With an agility and quickness that belied her previous state, she reached out her arms, pulled herself completely away from the casket, and stood up. By this time complete bedlam consumed the room. A couple of people raised their arms to praise the Lord, their voices loud in exaltation. Some fainted. Many raced from the room, perhaps convinced that the long forecast, television-prophesied, zombie invasion had begun. Others could do nothing but screech, with the rest of their bodies frozen in paralysis.

Barely able to hear his own voice, James took a step toward Janna. With a sense of wonder and awe, he couldn't help running his eyes up and down the body of his wife. "Is this real?"

She no longer appeared thin and emaciated. Her flesh had filled out with normal muscle tone, evident in the confidant way she stood.

She spoke for the first time, lilting and musical, loving. "Jesus asked me if I would come back here to do a further work for Him. How could I say no?"

"Oh, Janna!" James enclosed his arms around her, lost in an embrace that closed out the world so that he knew only her and nothing else.

Chapter 80

The next morning, media outlets, first locally, then nationally, blared the headlines: "Weeping Pastor Raises Wife from Death!" Internet sites ran the video taken by the reporter present that purported to show Janna being raised from the dead. More rain had fallen during the night and continued into the day. It didn't stop hordes of reporters camping out in the front yard, spilling into the street wanting to appropriate the story for themselves.

James, his arm around Janna, stood at the window, overlooking the jumble of people, cameras, cables, and news trucks. He pulled his newly-found wife closer and kissed her cheek. "You've become an overnight sensation."

She gazed into his eyes with a love he couldn't begin to fathom from anyone in a human body. "God is the sensation. We're here to give Him glory."

The doorbell rang. James gave Janna a helpless look and walked to the door.

The man held a portable microphone. Behind him, a cameraman stood with his equipment perched on his shoulder. "Mr. Glazier? I'm with CNN. Is it really true your wife was dead, and you brought her back to life?"

"Did you see the videos taken last night at the funeral home?"

"Sure, but what do you have to say about it?"

"Do you believe that Jesus Christ is the Son of God who brings salvation to all who call on His Name?"

Bafflement crossed the face of the reporter. "What's that got to do with anything?"

"Answer that question first in your own life, and then you'll know the true response to your question." James stepped back and gently shut the door.

"Hey, wait!" The reporter knocked repeatedly, but James had already returned to Janna's side.

Chapter 81

Washington, D.C.

"What is this garbage coming from that podunk town in Michigan?" President Luisa Parker raged and paced the length and back again of the Oval Office multiple times, unable to settle down.

"This incident disturbs you greatly, Luisa. Why does it do so?" Arnold Rickards sat back in his comfortable chair watching his friend. "None of it means anything to you. These foolish things come and go."

"I have a feeling. There's more to this than meets the eye, and I don't like it." The president's fist struck the open palm of her other hand. "These Christians! I hate them. When they're all rounded up and completely removed from my sight is the time I'll rest easy. I don't trust them one bit. They're sneaky. This pastor has something up his sleeve. I know it!"

Rickards laughed. "Oh, Luisa, you're so paranoid. Listen, you have pulled off the coup of a lifetime. You've done what Barack Obama only dreamed about doing. With the nature of his hundreds of initiatives and executive orders, don't you think he wanted to take full dictatorial control of this country? Of course he did. Fear got the best of him because there were still too many guns in the hands of the little people. He got the ball rolling, but you have taken the major step of gun confiscation and martial law. What's not to like?"

"If you were in my shoes, Arnold, you wouldn't rest easy either."

Rickards smiled gently, his head sadly turning side to side. "Listen, you castrated the military. There's not a single high-level officer who dares do anything but follow your orders. All the ones left value their careers above their convictions. The men and women in the ranks have been brought completely into line through the gender wars we've waged for many years. Every federal agency is armed to the teeth with willing, ready, and able agents to act on your word at a moment's notice. The unions, all loyal to you, are chomping at the bit to use those weapons at your command that you supplied to them. Local police have lost all independent initiative because of their fear of retaliation from the federal government. Any cops who disagreed and resisted have been drummed out of service. The only ones left give fealty to you. All of these groups hate the Christians as much as you do. Not only that, but they believe, because you've brainwashed them so effectively, that the Constitution is the enemy of a good, benevolent government that you happen to control. The ice you fear to walk on is quite solid, my dear."

Parker rubbed her face and sat next to Rickards. "I've heard of people being raised from the dead. Didn't believe it then, and don't believe it now. It's all a trick by this pastor to get into the public eye. And look how it worked! I'm telling you, Arnold, whatever this guy's reason for the PR, nothing but trouble will come from it."

"I will tell you truthfully, Luisa, where my one worry arises. That is from Abu Saif. Generally a vice president has little power. On the surface that would seem to be so with him. In this case, because he is a Muslim, it concerns me."

Parker eyed Rickards with puzzlement. "What do you mean?"

"Particularly beginning with the administration of Barack Obama, Muslims have infiltrated every level of government. The Muslim Brotherhood has been a close advisor, not only in every federal agency, but to the presidency itself. Think of the councils that advise you. Are they not largely comprised of Muslims? What if they believe you have done an injustice to Saif?"

With a wave of her hand, Parker dismissed the idea. "Nonsense. These people know who holds the reins of power. We've accommodated them and given them all they've asked for solely to keep them eating from our open palms. They are the loyal ones. Of that I have no doubt. Look at how we've given them so many things to keep them happy. They have their Sharia law courts right alongside our courts in every major city. At their request, Islam is taught in the schools and Christianity is ridiculed and dismissed. They have all this and more only through our benevolence. I wouldn't give them another thought."

"Do you hear yourself, Luisa? They have gained much power."

She shook her head. "It's the Christians who are the problem. We completely eradicate them and we'll have it made."

Chapter 82

Western Michigan

The morning of the elections, the first Tuesday in November, came and went with a whimper. With the imposition of martial law and the decree that holding the elections was too dangerous because of the Christian radicals who might terrorize the polling places, everyone stayed home. No elections were held. The sitting president remained in office with no electoral replacement.

Since the funeral, James and Janna had done nothing but enjoy each other's company. When they ventured out during the day, they traveled to isolated parks and nearby forest preserves to appreciate the wonder of God's creation around them. The coming of the rain had broken the heat at last, and chilly weather had begun to set in. They couldn't have cared less, hardly noticing anything but God's grandeur and each other.

At night they cuddled on the sofa, talking, reading, and praying, glorifying in the reprieve from the separation that death had imposed on them. It was a wonderful time of togetherness with little discussion of what lay ahead. For now, all that mattered was their reunion.

A week after the funeral, a couple of days after the non-election, James and Janna sat down to lunch. James prayed over the food. As they began to eat, the doorbell rang. He smiled at his wife and went to answer the door. A blast of cooler air rushed inside when he opened it.

"Gadi!" Genuinely pleased to see his friend, James invited him in. "We just began lunch. Would you like to join us?"

"I thank you, James, but I have something much more important than food. I hope you do not mind."

James brought his friend into the kitchen where Gadi hugged Janna. "I am so happy to see you well. It is indeed a miracle."

"There's nothing else that can be said about it." Janna gestured to Gadi to sit. "God is sovereign. He created us; He can heal us; He can restore us to life from the dead."

Gadi removed his leather jacket and hung it over the back of the offered chair before sitting. "Yes. That is what I wanted to speak to you about. I see that I am intruding on your lunch. I am so sorry."

"You're troubled, Gadi. How can we help?" Janna pushed her soup bowl away and waited patiently with her hands clasped before her on the table.

"This miracle." Gadi hesitated, clearly troubled, and plunged ahead. "You were dead, embalmed. There was no blood in your body. I asked the funeral director later, and he confirmed it. Yet here you are. That is impossible."

Janna nodded. "By human standards."

"That is the heart of the matter. James knows; he and I have had many discussions about faith. Perhaps he has told you that as a secular Jew I have been agnostic about the existence of God. My people have a long, rich history, a checkered history, of belief and apostasy. In this last week I read the entire Hebrew Bible, your Old Testament. I then proceeded to read your New Testament. One other time in my life, I read the Hebrew Scriptures and dismissed them as irrelevant. This time, for some reason, my eyes were opened. I saw the prophecies, hundreds of them. I read Isaiah 53 anew and wondered if this was a passage transposed from the New Testament. How could someone write so clearly about an historic figure seven hundred years before His birth? Isaiah describes Jesus as if he knew Him from personal experience. I saw that the entire Old Testament points to Jesus. That is the reason it was written: to prophesy about the coming Messiah, and that man was Jesus. And not only was He a man, He was God. Most amazing is that He is not dead. He rose from the dead, like you, Janna. Jesus came back from the grave to rule and reign for all eternity."

Janna placed her hand warmly on Gadi's forearm. "That is the difference, Gadi. Jesus rose to defeat death to bring us life. God raised me to serve and glorify Him. I am only a servant of the Lord Himself."

"I understand. What this has shown me—finally, definitively—is that God is real. Jesus is truly His Son. But there is more. God is loving beyond anything I can comprehend. That is so clear in the Scriptures, both Old and New. How could He not be? Jesus sacrificed Himself by going to the cross and taking on all of mankind's sins. It humbles me." Gadi bowed his head. In a voice little more than a whisper he continued. "I fear."

Once again James felt he'd had a heart transplant. He experienced the breaking heart of God for one of His lost creation, desperately desiring that this one become His child with all the privileges and responsibilities that entailed. In what was becoming common, James wept God's tears for Gadi. "What is it you fear?"

Gadi sat back and looked at the ceiling. He closed his red-rimmed eyes before he answered. "The wrath of God."

"It is a fearful thing to fall into the hands of the living God." James pushed back his chair and went to the sink to bring Gadi back a glass of water. He gratefully accepted it.

"Yes. That is the flip side of God's love. Many verses confirm that if we choose not to repent and trust in Jesus as our Savior, God will allow us to have our wish. If we don't want to love and cherish Him in this life, why would we want to be with Him for eternity? He is very accommodating. He has made a place of separation from Him, a place many choose to go." Gadi suddenly jumped up. "I do not want to go there! I do not want eternal darkness and separation from God, unending torment and despair at having made the wrong decision! I do not want to go to hell!"

Gadi fell to his knees before Janna. "You have seen Him, talked to Him. He brought you back, even from His very presence. Please. Can you intercede for me? Can you ask Him to deliver me from this living death?"

With a gentle touch Janna placed her hand on Gadi's head, then placed it under his elbow to encourage him to rise. He did and stood panting, helpless before her.

"God gives each of us the ability to ask Him ourselves, Gadi." Her soft voice caused him to lean forward, eager to hear what she had to say. "The only intercessor we need is Jesus. A priest, a rabbi, a pastor, me: none of us are necessary to hear your confession and bring you salvation. You only have to ask God yourself. Give Him your heart. Allow Jesus to do this work in it that you need. He will do it. At that moment He will also place Himself within you in the Person of the Holy Spirit. From then on, you have a direct pipeline to God from your spirit to His. God will live within you to help you walk out your redemption.

"It is really that simple?" Despite having read the Scriptures and accepted their truth, doubt showed on Gadi's face.

Janna took Gadi's hands in hers. "It's that simple. Would you like to pray for Him to accept you as His son through the blood of Jesus?"

Gadi's smile burst out like the sun after a rainstorm. "Yes."

Chapter 83

March 2029

The winter took its toll on the entire country. In those parts that were in the Snowbelt, they had accumulation without end. Multiple blizzards swept the continent from north to south, west to east. Many died in the harsh weather. Those areas not prone to snow received voluminous amounts of rain. Many thought this would be the year that California slid into the Pacific given the floods and landslides up and down the coast, along with the slipping of the tectonic plates that caused numerous earthquakes. Many a winter day had people pining for the years El Niño had swept the land bringing warmth in an otherwise cold season. Amidst the never-ending snow shoveling, the mountains of white that towered above many houses, and the daily torture of navigating treacherous roads, there were jokes without end about how global warming had finally won the day.

Despite the weather, reports came in from across the country of yellow-cross Christians rounded up and disappearing. Martial law had settled in. Most people felt little impact. They shrugged their collective shoulders and went about their business as best they could. Years of eroding freedoms had stripped away much awareness as to how the country was supposed to constitutionally operate.

Those who were politically aware noticed fewer freedoms each week. Every now and then, a report surfaced about armed skirmishes between government agents and those who resisted their disenfranchisement. James and Janna often talked about where all this might lead. They came to no conclusion other than God would use the situation to His glory.

It was rumored that secret facilities in every state had swelled with new arrivals of disfavored persons. The strange phenomenon for the Glaziers was the absolute absence of attention to them by the authorities. They wore the requisite yellow crosses, but remained unmolested by anyone with hostile intent. The lack of harassment led them to believe that God had strategically placed a hedge of protection around them for the time being. They had no idea how long it would last, but accepted and thanked the Lord for it every day. Several times James attempted to drive to Camp Grayling to investigate Bob Sanders' incarceration. Each time roadblocks and other governmental hindrances obstructed his way.

In this period Joe Bennett came calling on James. It seemed that Lighthouse Church had made adjustments to accommodate recent government mandates. It was still in business, and had reconsidered James' termination. "The allegations of sexual misconduct were proven false. The board has also agreed that, though somewhat unorthodox, your prayers were effective in healing Janna."

Sitting with the two of them in their living room, Bennett had retained his woolen hat. It surprised James that after five minutes of the man's twisting it around in his fingers, pulling and stretching it in nervous anxiety, that it wasn't full of holes.

After everything they had put James through, it took all of his fruit-of-the-spirit self-control to respond with grace. The time wasn't yet at hand to utter God's Words. He knew that Lighthouse Church had effectively come under state control in order to continue operations. It was the compromise required by churches to exist at all. "That's generous of the church, Joe. Under other circumstances, I might consider it. Unfortunately it's bad timing. God has called on Janna and me to take a little trip, so it's not something that will work for us."

"We'd be happy to hold the position open for you until you return."

"I know you've had a series of interim pastors these last few months. Is the search committee not having much success?"

Bennett scratched his chin. "Afraid not. We figured that after what you guys have been through, it's hard to find someone more qualified. We...uh...we made a mistake in letting you go—by giving you that ultimatum. That...uh...wasn't a real Christian thing to do."

"We all make mistakes, Joe. I forgive you." In his heart, surprisingly, James found he had no animosity toward Bennett or the church. "God has given us direction, however, and we won't disobey Him. You'll have to find someone else to fill the pulpit. Besides, I think with what I have to say and how the church has had to bend to new rules the feds have initiated, we'd have a lot of issues."

"Thought you might say something like that. I suppose you're right. I'm real sorry. Best of luck." Bennett shook their hands and left.

James rejoined Janna on the couch. "I think that closes the door for us here. The time has come. Are you ready?"

She jumped up. Janna's vigor and strength since her resurrection hadn't ceased to amaze James. "Let's get to it."

Hand in hand, they began their preparation for the journey God had set before them.

Chapter 84

Washington, D.C.

In the months following the arrest of his boss, Ibrahim Sufyan had plotted how to free Abu Saif and gain revenge for what the kafir president, Luisa Parker, had done. Sufyan had no way of knowing what Arnold Rickards had told Parker about the threat of the Muslim Brotherhood to her administration, but the truth he'd spoken was only the half of it.

Years of planning by the Brotherhood had paid off. Its stated intent was to infiltrate the United States and wage cultural jihad against this sworn enemy. Through multiple cover organizations, they had done so by cozying up to liberal, progressive types and duping them into thinking they shared a common goal: a tolerant, multicultural community free of Christianity with its exclusive, prejudiced message. By pushing Christians to the fringes, they'd made and won their case that Islam should be taught in schools and accommodated throughout the land because it was the open-minded thing to do. Despite the evidence in Muslim countries that Islam could not and would not coexist with homosexuals, the Brotherhood had accomplished the amazing feat of deceiving an entire group of people that Islam stood in solidarity with their struggle for recognition and equality. In the same manner, regardless of conservative efforts to demonstrate Islam's abuse of women and their relegation to nothing more than sex objects, feminists in the U.S. generally ignored all that and stood with their Muslim comrades against the tyrannies they perceived were perpetrated by Christians.

Above all else, they had completely infiltrated the government of the United States from the lowest to the highest levels. Those who weren't outright Muslims were either in-the-closet practitioners or completely sympathetic to the Islamic cause. The non-Muslim supporters, in the position known as dhimmitude, went along through either fear or admiration.

To the surprise of no one truly following the teachings of Muhammad, the Muslim Brotherhood had become a dominant force in the nation and was ready for the next step.

In a secret meeting place, Ibrahim Sufyan stood before three high level Brotherhood imams. The men nodded approvingly at his plan. "For too long we have been in Dar al Harb, the House of War. We have had to bow down to the kafir and suffer their infidel ways. With this one strike we will ascend to Dar al Islam, the House of Islam, and so take over complete control of this nation. We will make it great again, Allah willing. It will be the greatest victory of the caliphate yet known in the world. Because of our courage, soon the Mahdi will return and the glorious end will come."

The ranking imam among the three grinned. "Go in the peace of the Prophet. Do that for which we have worked long and hard. You have our blessing."

Sufyan bowed before them and went to complete his task.

Over the next several days, he contacted all the supporters he had cultivated during his time in his privileged position beside Abu Saif. He kept his mission hidden, indicating he needed only to conduct undisclosed business.

With a wink and a nod to those who saw him, he entered the White House late in the evening. Like a shadow, he proceeded to his destination and settled down for the night.

The next morning President Luisa Parker entered the Oval Office with an aide. After discussing several matters of national importance, the aide left the office and closed the door behind him.

Sufyan moved from his place of concealment and like a wraith, materialized beside Parker's chair where she sat in a pink pantsuit concentrating on the papers before her. Before she could say a startled word, he grabbed her hair and yanked back her head.

Her abject terror as she saw the long blade Sufyan held gave him much satisfaction. "You have taken a step too far. It is time for the rightful president to take his place. You infidels will no longer rule us."

It took only a moment to complete his mission. With a swipe of the sharp knife, he took her life. "Allahu Akbar!"

He then arranged things appropriately and withdrew his intelliphone, taking photos from a variety of angles.

Satisfied, Sufyan moved confidently to the door. He looked back once at the former president's head placed squarely in the center of the desk, her body slumped in the chair where he'd left it. The red of her blood clashed with her pink outfit. Sufyan thought it fitting.

He began to whistle under his breath. His next stop was the prison to free the new president of the United States.

THE END

ABOUT THE AUTHOR

Gary W. Ritter has written novels and short stories for many years, recently winning multiple short story awards through FaithWriters.com. Following a career in telecommunications and real estate, he became a pastor with a heart for the persecuted church and for missions. God has given Gary clear direction to use his talent for fiction writing to warn the nation and the Church that neither can continue ignoring His Word and expect to thrive. **Sow the Wind** is the first book in the planned *Whirlwind* series.

45752132R00220

Made in the USA
Middletown, DE
12 July 2017